Save
AETHER

Book Three of the Trinity Key Trilogy

L.M. Fry

ELEAH Enterprises
EDMOND, OKLAHOMA

ISBN 978-1530320158
978-1530320103
First Edition

Acknowledgements

This book wouldn't have been possible without these amazing people to whom I owe so much thanks:

To my husband and children, I love you all so much. You guys inspire me every day.

To my parents, who believed in me from day one.

To Megan, my best friend and fellow author. Without our writer's therapy, I would go insane.

To the wonderful editor Kay McAndrews. You are so very patient and kind. I appreciate the hard work you put into editing.

To my critique group Megan, John, Gretchen, Jess, and Lynn. You guys are a godsend.

To the people at West Texas Writer's Academy (too many names to list, but you know who you are.) You've all kept me going for the past few years. I wouldn't be where I am without your guidance and advice.

To the Deranged Doctors Team who designed the book covers for the series. They are amazing.

http://www.derangeddoctordesign.com/

Dedicated to
My Writer's Academy Family
There are too many names to list, but you know who you are.
Thank you for everything.

CHAPTER ONE

Julia

Julia's legs felt like petrified wood. She'd been standing in front of the Elder's tribunal for hours, and the pompous blowhards still hadn't decided what to do with the so-called "heretical girls." Julia didn't understand what the stink was all about. So what if Valera, Theo, and she had reunited the Trinity Key? At least they had saved Aether from Valera's lunatic uncle, Marcus. She glared at each of the Elders, mentally muttering– *you're so welcome.* Not to mention, technically speaking, that the Trinity Key belonged to the girls by right of birth. They were the direct descendants of Danu after all. However, the almighty Elders disagreed – strongly.

To prevent her feet from taking root, Julia lifted her left leg, spun her ankle, then repeated the same thing with her right. She suddenly realized the nasty plump elder, whom she had nicknamed Slammy Magee because of his loving his gavel so much, was staring at her little dance with his signature sneer. Wait for it… wait for it…

1

Bang, Bang, Bang...

And there it is, folks! His gavel shook the entire table. Julia resisted the urge to cover her ears with her hands. They were already ringing from his incessant objection to *everything*.

"Are we boring you, young lady?" He pointed the wooden hammer at her.

Of course she was bored. Listening to a bunch of unhappy geriatrics blab was painfully monotonous, but she bit her tongue to keep from telling him the truth. The last thing she needed was to give him another reason to hate her – he already seemed to have plenty. Instead, she bowed graciously, or so she thought.

"No, your honor. Just working out a few kinks," she answered.

He didn't seem too pleased with her response. "You are in grave trouble, so I suggest you take these proceedings seriously."

"Oh, but I do, your honor," she yawned.

Julia, please don't goad him on anymore. Just nod or something, Valera pleaded inside Julia's head.

Julia huffed. *Hey, I didn't do anything. It's not my fault that they can't agree, and my legs fell asleep,* she shot back with a scowl.

Still, Julia lowered her head with a sufficient amount of feigned humility. He appeared satisfied by her reaction. She furtively stuck her tongue out at Valera, and received a curt head nod in return. Rolling her eyes, she focused on the old lady who seemed to be in charge of the Elders. Theo had called her Parmelia, and she was the only one who had taken their side. However, if she knew that they planned on releasing Danu, then would she still fight so hard to free them? Julia doubted it.

Parmelia caught Julia looking at her and smiled. Julia quickly looked past her at the window and studied a crack in the glass. The first time she saw the Elders' tower, the building seemed like a stunning architectural masterpiece that stood far above every other structure in Pacifica City. But up close, small cracks and stains marred the walls. Even the massive glass dome that protected the city situated on the ocean floor had fissures that spread like fungus in the glass. They weren't deep enough to leak, but she had to wonder how much longer Pacifica would last. The citizens were living in the illusion of security. With one well-placed tap, the whole city would be *underwater*. Julia chuckled at her own wit, eliciting a frown from Theo.

Stop smiling like a freak. You're going to get us executed or something. We have to keep our heads low until this is all over.

Why are we even sitting through this? We could leave any time. It's not like they could stop us. Julia was enjoying this telepathic form of communication that the three of them shared. *Let's blow this joint and save Danu already.*

Theo's right. We need to be careful, Valera cautioned Julia.

Gah! You two are boring… you're worse than Slammy Magee over there. At least he has some spunk.

Theo's blank face broke into a smile. Julia had cracked the beast and she felt like she'd won a small victory, until Theo regained her composure a little too quickly. Now, if only she could make Valera snort or laugh.

At that moment a tickling sensation crept up Julia's neck as if a spider crawled on her skin. The old woman blathered on about something – not that Julia was listening – but she was also staring at Julia with a disconcerting intensity. Julia lost interest in teasing her friends. Something in the old woman's face felt familiar. Julia swore she'd seen the woman before, but strained to remember where. Parmelia had been the one who picked up the Trinity Key after the girls merged it, but the sense went beyond that. Julia just couldn't shake the feeling.

Now a bitter metallic taste formed on the back of Julia's tongue. The harder she thought about the old woman, the stronger the taste got.

Why do I taste metal? Do you guys taste it?

Theo shivered next to her, and her voice invaded Julia's thoughts. *You're holding aether. I can feel it, although to me it smells like the air before it rains.*

Valera tilted her head and frowned. *Really? To me it's saltier, like the ocean.*

Weird, Julia responded.

Along with the taste, she felt the smoothness of the energy. At her whim, it was as if aether slipped over her skin like cold polished river stones. Goosebumps formed on her arms. Aether danced around her, tempting her. A nudge from Theo warned her to let go. The energy that flowed through her was new and scary. She remembered Valera's rocky start with it, and decided to release it. Julia sighed and let it go, then turned her attention back to the proceedings.

Slammy Magee was driveling on again. "Separation is the only way to ensure the safety... blah... blah... blah... Dangerous... Impudent... Wild... Lock them away... blah... blah... blah..."

Julia smiled. He was right – she was dangerous, impudent, and wild. In fact, she prided herself on those very characteristics. *Well said, Slammy!* Her appreciation for the man's opinion was short lived. At the mention of her father's name, her temper sparked.

"She is daughter to the leader of the Azure Serpents, Lazarus Killian. Need I remind you of *his* crimes against Aether?

Lazarus was a plague upon us all. Are you willing to release his offspring onto the world?" He glared into the eyes of each person in the room, ending on Julia. A deep growl built up in her throat, but he simply sneered. "I… am… not! She will be the end of Aether as we know it."

Julia couldn't take his offenses any longer. If the Elders were going to lock her away for being a *supposed* deviant, she might as well give them what they wanted. She stepped forward. Theo grabbed her arm, but Julia pushed her off.

"No, Theo. I won't sit here and be disgraced in front of these… these pretentious snobs." A gasp went through the crowd, bolstering Julia's ego. "That's right, people. You think you're so righteous . . . the revered Elders of Aether who hole up in the depths of the ocean like sharks with no teeth. Do you feel good about yourselves, gumming on three innocent girls?"

Julia reached out for the cool touch of aether. It surged through her pores and into her veins. She held her hands over her head, preparing to unleash a torrent of pain and ice on the tribunal.

In a deadly whisper, she threatened, "I am not my father… I am far… more… dangerous."

Julia unleashed everything she had into the air, calling forth what she anticipated was a massive ice storm. The people in the room held their breath. Slammy Magee screamed, shrinking back like a coward. The air chilled around her, and then… nothing. No dark clouds. No ice. Not even a snowflake.

Someone in the crowd chuckled, which spread into a full-blown hysterical fit. Julia looked down at her hands in disbelief. She shook them and threw them forward again, screeching when nothing happened. Theo and Valera dragged her back in line. Slammy Magee's face turned the color of boiled lobster. Parmelia covered her face with her hands and shook her head.

"I don't get it," Julia whined.

"What were you thinking? Are you trying to get us killed?" Theo hissed.

After Julia's spectacle, Parmelia raised her hand to calm the tribunal. The laughter subsided.

"Clearly, these girls pose no more threat to Aether than any mule-headed teenager. The girls will return to Aetherland Isle..."

Julia watched Slammy Magee smirk, and then he licked his lips as if salivating. She forgot about her embarrassment. Suspicions raised, she nudged Theo and nodded toward the man. Theo frowned at his odd behavior. He grasped the gavel in a white-knuckled grip.

"The girls will remain under guard—

Slammy Magee hammered the table top, interrupting Parmelia's speech. He stood up and pointed the gavel at the old woman. For a second, Julia thought he was going to hit her with it. Everyone in the room chittered. The pit of Julia's stomach churned. She'd given him the incentive he needed.

"This is unacceptable!" He glared at the crowd. "Have they not proven their disobedience once before? Yet, here we are once again at the precipice of destruction, and Parmelia wants to release the girls upon Aether."

Heads in the crowd shook and a nervous chatter erupted in the room. Slammy Magee grinned.

"I call for a motion of no confidence in the Leader of the Elders," he shouted over the noise. "For the direct and purposeful endangerment of the people of Aether."

In unison, the grumpy looking twin members of the council chanted, "No confidence."

The last two, Parmelia and a middle-aged woman, gasped. Slammy motioned for a white robe guard to come forward. The man moved to stand behind Parmelia, overshadowing her tiny frame. The metallic taste flooded Julia's mouth.

"Parmelia, you are accused. What say you?"

"You can't do this. I won't allow it," Parmelia protested.

"This is absurd," the middle-aged Elder screamed.

"By right of the majority, I exile you and all defectors from Pacifica City. Get them out of here!"

The white robe took Parmelia's arm. She tried to fight him off, but her thin arms couldn't escape the man's grasp. The room erupted in chaos. People screamed and argued. Parmelia and the non-compliant Elder were dragged from the room, kicking and yelling. Julia felt Theo and Valera pulling on aether beside her. Julia aimed at the man holding Parmelia, but, before Julia could wield her power, something hit her in the back of the head. Pain burst through her skull and down her spine. She fell to her knees.

None of this made any sense. Parmelia's eyes bored through her as she teetered on the edge of consciousness. Julia tried to fight the darkness, but it overpowered her. She gave in to the agony.

*

Julia awoke inside a small room with shackles around her wrists. A massive lock tethered her chains to a blueish colored wall. A ray of light shone through a brick-sized hole above a thick metal door. The floor beneath her cheek was frigid and hard. She shimmied herself into a sitting position, groaning as her shoulders and arms opposed her every movement. From the stiffness in her muscles, she figured that she'd been out for a while.

The last thing she remembered was Parmelia being pulled out of the courtroom, and Slammy Magee banging his gavel and yelling. Julia tried to use aether, but the energy was beyond her grasp. Alone, confused, and hurting, she reached out to Theo and Valera.

Are you there?

I'm here. Theo's response was a beacon of hope.

What happened? Why isn't my power working?

Theo took a few minutes to respond, and Julia began to worry. She heard Valera arguing with someone on the other side of the wall.

"Mother, I'm not leaving Theo and Julia..."

The second person seemed to be Valera's mother, Victoria, and by the sound of it, she was unleashing an inferno of rage upon her daughter. Julia provided them the curtesy of not eavesdropping – on purpose. It wasn't her fault if their voices carried, especially when Julia's name came up. She cringed. The screaming quieted, and a door slammed. Julia felt bad for Valera, although, at least she had someone who cared. Julia didn't have anyone to come say goodbye to her. Gideon was it, and she didn't know how he was doing after crashing into the lake at Azure Springs.

Did you hear that? She sent out to Theo.

Yes... Victoria isn't happy. Theo sighed. *I can't use aether either. I don't know why... I can't even feel it in here.*

Where are you? Julia asked. *I'm in a blue cement box. I don't know where.*

I am too. Which direction was Valera's voice coming from?

I think I heard them through my left wall.

I did too.

If Valera were close enough to hear, Julia figured the cells were adjoined. She skootched across the room and tapped on the wall with her shackles. Pressing her ear against the cement, she waited for a response.

"I'm here," Theo said.

Elation surged through Julia. Theo and Valera were close by. At least she wasn't alone.

"Theo... I'm... glad you're there." Julia's voice shook.

"Someone's at the door." Theo went quiet.

Julia leaned against the wall and listened. A door opened and someone entered Theo's room. Chains rattled for a second, and then stopped. Julia waited for what felt like an eternity. Bile rose in her throat as she imagined the worst possible outcomes – Slammy Magee executing them one by one, or worse Slammy Magee torturing them before executing them one by one.

Theo? Julia hit the side of her cell.

It's my mom, Theo returned, and Julia released a long breath. *She wants to talk to us. Can you hear her?*

Marjorie's voice penetrated the wall a little muffled, but clear enough to hear. "I was worried sick about you girls. I thought for sure I'd never see you again."

"What happened to the others? Joe and Nessie..." Theo asked.

"Don't worry about them. They're fine. How are you? Are you okay, Julia?"

Julia didn't know how to respond. The fact that Marjorie showed any worry for her left her speechless. The cement cooled her forehead.

"Uh, yeah. I'm okay," Julia said as loud as she dared.

"They didn't give us much time. The remaining Elders won't listen. They said we could say goodbye before... before they make us leave." Julia could tell Marjorie was crying. "Someone will come to you soon. We're going to get you girls out one way or another. I promise. Just hang in there."

Theo's door opened again, and Julia heard a male voice.

"You can't do this. She's my daughter... you can't," Marjorie screamed.

"MOM!"

After some shuffling, the room became eerily quiet. Julia didn't know what to think. She tapped on the wall, but Theo didn't respond. The silence grew too heavy, and loneliness shrouded her like a suffocating cocoon. She curled up on the floor and waited.

A little later her cell door opened, and she was blinded by a bright light. A shadowed figure blocked the doorway. He lumbered into the room and unlocked her chains.

"Come with me," he ordered.

Julia's hackles went up. She didn't know this man. He could have been Slammy Magee's minion sent to assassinate her. She wasn't going to just fall into his trap.

"What if I don't?"

The white robe looked at her through half-lidded eyes. "Listen, kid. Just come on. I don't want to drag you out."

"I'd like to see you try. Do you know who I am? Do you know what I'm capable of?"

Her voice came out stronger than the confidence she felt. She hoped that he hadn't witnessed her useless display during the tribunal. She hoped that he didn't know aether was out of her grasp within the confines of the cell. She hoped that he couldn't tell how scared she was. A sly smile crossed his face. He yanked on the chains.

"Are you going to give me a sniffle? I saw your little display, so stop stalling and move."

She wasn't going to give in. "I'm the daughter of Lazarus Killian and a warrior of the Order of the Azure Serpent!"

When she stood her ground, he sighed. He reached for her arm, but she side-stepped him and elbowed his back. She didn't need her power to outwit him. He fell to the floor. She ran to the door, where a dozen white robes waited. She did a quick mental head count. There were too many of them. Defeated, she put her shackled hands in the air. The first man exited the room, holding his ribs and glaring at her.

"I'll go peacefully," she declared.

The white robe growled, picked up the chain, and pulled the chain hard enough that she fell to her knees. The others stood by and watched. She was on her own. Julia regained her footing and prepared for a fight.

"Halt! What is going on here?" Parmelia's raspy, but firm voice said.

"Ma'am. The girl has been called to the leader's office, but she is insolent and refused to come," the white robe mumbled.

His arms dropped to his side, and his face turned bright red. The others backed away. Parmelia squinted at the men. Julia was relieved to see that the woman still held some authority in the tower. Parmelia smelled like gardenias. When she touched Julia's cheek, a memory of white flowers in a woman's hair flashed through Julia's mind. Julia flinched away. The old woman sighed and turned to the white robes.

"I'm here to speak with the girl. You are dismissed." Parmelia shooed the men away.

The injured one hesitated. "But Ma'am... she's dangerous, and I was told to take her —

"Don't be foolish. She's a child. And I *will* speak with her for a moment."

The white robe handed Parmelia the chain and left. Parmelia put her hand on Julia's shoulder and ushered her back into the cell. Julia thought about fighting, but her instincts told her to stay and hear the woman out. Even if she could easily overcome the old woman, she didn't want to hurt her. Julia had no choice but to go along.

"We don't have much time. I called in a few favors to gain access to you, but once *they* find out I'm here... Well... we must speak quickly. There is much I need to tell you."

Parmelia dropped the chain on the floor without securing it. She also left the door open a crack. Sweat beaded Julia's brow, and her legs itched. All she had to do was knock Parmelia over and run. Julia could walk right out the front door, but she stayed.

"If you people think you can keep me locked up, you're mistaken." *Then what am I doing? Run, Julia.* She scolded herself.

Parmelia turned and chuckled. "You remind me of your mother. She was just as rebellious."

Julia's tough charade faded. She swallowed a knot in her throat. "You knew my mom?" Her mother was long dead; so how could this woman know her? Her curiosity sparked, and all thoughts of running disappeared. "Who are you?"

Parmelia took a deep breath. "I wanted to meet you under better circumstances, but... this is how it will have to be. I am your grandmother. My daughter, Juliet – your mother – married Lazarus." Parmelia wiped a frail hand across her face.

"Why should I believe anything you say?" Julia hissed.

Parmelia continued on, as if remembering a dream. "You should know that I was there the day you were born, and both your mother and father were so happy and in love with you."

Ha! Julia knew she had to be lying. "You must be confused. That doesn't sound like my father at all."

"He... changed soon after your birth. The previous leader of the Order, your paternal grandfather, was obsessed with Danu's power. That obsession poisoned Lazarus's mind and killed your mother. I was told that you and your mother died in an accident."

Julia paced the room. Her mind and heart were torn in several directions. She still had a family. She had a grandmother – who had believed for sixteen years that Julia was dead. The thought scared, delighted, and angered her at the same time. She stopped in front of the old woman.

"And you just believed him? Did you even try to learn the truth? Wasn't there a funeral or something? You could have asked to see the body, or... I don't know."

Parmelia looked small and fragile, wringing her hands. "There were no funerals. No bodies. After Juliet's death, Lazarus declared war on the Elders and shut us out of Subterria. Our spies discovered a plot to murder the families of Valera and Theo. Victoria exiled her family on Aetherland, and Marjorie chose to hide her family in the human world. Aether fractured. If I had known, I would have fought for you. You're my grandchild."

Parmelia stood on shaky legs and held her arms out. Julia hesitated. With one kick, she could escape the old woman and run away. She could hide in Subterria or live in the human world. She didn't owe Parmelia or anyone else anything. She was strong. She was smart. She didn't need anyone.

A salty taste touched her tongue. Tears streamed down her face. One step was all it took, and Julia fell into the woman's arms and cried.

The footsteps outside the door came too soon. White robes flooded the room and split Julia and her grandmother apart. Griping the doorframe, Parmelia fought to stay a few seconds more. The men took her away and locked Julia inside. Her grandmother's voice shouted in Julia's thoughts.

We're going to fight this. We'll get you girls out as soon as we can. Watch over each other...

CHAPTER TWO

V*alera*

Without the other girls, Valera felt lonelier than ever. When her mother had come to her, she thought that everything would be okay. She was wrong.

"You are coming home with me." Victoria had grabbed her arm and rattled the chains around Valera's wrists.

"But, I though… I'm a prisoner. They aren't just going to let me go…"

"I've made a deal with the Elders. We're leaving."

Valera's hopes grew. She hugged her mother, although Victoria didn't return the gesture right away. Valera didn't care. Her mother was there to save them. Valera, Theo, and Julia still had a chance to be free. Victoria patted Valera's back and stepped back.

"Now that this nonsense is over, everything will get back to normal. We'll get you back to Aetherland and put this whole mess behind us."

Valera wasn't exactly eager to go back to the way things were, but maybe she could change her mother's mind about keeping her locked up on Aetherland Isle. She'd been set free once, and didn't want to lose it. Besides, she had Gideon and the girls now. If anything her time away proved that she was just as capable as her brother Victor. She'd survived being kidnapped. She'd been to the human world and come out unscathed. She'd helped take down Marcus.

"Yeah, back to normal. Theo will be with her parents again, and I bet Julia will like the island, if she'll give it a chance."

Surely, Julia would see some merits to Aetherland Isle. She'd be free to do as she pleased, within reason of course. The three of them could learn to control their powers together.

"Theo? Julia? You misunderstood me. *We're* going home. Those other two are not my problem."

"We can't, Mother —

Victoria lifted Valera's tangled hair from her shoulder and scoffed. "What an unruly mess. When was the last time you brushed it?"

Valera pulled away from her mother, yanking her own hair in the process. "Mother, listen to me —

"Really, you need to learn to take care of yourself. Look at your clothes. You're beginning to look like an airship pirate. You'll be wearing proper dresses from now on." Victoria pinched the stained white fabric of Valera's sleeve and scrunched her nose up as if it were a dead skunk.

Pressure built up inside Valera. Her hopes unraveled. Her mother had no intention of freeing her. She wasn't there out of love and concern. She just wanted control over Valera's life. Valera pulled away from her mother's grip, mussed up her curls, and erupted.

"Mother, I'm not leaving Theo and Julia behind! They're my sisters.... And... I like dressing like a pirate... I am a pirate... a deviant... criminal... PIRATE! And I won't put my hair into scalp-numbing buns ever again. I like my wild hair. It suits me, Mother. Why can't you see who I really am?"

Victoria's fair-skinned face went from pink to red to purple. Her jaw clenched, and her hands fisted up. Valera had pushed her mother too far. She retreated to the back of the cell. After a few sharp, hard breaths, Victoria's natural color returned. She adjusted the high collar around her neck and smoothed out her bun.

"If you turn your back on your family again, I won't help you. I'm leaving in an hour. You have until then to change your attitude, or I'll leave you here to rot with those other two." Victoria's voice was cold and rigid.

Valera opened her mouth to say something, but the words caught on her tongue. How could her mother do this to her? She knew she had made some questionable choices lately, but she never imagined her mother would abandon her.

"Think carefully, young lady."

Her mother refused to look into her eyes. Victoria yanked on her black gloves until her fingers were so far into them that the fabric strained against her nails, and stormed out of the room. The reality of Valera's situation came crashing down on her. Being free and releasing Danu became distant memories. She was in chains, unable to reach aether, and alone. Slinking down the wall to the floor, Valera curled up in a ball. The shackles around her wrist made her skin itch. The chill of the cement floor seeped through her bones. She cried.

Valera, are you there? Theo whispered in Valera's mind.

A spark of hope rose within her. Valera sat up and closed her eyes. Aether was out of reach, but her friends weren't.

I'm here! I'm so glad to hear you.

After all that yelling, you were so quiet that we thought your mother murdered you or something. Julia quipped.

Valera wiped her face with the back of her hand. A twinge of embarrassment shot through her. They must have heard the argument.

How much did you hear?

I stopped listening after you yelled pirate. I'm not a snoop, you know, Julia laughed.

Yeah, right. You're hilarious, Julia, Theo added, joining in. *We didn't hear much, Valera. Is everything all right?*

Valera sighed, *No, she may as well have murdered me. Then I would have been better off. She wants to take me back to Aetherland.*

Danu's ass, how does she plan on doing that? Julia swore. *Parmelia said we're stuck in here.*

You are stuck in here. She made a deal with the Elders, but it only extends to me. I told her I'm not going.

Are you crazy? You have to go. Both Julia and Theo's voice screamed in her head.

No, I don't. I won't leave you behind.

Valera was growing tired of having people tell her what she *had* to do. She knew they meant well, but it didn't matter. She would make her own decisions from now on. Still, having Julia and Theo with her lifted her spirits. Together, they'd find a way out of the situation. The girls grew quiet. When her mother came back in, she'd try to reason with her. Surely, she'd see the logic in keeping the girls together. Either way, Valera's mind was set. She was staying.

The hour passed in a blur of voices from the other two cells. Valera was too busy organizing her thoughts to listen in. When her door swung open and her mother again filled the frame, Valera stood up and faced Victoria. She crossed her arms and prepared to have a calm, adult discussion with her mother. But before Valera could open her mouth to speak, Victoria shook her head. She didn't even ask Valera what she'd decided.

"Your mind is made up then? So be it."

The door slammed shut and her mother left. Just like that, Valera was forgotten.

She just left me here... no goodbye... no 'I love you'... nothing.

I am sorry, Valera. This is my fault. If I hadn't lost control...well you know. Julia almost sounded sympathetic and remorseful – almost. Valera heard a quick chuckle, and then Julia quipped, *Welcome to Alcatraz!*

What's Alcatraz? Valera asked.

A human prison in Califor– . . . never mind, a bad place, Julia groaned.

Valera looked at her chains and huffed. *Well, Alcatraz or not, this sucks!*

Valera, you almost sound human! Theo chirped.

Oh, no, don't even go there. Valera laughed. *It's pretty clear that I'm meant to stay in Aether. I didn't do very well in the human world.*

That's the truth! Julia's voice chimed in. *Considering you nearly burned down Colorado, maybe it's for the best that you're locked up.*

Funny, Julia. Valera yawned. *Hey, how are we able to talk, but I can't touch aether?*

I've been trying to figure that out since we got put in here... so far, I have no idea, Julia grumbled. *Oh well, I don't know about you two, but I'm tired.*

Valera lay on the floor and tried to get comfortable. The cold made her muscles sore and her bones ache. The metal cuffs were like ice blocks around her wrists. She tried in vain to soak in aether and feel the warmth that it brought. Whatever curse was on the cell made it impossible. She fell into an exhaustion-fueled trance, where she dreamt of the great white tundra. A familiar voice called out to her as it did most nights.

Daughter, release me… So much pain…

Then, a new image flickered in her mind. Danu showed her a united Aether, rejoicing that the goddess was free. Valera felt an overwhelming sense of peace and joy. In her dream, the sun rose above the horizon, blinding her eyes. A pain shot through her thigh.

"Wake up. Dr. Lawless wants to speak to you," a white robe grumbled inside her cell.

The door was open, flooding the cell with light. Valera rubbed her face with her hands. The white robe grabbed her arms and pulled her to her feet. She shrugged out of his grasp. Taking a deep breath, the salty smell of aether washed over her like a wave of warm water.

"No need to be a jerk," she griped, soaking all of the warmth from aether that she could.

A loud thud came from the hallway, and another white robe flew backward across the doorway. Valera smiled. They must be trying to wake Julia up as well. And, this guy thought Valera was grumpy in the morning. Ha! He left the room for a second, and Valera heard a ruckus. Purple sparks lit up the room. Theo. Valera stepped into the hall. With the aether overflowing within her, she heated up the chains around her wrists until the metal became pliable. They fell to the ground with a plop. White robes surrounded her, and she prepared to attack.

"Fascinating!" A man's voice cooed behind her.

She swung around ready to fight, but the man held his hands in the air and smiled. He wasn't a typical white robe. He wore a lab coat instead of the robes, and his greying hair stuck out in all directions. The white robes moved in around her.

"Stay back. I warn you," Valera muttered.

"Enough, of this. Leave them be," the man in the lab coat ordered.

The white robes backed away, but stayed close. Theo and Julia came to Valera's side and stood facing opposite directions. Sparks crackled from Theo's hands, and Julia's fists turned white. The man seemed thoroughly intrigued.

"May I?" he asked, pointing to Valera's hands.

Valera looked at her wrists – nothing seemed remarkable to her. The man held his hand out palm up and stepped toward Valera. Julia nudged her side.

"Don't trust these people," she hissed. *We should try to get out.*

Theo retorted, *And go where?*

Oh, I don't know… to release Danu like we planned, Julia snapped.

I want to release her and stop the nightmares as much as you do, Julia. But we don't even know where the tomb is.

Valera smiled, remembering her dream.

What are you grinning at? Julia hissed.

Last night I dreamt that Danu united Aether. It felt wonderful, Valera sighed.

Listen, Theo groaned. *I've heard of this guy before, he could help us. I think we should go along with it.*

Why would we do that? Julia scoffed. *We can't trust him or anyone else in this place.*

For one, he called off the guard. Valera held her hands out. "I guess."

He held her forearms and examined both sides. Pulling a pair of thick spectacles over his eyes, he got a closer look. He grinned and released her.

"Absolutely, amazing!"

Valera frowned. "What?"

Thinking she had something on her, she checked her arms. There wasn't anything on her skin.

"You didn't burn! Not even a scorch... simply fascinating."

Julia scowled at the man and took a step forward. The smile faded from his face, and he stepped back. Even he seemed afraid of her. With her fists high, she blocked him from Valera.

"Who are you?" she seethed.

His shoulders dropped, and he cleared his throat. "I am Doctor Ellwood Lawless, of course."

"You study Danu," Theo muttered.

You know him? Valera asked.

The man perked up, put a hand on his hip, and puffed out his chest. "Yes, you've heard of me then. I'm not surprised really, my exploits are known far and wide. Why even some among the human..."

He droned on, but Valera stopped listening.

Theo's voice popped up in her brain. *His apprentice was my "trainer" in Aetherland, while you two were gallivanting all over the world. That guy was annoying, but this guy could help us find the tomb's location.*

Theo raised an eyebrow at the man. "Something like that. What do you want?"

He crossed his arms and smiled. "I have a proposition for the three of you. As the first full-fledged Trinity in generations, I'd like the opportunity to study you."

"Full-fledged? You mean we're the traitors who broke Elder law, and you want to use us like lab rats." Julia spat. "What do we get out of it?"

He smiled and nodded toward a fresh group of white robes. "Trust me, you won't be disappointed. Play nice this time, and you'll see what I mean."

The white robes approached the girls. It took three of them to walk a shackled Julia away, and two more for Theo. When one of them came for Valera, he peered at the mass of metal on the floor and at her arms. She was glad to be rid of the metal bracelets. He frowned at her, and she shrugged back.

"They fell off," she offered. She wasn't going to be put in another pair either.

To her surprise, he put a hand on her shoulder and led her away, shackle free. They were escorted back into the round courtroom where the debacle of a tribunal was held the day before. This time it was devoid of spectators, and Slammy Magee sat smugly in Parmelia's spot. Julia glowered at the man. His penchant for the gavel hadn't simmered since their first trial. He slammed it until Valera thought for sure it would break. The old panel of five Elders was down to three.

"I hope your overnight stay in the cells have tempered your attitudes. As you can see, there's been a change in management around here. We are the True Followers of Danu," Slammy rambled.

Valera rolled her eyes. It was bad enough they'd had to deal with the Azure Serpents and Elders, now there was a new bully in town. From the sound of it, they were as delusional as all the others.

Here we go again, Valera moaned.

Let's hear them out, Theo said.

Julia groaned, *Let's blow them out of the water instead.*

Julia, please behave, Theo begged.

"True Followers?" Leave it to Julia to open her mouth.

Bang… bang… bang… Slammy loved his gavel.

"You will not speak unless spoken to… but yes, we are the True Followers. Our sect has been hiding in the ranks of the

Elders for an eternity, but now *we* rule. And you will do as you're told —

"I'm here... I'm here."

He was interrupted by Dr. Lawless, who shuffled into the room like a whirlwind. He bowed to the panel with flourish. Although, Slammy snorted and seemed miffed, he didn't say anything. Dr. Lawless walked past the three girls with a wide grin on his face. Before he turned toward Slammy, he winked. Valera didn't know what to think about the man. She peeked over at Theo and Julia, who both appeared as confused as she was.

"Master Elder." Dr. Lawless bowed again this time in front of Slammy.

"You're late," Slammy sneered. "This is Dr. Ellwood Lawless of the True Followers. He will be studying your abilities, and preparing you for the return."

"Return to what?" Valera asked.

Slammy huffed, "The return of Danu of course. You three are the key, and you will bring her back."

CHAPTER THREE

*T*heo

I don't like the way he said that. What should we do? Valera asked Julia and Theo.

Julia continued to scowl at Slammy. *I don't trust them. Look at the way he's leering. He's not telling us something.*

Of course, he's not telling us everything, but I think we should go along with it. At the very least, it will buy us some time. Theo added.

We may not have a chance like this again. We should escape now, while we can, Julia argued.

He may be odd, but I think Dr. Lawless can help us learn about our abilities.

Fine, but don't say I didn't warn you, Julia spat back.

The white robes came back and took the girls back to the cells. When the guard holding Theo turned down a different corridor, she panicked. She began to doubt staying. Aether slithered its way under her skin, and she held it. She resisted the white robe's shoving, and in turn he pushed her harder. A second white robe yanked on the chains around her wrists.

"Where are we going?" she asked.

"Just move," the man behind her huffed.

He jabbed her hard in the ribs. Her anger sparked. Aether broke loose from her grasp, and she forced him away from her. He yelped. The man holding her chains received an equal jolt of electricity through the metal. He released her restraints. A boisterous laugh came from behind her. Dr. Lawless rushed down the hall.

"You men are going to have to learn not to manhandle these girls. They're a thousand times more powerful than you could ever imagine." He patted the white robe on the back. "You can go. Theo and I can manage on our own. First, have the decency to remove the cuffs."

The white robe grumbled, removed her chains, and left. Dr. Lawless held an arm out and let Theo continue down the hall on her own. They walked through the Elders' tower to what looked like a ballroom with grand crystal chandeliers, a monstrous stone fireplace, and a long inlaid wood floor. An ornate tea table and two rose colored velvet armchairs sat near the door. Dr. Lawless sat in one seat and gestured to the other. Theo lowered herself to the edge of the cushion. He poured tea from a flower-covered tea set and offered a cup to Theo. She refused.

He'd left the ballroom doors open, which seemed odd. He wasn't trying to trap her. Floor-to-ceiling windows surrounded the room – glass she could shatter with a thought. She tested aether and smelled the fresh rainy odor. He had to have some trick up his sleeve. Perhaps he was trying to get her to let her guard down. She nodded to herself. *I'm not falling for it, Doc.*

Dr. Lawless leaned back in his chair, grinning. He slowly pulled a notebook and quill from his pocket and placed them on the table. He sipped his tea and sighed.

Theo? Are you okay? Valera's voice interrupted her thoughts.

I'm fine… I think. I'm in a room with that doctor.

When I saw them take you away, I freaked. I may have knocked a few of their teeth out. Julia sounded out of breath, but energized.

I'm okay. Just sit tight. I'll let you know later how things go.

She clasped her hands together and rested them on the table, trying to appear at ease. He nodded in approval. She steadied her breathing and kept herself open to aether. If he tried anything, she'd be ready.

"I chose to work with you first since you've already worked with my apprentice. I've read his notes and found them very… curious."

"He was a pompous know-it-all who knew *nothing* at all," she said matter-of-factly.

Theo knew it wasn't the best way to start whatever this was, but she wasn't going to sit back and be treated like an imbecile. He chuckled and crossed his arms.

"Yes… he is. Actually, I was supposed to go to Aetherland to help you, but I was detained here." He frowned and cleared his throat. "I want you to know I trust you, and I hope you'll come to trust me as well. I am very excited and only want what's best for you girls. You should understand we have never had the chance to see Danu's power first hand."

"We who?"

"The True Followers, the Elders, no one really. We've waited a long time for this. However, we aren't here to discuss that. I want to know more about you."

He opened his book and licked the tip of his quill. Positioning the pen above a blank page, he waited. The man confused her. Why was he so interested in their abilities? What did he really want from them? What did the so called True Followers plan to do with them? She didn't trust him, but she also didn't think he was a threat. So far, he was the only one who seemed to want to help. Theo didn't know how to start. After a minute, he sighed.

"Let's begin with your upbringing. When did you first know you had a connection to Danu?" he asked.

"I didn't know. Not until I came to Aether."

"Yes, but did you *feel* that there was something inside you."

"No." She shrugged. "I was actually pretty unremarkable for most of my life."

From the frown on his face and the clenching of his jaw, she knew it wasn't the answer he wanted. His pen still hovered about the page. Theo watched a drop of ink hanging onto the tip of the stylus, threatening to fall. One small jiggle, and the blank page would be ruined. She felt the thrill of anticipation. Any second now... he tapped the stylus with a finger, and the ink exploded on the page. The splotch looked kind of like an elephant. Theo chuckled.

"Is there something funny about my notebook?"

She looked into his cold blue eyes. He wasn't as bemused by the spot. Then again, she'd been cooped up in chains for two days. Anything was more exciting than sitting in a cell.

"Oh, uh... no. Sorry, what was your question?"

"Perhaps we should start with a demonstration."

"Like what?"

He tapped his chin with the black feather of his pen. "Perhaps just a small display."

Theo shrugged. She touched aether and formed a spark between her fingers. The sensation of the energy flowing through her rejuvenated her. The spark jumped from hand to hand as if she were juggling. Dr. Lawless squealed in delight and began scribbling in his notebook, writing right through the ink elephant. Theo spun aether into a cloud above her hand, twirling it into a palm-sized electrical storm. Dr. Lawless' pen swept across several pages, and then he dropped the quill. He reached out with a finger toward the cloud.

"I wouldn't do that if I were you," Theo warned.

He didn't listen. His finger got too close and a miniature bolt shot out and singed his hand. He yelped, bringing in a swarm of armed white robes. They were waiting right outside the open door just out of sight – so much for *trusting* her. She snorted. Dr. Lawless sucked on his damaged digit, and waved the guards away with his other hand. They reluctantly left the room. The doctor wrote another note in his book: *The manifestation of electrical charge is palpable.* Theo grinned.

"I told you it was a bad idea."

"Indeed. Where does the flow of aether come from? Is it only settled in your hand, or is it more widespread? What does aether feel like? Can you always sense it around —

"Whoa, slow down, Doc."

"Forgive my eagerness. I'm just… curious about how it feels to hold the power of Danu in your hands."

His eyes turned glassy as if he were in a faraway place, and he bit his bottom lip. His change in demeanor creeped Theo out, but he recovered quickly and seemed to brush away whatever dream he fell into. She figured he was just eccentric. He must have sensed her discomfort.

He softened his voice and asked, "Do you feel pain when you use aether?"

Theo shrugged. "No, there's no pain. It's more like a … tingle." She omitted the fact that using it in excess was exhausting, or that it could become uncontrollable at times, especially when she got emotional. "Most of the time, I feel aether all around me. It has a smell to it like rain, but it's different for all of us."

"You say most of the time?"

Theo groaned, "Yeah, those cells you put us in weaken it somehow."

"Aha! Professor Scrod was right. She created a paint that she believed would block aether from the room. She'll be glad to hear it works," he gushed.

"Good to know," Theo grumbled. "Although I have to wonder what made you create such a thing in the first place. Were you expecting to lock us up?"

He looked surprised and hurt. "No. Well, *I* never intended to lock you up. I can't speak for the other True Followers."

"I see," Theo deadpanned.

His excuse seemed all too convenient to her. She reached out to Julia and Valera.

There is a substance painted on the walls of the cells to keep the aether away.

Roger that, Julia shot back. *I'm going to try and scrap it off.*

"Where were you just then? You looked like you were focusing on something," Dr. Lawless pounced.

"Nowhere. I was just thinking."

"Theo, you can trust me. I'm on your side."

"Trust you? You're a part of the True Followers... or is it the Elders? I can't tell the difference. Either way, you have us locked up in aether-proof cells. How can I trust any of you?"

He looked back at the door and leaned closer to her. "The difference is that the True Followers believe Danu's spirit can be released, giving them power. They want to *use* you. The Elders maintained their rule by withholding the truth from the people. They want to stop you from fulfilling your destiny.

However, I and a few of my colleagues just want to learn from you and help you."

"Then help us get out of here," Theo hissed. She was growing tired of all the people who wanted to use them.

He nodded. "I'm working on it. We have to be careful. There are spies everywhere." He leaned back and spoke in a louder voice.

"Well, that was enough for today. Good job, Theo."

The white robes returned. Dr. Lawless stood up and put a hand on her shoulder. He squeezed her arm and nodded. She smiled in return. There wasn't any harm in playing along - for a little while. The white robes escorted her back to her cell. The cuffs were gone, but the click of the door echoed in her mind. She hated feeling trapped.

CHAPTER FOUR

Julia

Julia paced across the small room. The chains around her wrists dragged along the floor. The muscles in her arms ached from scratching at a corner wall with the metal, trying to remove whatever the Elders, or True Followers, or whatever they called themselves, had coated them with. She hadn't had any luck. The stuff was like solid tar. Theo's door slammed shut.

Are you there? She asked through their telepathic connection.

Yeah, I'm back.

Valera chimed in. *What happened?*

Nothing really. We just talked. I made a few sparks. Lawless says he wants to help us.

What does that mean? Julia snapped. She didn't trust anyone; let alone some random doctor she didn't know.

He said he's going to get us out of the cells, and I think we can trust him. He's not with the True Followers. He wants the same thing we do – to release Danu. We can't trust Slammy and the rest, so I say we see where this goes.

Julia slapped the wall. She didn't want to just go along and wait. Sinking to the floor, she put her head between her hands. She'd never been in a position like this, and she didn't like it. It made her feel weak.

With a click, the lock on her door disengaged, and a white robe appeared. Julia stood up, and he flinched. His reaction made her smile. At least, they knew she was dangerous. And, in return, it gave her a modicum of confidence. He picked up the chain as if it were attached to a viper and unlocked the cuffs from her wrists. She rubbed her chaffed skin.

"Dr. Lawless would like to see you," he muttered.

My turn, she said to the Theo and Valera.

Theo shouted, *Don't do anything stupid, Julia. This may be our only way out.*

You wound me, Theodora. Have a little faith. Julia grinned.

"Well, by all means, my good man, lead the way," she quipped to her escort.

The guard frowned, in what she supposed was confusion, and held the door open. She followed him down the hall, noting the seven other white robes who just happened to be standing around nearby. She tipped an imaginary top hat to them and smiled. They all seemed to become distracted by invisible tasks.

The guard took her into a ballroom, where Dr. Lawless stood up from a small table and held out a hand. She took it and gave it a solid shake. Dr. Lawless gestured toward the empty chair. Julia sat down and leaned back. Crossing a foot over her knee and her arms across her chest, she assessed the man. He was scrawny, and his slim, long fingers creeped her out.

"It's good to see you again, Julia."

She nodded, but kept quiet. The Academy had taught her to disarm her opponent through silent intimidation. An enemy ill-at-ease is easy to manipulate. He cleared his throat – a sign she was winning – and sat down.

"I'm here to assist you in developing your abilities and to guide you to the true path of Danu," he droned. Once the guard left and closed the door, Dr. Lawless leaned forward and whispered, "I'm here to help you."

"I know. Theo told me."

His brows dropped, and his mouth popped open. His confusion delighted Julia. Clearly, Theo hadn't mentioned their telepathy. Perhaps the expert of all things Danu wasn't as smart as he thought.

"How? I just spoke with her," he muttered.

"We have our ways." She winked. "So, Lawly – can I call you Lawly? Good. What's the plan?"

He sat back and scribbled in his notebook. Apparently he found something she said worth noting, but what? She tried to maintain her composure. When his hand stopped, he looked up at her and took a deep breath.

"First, I'd like to assess your abilities. After Professor Scrod is done archiving the artifacts acquired from *The Vault*, she'd like to discuss them with the three of you. I've been told there are some very interesting finds."

Julia couldn't believe what she was hearing. Slammy Magee had stolen the artifacts. "You have the artifacts here? Those belong to the Order... to my father. What right do you have—

"The artifacts are on their way here, yes. And I promise they will be treated with the utmost respect. Better that they come here and be studied than to remain unprotected in the human world."

That was not the answer she wanted to hear, but fighting about the artifacts was futile. These people would do what they wanted, and there wasn't anything Julia could do. Her abilities were pathetic. She drew in aether and chilled the air in the room. He pulled the collar of his jacket together and rubbed his fingers.

"Is it cold in here?"

"Not really."

She grinned. Her powers might be weak, but not for long. She'd play their little game, and soon she'd be stronger than Theo and Valera put together.

He cupped his hands and breathed into them. "Oh, okay then, let's get straight to it. Let's focus on the flow of aether. Tell me how you reach out for it."

"Well, Lawly, it's just there."

He scowled at the nickname and sighed, "In detail please."

"I think about it and boom." She snapped her fingers for effect. "It's there."

The doctor groaned, "Fine, fine. Gather it up, and I want you to focus on this pen."

She did as she was told. The metallic taste filled her mouth, and she aimed at the quill in his hand. Even though she put all of her energy into it, the only thing she created were wispy snowflakes that floated from her hands and dropped onto the table. The doctor touched one of the flakes, melting it between his fingers.

"Ice, of course, that explains it." He raised an eyebrow and tugged on his coat as if just now realizing why the temperature dropped.

He grumbled under his breath. Although, Julia's performance was less than spectacular, she grinned. She enjoyed his frustration. A sly smile appeared on his face, and she grew suspicious.

"You seem to be inhibited." He scribbled in his notebook. "It's not surprising really."

"What's not?"

"Well, simply said, Theo's powers are clearly more… advanced than yours." He tapped his chin with the pen. "Perhaps it's an intellectual variance?"

"Are you saying that she's smarter than I am?"

He shrugged. The steely tang overwhelmed her tongue, and the room became a freezer. Once again, she lashed out at the target, producing more snow. Frustration gripped her, and each time she tried to create ice, she got weaker. This was unacceptable. Theo was not smarter than she. Julia was just too stressed.

"Stop, stop. You're going to burn yourself out," Dr. Lawless said.

"My inability to perform has nothing to do with my intellect. How is anyone supposed to work in these conditions?" She threw her arms wide. "I've been locked up in a tiny cell, without proper amenities or food."

Yes, she was in a grand ballroom. Yes, the cuffs were gone. Yes, Lawly over there was treating her with *some* respect. Yet, she was being held against her will by strangers – the irony of it all. She'd have to remember to apologize to Valera… when it suited her.

"I apologize for the accommodations. I'll speak with the True Follower's council about it post haste. I'm sure we can come to a more amicable solution, although it may take some convincing. You girls are somewhat… unpredictable."

"If you can get me out of the cell, and provide some fresh clothes and a bath, then I'm sure my abilities will progress much faster."

She wasn't expecting him to give in so easily. Not that she trusted him, but her resolve was slipping. She rubbed her palms on her pants, crossed her arms, and then dropped them to her lap. He scribbled another note and closed the book.

"I think we've done enough for today. The guard will return you to your cell. Hopefully, we'll have you better situated soon."

The guard ushered her back without ever touching her. She slunk to the ground in the gloom of her prison. A migraine rotted a hole through her skull, and all she wanted to do was rest. Within minutes, the voices started up in her head.

How'd it go? Theo asked.

What if I'm next? Valera interrupted. *What happened in there? Was it awful?*

Valera, you're giving me a headache. Please, shut up. Julia snapped. *Everything is fine. Lawless* says *he's going to help. We'll see.*

Julia closed her eyes and drifted. Once again, the image of Danu floated around her thoughts. Her voice called out for help. No matter how many times Julia pushed the dream away, it always returned.

I think... I think someone's at my door, Valera shrieked, waking Julia from her tormented doze.

Julia heard several voices outside the cells. One of them was Dr. Lawless. Her door opened.

"The True Follower's council would like to speak with you." Dr. Lawless poked his head into the dismal space. "And I am here to escort you."

The guards were gone, although Julia suspected they were close by. She was glad to see Valera and Theo waiting in the hall. Dr. Lawless' grin widened.

"There something… mystical about seeing all three of you together. It's like the reincarnation of the sisters themselves. Shall we?" He waved an arm toward the courtroom.

Slammy was on his perch, as snobbish as ever. He eyed the girls from over his upturned nose. Julia automatically went to the middle, but Dr. Lawless cleared his throat and ushered her over to the spectators' chairs. When she opened her mouth to speak. His finger went to his lips.

"Just be quiet and behave." He winked, and then began, "Grand Elder, we humbly beg your pardon."

Julia rolled her eyes, but kept her mouth shut. Lawly's pageantry seemed to make Slammy extra portentous. He placed his hands on his belly and leaned back. His chair creaked under his weight.

"I'm listening."

"After spending time with the girls and explaining the true path, they've decided to honor Danu and join the True Followers in our quest."

What? Wait a second, I didn't agree to this.

Just go with it, Julia. Theo snapped back.

"Well, isn't this a fortunate turn of events. I wasn't sure these… children could be reasoned with."

"Yes, fortunate indeed. As initiates of the True Followers, I ask that they be moved to the chambers tower. They will remain under my guidance of course."

Slammy rubbed his chin with his over-stuffed sausage-like fingers.

"I will grant your request, if… they vow allegiance to me."

Hell no, Julia spat. *Let's bust out of here and free Danu ourselves. We don't need Dr. Lawless or anyone else.*

We're not actually going to swear fealty or anything. We need the help, especially you Julia. Keep the goal in mind.

Theo's assertion that Julia needed help from the doctor unnerved her. Julia knew her skills were weak, but she could learn on her own. *Slammy turned on my grandmother. That's her chair he's crushing up there.*

Valera chimed in, *I don't know, Theo. This seems kind of... wrong.*

He'll pay for what he did to your grandma, Julia. But right now, we have to play his game. We can't free Danu on our own.

Julia hated to admit it, but Theo was right. They didn't know where Danu's tomb was. They needed the artifacts and the Trinity Key, and they didn't know where they were being kept They had little choice.

Julia sighed, "I swear allegiance to the True Followers."

"I do too," Theo and Valera said in unison.

Slammy Magee lifted his gavel and slammed it. Julia covered her ears. He needed serious psychological help for his gavel fetish.

"You are dismissed," Slammy proclaimed. Before he left the room, he turned to the girls. "However, understand this – one misstep, and you'll regret it."

He lumbered from the room as if he were the king of Aether. Julia hated him, and she wasn't so fond of the doctor either. Dr. Lawless bowed in front of the girls. He seemed awfully proud of himself. He may have gotten them out of the cells, but they were still captive. However, Julia *was* one step closer to getting out.

Dr. Lawless took the girls through a skywalk to a second, smaller tower. The three-story glass building held the white robes' living chambers. The whole building was like a giant atrium with three levels of rooms surrounding a central corkscrew staircase. At their arrival, white robes looked over the railings and watched Theo, Julia, and Valera ascend the stairs to the last floor.

"Don't wander around the chambers tower without a guide. Things are in a state of chaos with the new leadership change. Not everyone agrees with the beliefs of the True Followers, and you may end up being a target of their discontent. I've taken the liberty of acquiring three rooms, which were recently vacated by deserters who found themselves on the wrong side of the coup and refused to accept the new authority."

"In other words, they were tossed out along with Parmelia," Julia muttered.

Dr. Lawless cleared his throat and ignored the gibe. "There is a communal bathroom at the end of the hall. You'll find a change of clothes in the closet."

Julia walked into her worst nightmare. It was bad enough that she was in a strange city, but they put her in a room with pink flowers on the walls and frilly bedding. The goody-two-shoeness of it made her teeth ache. Worst yet, the room smelled like roses. She was a parrot in a fancy birdcage.

Her academy instincts kicked in. She rummaged through the drawers and closets, looking for anything useful. All she found were clean undergarments and a plain white robe in the dresser. If these were the clothes Dr. Lawless spoke of, she'd stay in her stinky old leathers.

"This is worse than the academy," she spoke aloud to the empty room. "What I wouldn't give for a cot and cold stone walls."

"I don't know. . . I kind of like it," Valera chirped, poking her head in the door. "It reminds me of home."

"You would," Julia groaned.

Theo walked in behind Valera and cringed. "I'm with Julia on this one. It's over the top. Mine is pretty much the same except in yellow."

"I don't know why you are complaining. At least we are out of those nasty cells, and we've got all the necessities up here," Valera huffed.

Julia shook her head. "I don't know about you, but all I need is a shower and sleep."

She saluted the girls and marched to the communal bathroom. Copper pipes lined the sterile white tile walls between shower stalls. The room reminded her of the academy bathrooms. It seemed that ugly tile and tiny showers were a staple in all institutional dormitories – even the human high school had a similar looking locker room. Fresh white towels sat on shelves, so she took one and shed her clothes. She washed the last few days of grime from her body, spending a luxurious few extra minutes under the hot water. Wrapping the towel around herself, she went to get her clothes. The pile she'd left on the floor was gone.

"Hello?"

No one answered.

"Damnit, who took my clothes?"

Still no answer. She snuck out into the hall, wearing only the towel. Her own room was empty, so she knocked on Theo's door.

"She just went to have a shower," a white-robed Valera called from her doorway.

"Someone stole my clothes!" Julia growled.

"No one stole them. A nice woman came by and collected all our clothes. She said she would clean them and bring them back."

Julia grumbled, "What am I supposed to wear then?"

Valera gave her a dubious look. "They gave us robes."

Julia shook her head and grumbled, "No way! They're trying to convert us, Valera. And you're just going along with it?"

Valera put her hands on her hips. "You can go around naked if you prefer, but I'm going to clean up and stay comfortable. So if you'll excuse me."

Valera headed for the bathroom. Julia stood in the hallway wrapped in her now damp towel and shivered. A group of white robes walked past her hall and stared at her.

"What?" she huffed.

They whispered to each other and passed by laughing. Miffed, Julia slipped into her room and slammed her bedroom door.

"What a bunch of jerks," she said to herself.

"You must be Julia," a male voice said behind her.

She screamed and spun around. Julia suddenly felt like she'd eaten a spoonful of peanut butter. Her tongue stuck to the roof of her mouth, and she couldn't speak. A strange guy looked at her up and down, tilted his head, and smirked. She stared at his soft brown eyes unable to look away. He crossed his well-muscled arms across his chest, and leaned against the wall, a white robe slung over his shoulder.

"Are... you... Julia?" he spoke very slowly, as if she didn't understand English.

His sarcastic tone lit her fuse. The spell withered. She broke eye contact with him and scowled.

"Yes, I'm Julia. Who are you and what are you doing in here?"

His smirk never faltered. In one smooth motion, he stepped forward and held out a hand twice the size of hers. "Eli Jones, at your service."

"Good for you. Now get out!"

She looked down at his hand, raised an eyebrow and turned away from him. She became very aware that she was wearing nothing but a towel. Keeping hold of the suddenly too-tiny cloth in one hand, she scrambled for the white robe with the other. He let her grab it, but didn't leave.

"Do you mind?" She yelled.

"Not at all," he quipped, still not leaving. "I won't look."

He turned around and faced the wall. She slid the robe over her head, then shimmied into the nearby undergarments, all while hiding in the tent-like muumuu. He turned back around and chuckled. She refused to give him the satisfaction of knowing how annoyed and vulnerable she felt. The door was unlocked if she needed to make a quick getaway. She sat on a chair and assessed his physique, trying to ignore the soft brown eyes boring into her forehead.

"Not much of a talker, are you?" His voice sent a spark through her nerves.

He sat on the edge of the bed with his ever-present smirk. A loose strand of dark hair slipped from the leather thong tied at the base of his neck. Hanging close to his eye, that one strand of hair made her own eye twitch. She wanted him to do something about it, but loathed the idea of revealing anything about herself. Casually brushing her damp hair behind her ears, she pretended he wasn't there. He leaned back against the headboard, stretching his long legs in front of him and crossing his black boots on a crisp duvet.

"Ugh."

She eyed his dirty boots and rolled her eyes. He ignored her disgust and stretched his broad shoulders. The movement tugged at the unclasped collar of his shirt, giving a hint of the firm muscle underneath. She tried not to gawk, but his presence was intrusive and impossible to ignore. Questions flew through her mind. Why wasn't he wearing a white robe like everyone else? Why was he here? What were his intentions? Why did he make her feel so self-conscious?

She settled for something simple. "Why are you still here?"

"Parmelia, the leader of the Elders, sent me." He seemed pretty smitten with himself. "I'm supposed to keep an eye on you. You know, make sure you stay out of trouble." He closed his eyes and murmured, "Although you hardly seem worth the trouble."

"Excuse me?"

"This seems like a waste of my talents. I mean, come on, look at you. You're what? Fourteen? You're just a kid."

Her jaw dropped. "Fourteen? Not even close."

His eyes opened and he looked her over. "Oh, sorry. Twelve?"

"Ah... What? Uh... No. I'm almost seventeen, thank you very much." She looked him over and determined he wasn't much older than she was. "And who are you to call me a kid? How old are you? From the looks of you, I'd say no older than twenty."

"Nineteen – next month."

She didn't know whether to be insulted that her grandmother sent a *boy* to look after her, or happy. He'd certainly be easy enough to slip if she needed to. Although, she had no idea why Parmelia had sent someone so... conceited.

There's some guy in my room named Eli Jones, claiming that Parmelia sent him. Julia reached out to Theo and Valera.

What? Oh, no! Ow! Valera shrieked.

Are you all right, Valera? Valera...

No... no I'm okay. I just got soap in my eye.

Good grief, you sounded like someone was stabbing you to death, Julia snapped.

Theo chuckled. *Parmelia probably thought we could use a little help. Is this Eli person trustworthy?*

I don't know. He's a sarcastic pretty boy, but harmless enough... I think. Get this. He's only nineteen. And he's one of the most arrogant, annoying, rude people I've ever met.

Valera chimed in, *Sounds like a perfect fit then.*

Laugh it up, Valera.

Eli cleared his throat. "You're weird. Do you always stare blankly at people or is it just me?"

His laugh disrupted the connection between the girls. Julia hadn't realized she was staring straight at him as she spoke with Theo and Valera. Her cheeks burned. She hid her embarrassment behind her hands.

"You're so... annoying... and I'm not weird," she hissed.

"Touchy, aren't we."

"Shut up."

"So what did you do anyway? I mean it must've been bad because the Elders split and the city is in complete pandemonium," he quipped.

"Shut up."

He sighed, "We might as well get to know each other since we're stuck together."

She glared at him. "Shut up."

"Okay, fine. I'm going to check out the place. If you need anything—

"I won't."

Eli left the room, and Julia slammed the door behind him. He was undoubtedly the most insufferable person she'd ever met; and yet she couldn't stop thinking about him.

CHAPTER FIVE

Valera

Julia? Are you still there? Valera asked.

When Julia didn't respond, Valera decided to sneak over to her room. In the hall she ran into an over-sized mass of muscles. He smiled down at her and bowed. His manners didn't seem so horrible to Valera.

"Well hello, I'm —

"Eli Jones, I know." Valera tapped her bottom lip with her finger. "Hmm, I don't see why she was complaining. You seem nice enough to me. You'll have to excuse Julia's behavior. She can be a little prickly. I'm sure I'll see you around."

Valera waved to the confused looking man and skipped over to Julia's door. He wandered down the hall shaking his head. Poking her head into Julia's room, Valera inched her way in.

"What do you want?" Julia hissed.

"I'm just checking on you. I saw Eli in the hall. He's kind of cute," she chirped.

Julia glared at her. "Traitor."

"Who's a traitor?" Theo walked in and plopped onto Julia's bed.

"I am, because I think Eli is cute."

"Oh, is he?" Theo asked Julia.

Julia huffed and ignored both of them. Valera sat next to Theo and winked. Julia paced the room. Her face hardened, then softened several times over, and Valera deduced that Eli had something to do with it. Although, she was surprised that someone could affect Julia in such a way. Theo elbowed Valera in the ribs, and they both giggled.

"Will you two stop acting like children. This isn't a sweet sixteen slumber party you know. We're in a serious situation," Julia ranted.

Valera's cheeks hurt from forcing the smile off her face. Julia was right. They were in a precarious predicament, albeit an amusing one. She clasped her hands around her knees. Julia stopped pacing.

"So... I found out that the Elders have the artifacts from my father's vault," she spouted.

Valera figured it was a tactic to change the conversation. She would go along with it – for now. It was nice to see Julia so befuddled for once.

"That means they have Danu's relics. I'd love to get my hands on Aeda's Sextant."

Julia seemed to ease up. Valera grinned.

"Dr. Lawless said he'd let us take a look at them after he *assessed* our abilities."

"I'm guessing it's my turn tomorrow," Valera mused.

"Put on a good show." Julia rubbed the back of her neck and muttered, "I... uh, struggled today."

Valera stood up and stretched. "I feel like I haven't slept in weeks," she yawned. "If I'm going to make an impression on the doc then I need rest. Night, Theo... and sweet dreams, Julia." Valera waggled her brows. *Of Eli,* she said in their telepathic link.

Julia threw a chair pillow at her, hitting Theo instead. Theo screeched and threw it back at Julia before slipping out of the room. Valera could hear Julia ranting behind the closed door. Served her right for all the times, she teased Valera. Crawling under her covers, she luxuriated in the soft, warm bed. Within minutes, she drifted to sleep.

*

Daughter... help me...

Valera sat up and peered into the pitch black of night. The hour hand of the alarm clock inched past three. She'd been asleep for hours, and yet she felt like she'd just lain down. She swore she'd just heard her mother's voice. For a second, she thought her mother had come back for her.

"Hello? Mom is that you?"

She waited for a response. The clock ticked. Water rushed through pipes in the walls. Prowling night owls echoed through the halls. Her mother wasn't there. She lay back down and pulled the covers under her chin. The room felt cold and lonely. Closing her eyes, she tried to find sleep.

A woman screamed, and Valera's head erupted in pain. She grabbed her temples and curled into a ball. Behind her eyelids, she saw a woman suspended in air. Metallic snakes wrapped around her and squeezed the life from her. Something moved at the end of Valera's bed. Her blanket rippled, and she felt the cold, scaly beast wrap itself around her legs. Every muscle in Valera's body trembled. She slipped free, and threw her legs over the side of her bed. The floor writhed in the darkness, hissing. Hovering above the pit of snakes, a woman reached out to her.

Daughter, help me. Please. Hurry.

Valera screamed. The vision disappeared. Her headache ebbed. She threw her blankets back and found the bed empty. The floor was clear. She stood up, but the movement made her queasy. Her legs shook beneath her weight. The image had made her feel as if she'd just run a marathon. Her heart thumped in her chest and her muscles burned, leaving her breathless. She stumbled down the hall to the bathroom. After splashing water on her face, she reached out for the only people who would understand her strange vision.

Theo, Julia, are you there? Even in her mind, she sounded breathless.

I just had the worst nightmare, Theo responded.

I did too, only I wasn't sleeping. Valera sucked back the tears in her eyes. *It was Danu.*

I have the same dream every night, and they're getting worse, Julia added.

Should we tell Dr. Lawless about them? Valera asked.

Theo sighed. *It couldn't hurt.*

I don't care one way or the other, Julia said. *I'd just like to get a good night's sleep.*

Valera slunk back to her room. In the back of her mind, she could still see the snakes on her floor. She took a deep breath and hopped across her room, leaping onto her bed. Pulling the covers over her face, she closed her eyes. Sleep evaded her. All night long the distant cries of Danu haunted her. Even the warmth of aether couldn't drown out the goddess' torment. Valera spent the night churning under her blankets.

The morning came with a knock at her door. An Elder servant brought in a fresh white robe and slippers. Valera groaned and begrudgingly got out of bed. Shortly after dressing, Dr. Lawless appeared.

"Good morning," he chirped.

"Ugh."

The man was far too chipper for Valera's liking. He led her to the ballroom that Theo and Julia had described from the day before. She plopped into the chair and put her forehead on the table.

"Is everything all right, Valera. You seem fatigued," he asked.

She groaned, "Bad dreams."

"I see. Could you describe these dreams?" He pulled out a notebook and quill.

She looked up at him and yawned. "Danu is surrounded by snakes, begging for help. Last night was the worst one yet, though."

"She comes to all of you?"

"Yes, Julia, Theo, and I have the same nightmares. She calls out to us for help, but there's nothing we can do."

His face morphed into a twisted smile that alarmed Valera. He'd always seemed so composed, but the way his teeth gleamed made her think of a wolf baring his fangs. The grin disappeared, and he cleared his throat. Valera wondered if she imagined it all.

"Interesting, she actually speaks to you." He scribbled in his book. "We will delve into these dreams another day. Right now, I'd like to see your abilities."

Valera shrugged and pulled on aether. Tired as she was, controlling it was difficult. She formed flames on her palms and held them up. Dr. Lawless oohed and put the tip of the quill in the flame. The end of the feather shriveled, and a burnt hair smell wafted up to Valera's nose. She merged the two flames in her hands together. Julia said to create a show, so she did. The fire curled into a ring and swooshed around in a circle above his head. His eyes widened, and he shrunk away.

She extinguished the flame. "Sorry. I got carried away."

"No, no. It's just a little overwhelming. I should have known since you melted those shackles without much effort. Are there any other... powers that you've discovered?"

Valera wasn't sure what exactly the other two had told him. They had agreed to trust him, so she figured he may as well know all of it.

"The three of us can talk to each other... telepathically. We can also use aether as a kind of shield. Theo and I once combined our powers and it created a barrier. That's all I know... so far."

Dr. Lawless' hand flew across his page. "This is amazing... absolutely amazing. And you can hear Danu herself!"

"I don't know if it's Danu. We just have vivid dreams about her."

He looked up from his writing. His eyes ripped into her. His lips again split into that twisted grin. He lifted a finger and pointed between her eyes. He licked his lips. She surrounded herself in aether, wishing she could leave.

"Danu is *inside* of you. You are a very lucky girl, Valera." He inhaled sharply. "What I would give to bathe in her essence."

Valera flinched. The way he looked at her made her think he wanted to crack her open like a melon. He smoothed down his hair and tugged on his collar. She rubbed her eyes, wondering if his change was all in her head. She was exhausted, so maybe her eyes were playing tricks on her. When she opened her eyes, he was back to normal.

"I think it's time for you three to meet Professor Scrod. I know she's been looking forward to speaking with you. Shall we?"

He held his arm out. She reluctantly took it. They went back to the chambers tower and found Theo and Julia in the lobby. Eli lingered nearby, and Julia watched him from the corner of her eye. When he moved, she moved away. Theo was in the middle of this dance and seemed amused by it.

"Good morning, girls. I've got something rather exciting to show you." Dr. Lawless frowned when he saw Eli paying close attention. "Excuse me young man, but who are you?"

Valera frowned. Dr. Lawless didn't know about Eli, which meant Dr. Lawless hadn't spoken to Parmelia. Eli looked the doctor up and down. He smirked and put an arm on a startled Julia.

"Hey, Doc. I'm a friend of the girls." He winked.

Julia shrugged him off and brushed her arm as if an insect had been on her. Eli chuckled. Dr. Lawless' eye twitched. He cleared his throat.

"Well, I suggest you find something else to do. The girls have an important and *busy* day ahead of them." He stepped between Eli and the girls. "Follow me, ladies."

They left Eli in the lobby. As they neared a stairwell, Eli called back to them.

"See you later."

Theo giggled. *I don't know why you don't like him Julia. I think he's charming.*

Julia rolled her eyes.

Dr. Lawless is taking us to the relics. Guys, I am not sure about him. He kind of scares me. He was acting... weird earlier, Valera blurted.

He is a little weird. But he got us out of the cells, and he's helping us. Don't be such a yellow belly, Valera, Julia hissed.

Valera huffed at her. She crossed her arms and sulked all the way to the basement. On the lowest level of the building, they walked down a long dark corridor to a swinging double door that opened into a massive room. Dark splotches covered the peeling paint where water seeped through deep cracks. Puddles of water dotted the floors. A musty, briny smell filled the space. Rows of tables held equipment and the artifacts from *the Vault*. Several lab-coated researchers looked up from their work as the group entered. From the very back of the room a crazy-haired petite woman in a stained lab coat that was five sizes too large shuffled toward them. She pulled bright red glasses over her aqua-colored eyes. They covered half her face.

"Professor Scrod, I'm pleased to introduce you to the three sisters of the Trinity- Theo, Julia, and Valera," Dr. Lawless gushed and bowed to the woman.

"Oh, my, we weren't expecting you till much later. Ellwood, you naughty boy. You should have told me *they* were coming." The woman performed an awkward curtsy. "Welcome to our labs, oh, wondrous descendants of Danu. I am Professor Rowan Darmody Scrod, lead director of archeology."

She pulled her glasses to the edge of her nose. Her bright aqua eyes shone. A block of curled hair fell in front of her face, and she blew it out of the way. Her outstretched hand peeked out from under her ink blotched lab coat. Valera took it and the tiny woman shook the life out of Valera's arm.

"I'm honored to meet you girls. There's so much I'd like to ask. As you can see we've been archiving these items." She continued to shake Valera's hand, but turned to speak to Julia. "I assure you we are giving them the utmost respect that they deserve. Your father had quite an impressive collection."

Valera's arm ached. Using a little force, she pulled it away from Professor Scrod. The woman seemed surprised, and then jumped.

"Of course, you want to get right to work."

She spun around and scuttled back toward a room encased by filthy, cracked, glass walls. The girls followed her. At the entrance, Professor Scrod turned four dials and pulled a lever, and the rusted door creaked open.

With an excited grin, she proclaimed, "Behold the relics of Danu."

CHAPTER SIX

Julia

The three relics were displayed on a table. Now that she had her power, Julia hoped that the Sword of Ealga would respond to her. The crazy professor ushered them into the room. She reminded Julia of a nutty squirrel. Julia's eyes flicked over to Lawly, who seemed even more intense today. Valera was right, he was acting oddly. He gazed at the relics with a longing in his eyes that gave Julia an unsettled feeling.

"So far we've only examined the markings and materials of the relics. Unlike the other artifacts, they've been dormant. Unfortunately, we've had no luck activating them. According to legend, they hold great power. We're hoping perhaps you three can provide some insight." Professor Scrod tugged on a mass of curls.

"Julia, as the descendant of Ealga, why don't you try the sword," Dr. Lawless offered.

A twinge of nervousness niggled at Julia. Valera nudged her in the side and smiled.

Go ahead. You'll do great!

Julia stepped to the table edge and went to reach for Ealga's Sword of Ice.

"WAIT!" Professor Scrod yelled.

Everyone in the room jumped.

"What's wrong?" Julia yanked her hand away as if she were about to touch a porcupine.

The professor patted her lab coat and looked around the room franticly. "I need my notebook. I must notate everything!"

Julia shook her head. The woman was kooky. A notebook sat on the table in front of her. Julia cleared her throat and pointed to the book. Professor Scrod picked it up and hugged it like an old friend. She felt around her head of wild curls and pulled out a long pencil. Julia couldn't help but wonder what else she was hiding in that nest atop her head. Professor Scrod opened her book and flattened out a smudged page. She held her pencil at the ready. Everyone seemed to stop breathing, Julia included. Picking up the sword, Julia held it out in front of her. Everyone waited. And waited. And waited. Nothing happened. Julia swung the sword a couple of times. Nothing.

"I don't understand. I thought for sure..." Professor Scrod scribble in her notebook.

"What am I doing wrong?" Julia whined.

A crowd of watchers gathered outside the glass walls. She held it like a warrior about to strike, but nothing happened. The only thing that changed was the metal cooling in her hand. She put it back on the table and shrunk to the back of the room.

"According to the lore, Ealga's sword froze an entire lake with one touch." Professor Scrod frowned. "Perhaps one of the others might work."

Valera reached out for Aeda's Sextant. Julia felt the aether pull away from her. Valera held the Sextant up to her eye and looked through the eyepiece. However, without the sun or stars, all she saw was the dark. Once again, the room deflated with disappointment.

Dr. Lawless grew agitated. "Theo, why don't you try. You seem to be the strongest."

The barb incensed Julia. Theo wasn't the strongest, she'd just had more practice. Without realizing it, she'd gathered aether and cooled the room. Theo looked at her and smiled.

Don't listen to him, Julia. You've just turned the room into a freezer. She winked.

He better watch out. One more insult and I swear...

Ignore him. We're a team, Valera chimed in.

Julia's nerves calmed, but she glared at Dr. Lawless. She would show him. Theo touched Maera's Scepter with one finger. Julia startled at the loss of aether. Theo looked at the scepter as if it were a sleeping cobra. When nothing happened, she picked it up. At first, it seemed that the experiment was a failure. Julia felt vindicated, but then the scepter flickered. Theo seemed to concentrate on it even harder, and a spark erupted from the Aquamarine jewel.

"Don't stop! It's working! Look, how beautiful." Professor Scrod perked up and reached out to touch the jewel, and then seemed to pull back.

"Good job, Theo!" Valera cheered.

"Focus harder," Julia shouted. The excitement overpowered her resentment.

Theo bit her lip and squinted her eyes. Gripping it with both hands, she forced aether into the metal. Julia's hair lifted off her shoulders as did everyone else's. A static charge built up in the air. Theo let the staff touch the floor. The air sizzled and filled with bright white light.

Theo closed her eyes. The glass crackled all around them. Julia thought the walls were about to shatter. When Theo opened her eyes, the old cracks in the glass melded together and the filth burned away. The scientists outside the panes of crystalline glass gasped. Their hair began to rise as well. Julia felt Theo push the energy of the scepter beyond them. The massive room buzzed with life. All of the other artifacts in the larger room switched on at once. The room buzzed with noise and lights. When Theo's light touched the walls of the room, the stains disappeared and the fractures closed. The puddles on the floor boiled away.

Then all at once, Theo collapsed on the floor. Professor Scrod picked up the Scepter and placed it back on the table, muttering her amazement. Julia and Valera ran to Theo's side. Julia patted her cheek.

"Hey there, you still with us?"

Theo's eyes fluttered open. Julia smiled.

"I'm here. Just feel a little drained."

No wonder... You just had to show off. Julia laughed.

"Well you know me," Theo coughed.

The girls helped Theo get to her feet. They seemed to be the only ones concerned for Theo's wellbeing. Dr. Lawless and Professor Scrod jabbered to each other, smiling and laughing excitedly. The crowd outside cheered and examined the fixed walls.

"That's enough for today, Lawly. Theo's exhausted," Julia commanded.

Dr. Lawless frowned and grumbled. His anger frustrated Julia. Clearly, Theo needed to stop. Any trust she had for him disintegrated. Professor Scrod touched Lawly's back. Her brows furrowed, and she at least appeared concerned for Theo.

"Ellwood, they are young. We don't want to burn them out." She turned to the girls. "Get some rest. It was an honor to meet you, and please come see me anytime. I've so much to ask."

Julia ushered Theo and Valera toward the door. She wouldn't risk giving Lawly a chance to stop them. Professor Scrod opened the relic room door, and the crowd of technicians parted to let the girls through. Each of them bowed as the girls passed them. It was a strange feeling – to be acknowledged, to be given respect, to be adored. Most of her life had been a struggle for her father's attention, which he never gave her. Even though she hadn't performed like Theo, the people didn't discriminate between the three girls. Theo, Valera, and Julia were one.

With one final look back, Julia saw Lawly still inside the relic room, arguing with Professor Scrod. Julia thought it odd, but kept it to herself. She may not have a handle on her powers yet, but she was still the strongest of the three. In the end, she'd be the one to protect Valera and Theo. She helped Theo to her room.

"I'll just lay down for a little while," Theo murmured.

"If you need me holler. I'm just going to hang out in my room for a while," Julia said. Their time in the lab had taken a toll on her as well as Theo. Before leaving, she added, "Good job in there."

Theo smiled, and Julia went to her room. Sitting on the edge of the bed, she bathed herself in aether. Theo had shown her just how powerful they all were, and now all she needed to do was tap into that power. She just needed practice. If Theo and Valera could do it, then so could she. She was as intelligent as Theo and Valera – regardless of what Lawly thought.

She focused on aether and waved her hands around. Her breath came out in puffy white steam. The room cooled.

"Ice… Ice… Ice…" she chanted.

The tips of her fingers turned an iridescent blue. She was doing it. Redoubling her efforts, she envisioned icicles. A small crystal of ice grew out of her hand. She squealed and nearly lost her concentration. Then, her doorknob turned and Eli burst into the room.

"Hey there… whoa it's freezing in here!"

The ice fizzled into nothing. Angry, she threw a pillow at him. He caught it.

"You just ruined everything!"

"Chill, I didn't mean to interrupt… whatever this was." He smirked.

He thought he was so witty. He was an egomaniacal dimwit.

"Do you always just burst into people's rooms? Who do you think you are?" She ranted.

He shut the door. "Parmelia told me to keep an eye on you, remember?" He shrugged, "Besides I heard that you had some trouble in the lab. I just came to give you a message."

"Who told you that? I didn't have any trouble." She sat up and crossed her arms. "Well? What's the message?"

"Dr. Lawless wants to see you in the ballroom in twenty minutes. He said you need extra help."

She was tired of Dr. Lawless. He made her feel so… pathetic. Besides, she was doing better alone in her room. And who was Eli to Dr. Lawless? She thought Parmelia sent him, but now he's all buddy-buddy with Lawly? Her suspicions were on full alert.

"What, are you Dr. Lawless' lackey now?"

Eli sighed and crossed his arms. "I'm not *anyone's* lackey. Are you always this stubborn?"

Julia gripped the bed covers and clenched her jaw. She refused to answer his insulting question. If he wanted to play games, then fine. She was above such childishness.

"Well, I'm not feeling well. I'll have to miss the meeting," Julia feigned, flopping back on the bed and pulling a cover over her.

"Nice try. You're going," Eli stated. "I'm not going to be the one to tell Dr. Lawless you're too pigheaded to go."

Julia glared at him. "Don't you have anything better to do than hover around me all the time. Go bug one of the batty-eyed girls in the lobby."

She knew that needling him was a mistake, when that annoying smirk returned. He plopped on the bed, smushing the mattress and forcing her to roll toward him. She shuffled away from his side. He grabbed a corner of the blanket, acting as if it held some interest.

"Of course, I have better things to do than watch a spoiled brat, but I've been ordered to protect your petulant fanny. Not many could handle the task, that's for sure. I drew the short stick." He stood suddenly, taking the blanket with him. "So up you get. Time to train."

Even though she was fully clothed under the covers, she suddenly felt very vulnerable. She yanked the blanket back, but he had a solid grip on it. They ended up in a one-sided tug-of-war.

"Come on it's not fair..." she whined. "I'll do better practicing in here by *myself*."

Eli didn't even struggle. With one yank, he could pull her right off the bed. He held tight to the blanket and laughed.

"Why do you care if I go? You know if you did me the favor and tell him I'm sick, I'll do you a favor in return." She gave up the fight and released the blanket.

"Are you flirting with me? Julia, I'm shocked," Eli quipped.

Her jaw went limp. She wasn't flirting... was she? He was the most detestable, obnoxious, cretin she'd ever met. Besides, she didn't flirt. Somehow the ability to speak clearly escaped her.

"No... of course not... you're so not my type... you're like the opposite of my type... you're so... so... not..."

"Uh, huh," he smirked. "Whatever you say."

"Danu's ass! You're so annoying!"

"Language, Julia. What would your parent's think?" He laughed.

The mention of her parents stung. Clearly, no one bothered to mention to him who her parents were. All of this training and running around had made her soft. Tears stung her eyes. Her shoulders slumped. She stared at her hands, trying to keep her cool. The last thing she needed was for Eli to see her weakness.

"You okay?" His voice softened.

Julia took a deep breath. "Yeah."

For such an oaf, he was well tuned-in to her emotions. She felt his hand on her shoulder. He dropped the blanket and knelt down in front of her. She was surprised that he seemed genuinely concerned about her.

"Sorry, I didn't mean to say something offensive."

Julia scoffed. "When have my feelings ever stopped you?"

"Seriously, I'm sorry."

"It's okay," she sighed. "How are you supposed to know? No one told you about my parents."

She didn't know why she was still talking to him. She should kick him out of her room. She should condemn him for butting into her personal life. She should yell and scream and curse at him, but something in his brown eyes made her *want* to talk. He sat beside her.

"I wasn't told anything. Things must be pretty bad though. With your parents, I mean."

She nodded. "They're both dead. My father... he was not a good person."

Eli tensed up. "Sorry. I know how that is. My parents are dead too. They died when I was little. The Elders took me in and raised me. As you can imagine, it was *loads* of fun," he grunted.

She smiled. "I was raised in the academy of the Azure Serpents... *loads* of fun."

"Whoa, Azure Serpents, that's formidable. You must be a real rogue, then." He nudged her side, making her grin. "Was that an actual smile? I must be growing on you."

"Yeah, like a fungus."

"But an extremely good-looking fungus." He waggled his eyebrows.

Julia punched his arm and got out of bed. Their conversation was making her nervous. The last thing she needed was to get muddled up with a guy like Eli. As much as she didn't want to, she had to go see Dr. Lawless. She had to prove that she was just as good as Theo and Valera. She also wanted a chance to prod Lawly for more information and to see what his real intentions were. Eli escorted her down to the ballroom, where Dr. Lawless waited for her by the door. He frowned when he saw Eli close behind her.

"You may go now. She's in good hands," Dr. Lawless grit through his teeth.

Eli didn't move. He smiled at Julia and leaned against the wall outside the door. "I'll wait here for you."

She nodded to him. Dr. Lawless grumbled and ushered Julia inside the room before closing the door on Eli. Julia sat in the same chair as before. Lawly plopped down across from her.

"It's good to see you, my little ice queen," Dr. Lawless quipped.

She cringed. She was not an ice queen, and especially not *his* ice queen. She questioned his game. He meant to put her in a place of discomfort. She squinted at him. *Okay, I'll play it your way.*

"Hello, Lawly," she said, drawing out the nickname so she sounded like a cowboy.

His brows dropped. Julia could get under his skin too. She smiled. She tapped her fingernails on the table. He stood up and paced the room.

"I'd like you to tell me about the dream you girls have been experiencing. Valera told me you've been having nightmares."

Julia shifted in her seat. Even though they'd agreed on telling him about the dreams, she didn't like talking about them. Every time she closed her eyes, she could see the vision of Danu ensnared by snakes. She saw him smile out of the corner of her eye. This was all part of his game. *Bold move, Doc.*

"It's the same thing every night. Danu is being squeezed by snakes. She calls for help. I wake up."

At the mention of Danu's name, he rubbed his temples and shuddered. The dreams seemed to agitate him as much as it did her, but she didn't understand his reaction. Julia stood up, needing to move.

"She's suffering... suffering..." he whispered under his breath.

Julia stepped away from him. He was losing it. "Did you say something, Doc?"

"No... no... I'd..." he mumbled.

She decided to switch topics. His muttering was unnerving. "I managed to make an icicle in my room," she chirped.

"Well done, uh... I think... we're done for today, Julia. You may leave."

Her time in the Academy hadn't prepared her for this. She couldn't figure out his plan. First, he called her down to train. She didn't want to come, but she did. And now he dismissed her as if she were a child. She put her hands on her hips. She was done playing.

"I thought you were going to help me?"

"Tomorrow perhaps."

"No, not tomorrow... Now."

He spun around and charged at her, stopping inches from her face. Julia stood her ground, but fear bubbled inside her. The intensity in his eyes felt accusatory and dangerous. She could smell fish on his breath and the sweat on his skin. She clenched her fists and the hair on her arms spiked.

"I say when and where you train," he hissed. "Go back to your room."

An intense iron taste filled her mouth. Aether oozed into her pores. He had no right to treat her this way. She was one of the Trinity. She straightened her backbone, ready to lash out at him. His eyes widened, and he stumbled back a few steps. Suddenly, the door opened and Slammy Magee entered the room with a host of white robes.

"Remove her from the room," he ordered one of his men.

Two white robes stalked toward her. She remembered one of them from when Parmelia came to her cell. His swollen eye looked painful. A sly smile spread on his face. She prepared to fight. Before they reached her, Eli trotted through the door. He approached her and touched her arm.

"You heard the man." He winked. "Let's go."

The bruised man exhaled like a balloon losing its air, and his leer was replaced by a frown. She followed Eli out. Another white robe, slammed the door behind them. Instead of leaving, she stayed behind and put her ear to the door. Eli kept watch.

"I've been informed that you let the girls speak with Professor Scrod, and that those... deviants touched the relics. What were you thinking?" Slammy yelled at Dr. Lawless.

Eli touched her elbow. "We shouldn't linger."

"One minute," she whispered, holding up her palm

Before Dr. Lawless could answer, Slammy continued, "Do you know what they could do with those relics? It would be the end of us! We have to control them until it's time—

Eli took hold of her elbow. "Someone's coming."

This time she nodded, and they headed straight for Theo's room. Julia stormed into the room, fuming. Eli slipped in behind her and shut the door. Julia's nerves were on fire. She walked around the room, cracking her knuckles.

"What happened?" Theo asked from the bed.

"He asked me about the dream. I told him, and then he got all... creepy. He dismissed me and threatened me when I questioned him. Then, Slammy came into the room and ordered me out. I don't know, you guys... this seems to be getting weird. Lawless really freaked me out, and Slammy seems pretty pissed that we were in the labs," Julia railed. "He said they had to *control* us."

"What does that mean?" Valera asked from the chair, startling Julia. "Why is it so cold in here?"

Julia hadn't realized Valera was in the room, or that she was still holding aether. Eli wrapped his arms around his body and breathed out mist.

"Okay, okay, Julia, ease up. I'm turning into an ice cube," Eli chattered through his teeth.

Julia smiled, but released the cold.

Valera bit her nails. "What if we can't get back into the lab? I barely had a chance to study Aeda's Sextant."

"I have an idea. We should sneak downstairs at night, so you can use the relics on your own," Eli suggested.

Julia raised an eyebrow at him and grinned. "Aren't you supposed to keep us *out* of trouble?"

He laughed. "I figure it's better to help you learn to control your power, than to end up an icicle."

Theo and Valera giggled. Julia couldn't find words to express her feelings. No one had ever made her feel so confused before. She could feel her cheeks burning.

"I, uh... He's right. We need to practice on our own. What do you say?" Julia blurted.

"Let's do it," Theo nodded.

"Tonight," Valera said.

With that, Julia escaped to her room. She tried to stay awake to avoid the bad dreams. She practiced holding and releasing aether, but her thoughts drifted to Eli and his insufferable smirk. She refocused on ice and cold air. Her eyes stung from fatigue. She yawned, closing her eyes for just a moment.

Danu was there, calling out to her. Julia felt her pain. She was aware of everything around her. She tried to wake up, but was pulled deeper into the nightmare.

"Wake up, Sleepy," Eli whispered, gently tugging on her arm.

Groggy, she wiped her eyes and peered into the dark. A small light appeared in front of her. Eli hovered over her, grinning.

"How long was I out?" she asked.

"A few hours. I think we're good to go. I checked the halls, and everyone seems to have gone away."

Julia's body protested her late night wakeup. She reconsidered their midnight practice session, but had little choice. Eli took both her hands and hauled her to her feet. She groaned and followed him out the door. Theo and Valera waited in the hall. They slipped down the empty corridors, avoided the few straggling night owls, and snuck into the labs.

The scientists had left the lab open, but had locked the relic room.

"Damnit," Julia huffed.

Eli just grinned and moved the four dials. With a bow, he pulled the lever and the door creaked open. Julia clapped.

"I happen to be a very observant person with an excellent memory. Not to mention, Professor Scrod doesn't exactly keep the combination secret. After a drink or two, her technicians get chatty."

Theo and Valera clapped. Julia groaned. Why did they have to encourage him? It was bad enough he was boasting about taking technicians out on dates. Not that Julia was jealous. Valera gave Julia a nudge into the room. Ealga's Sword of Ice was still laying on the table. Before touching it, Julia opened herself to aether. The room grew cold.

"You can do this, Julia," Theo said.

"I should have worn a coat," Eli teased.

"Shush, I'm focusing."

She waved her hand over the blade of the sword and felt a tingling sensation. It was a start. She gripped the worn leather hilt and converged all of her energy into the sword. Although, nothing spectacular happened, she could feel a bond with the weapon. It wanted her to pick it up. Theo, Valera, and Eli shivered in the corner.

"Maybe work with something else without a blade. See if you can control your power before trying to use the sword." Steam rose from Valera's mouth as she spoke.

Julia didn't want to release the relic, but Valera was right. She needed to conquer aether before wielding Ealga's sword. Replacing the blade on the table, she faced the others. In her mind, she formed an ice mound. Holding her arms in front of her, she centered aether in one spot on the floor. When she opened her eyes, a knee-high blob of snow sat in front of her. She stomped her foot, and the pile melted into a puddle.

"This is not what I pictured in my head. I don't understand."

"Try to relax a little," Theo suggested. "You're so tense."

"Yeah, let aether flow. Don't force it," Valera added.

Their advice frustrated her even more. She knew she was tense. Her jaw ached because she was so tense. How could she not be tense? Eli came out of the corner and touched her shoulders. Theo and Valera suddenly disappeared into the background as if they weren't even there.

"You can do this," he whispered.

She looked into his soft brown eyes. The air swirled around them and grew frigid. The puddle froze beneath her feet. The urge to be closer to him moved her forward, but her foot slipped on her icy creation. She stumbled forward. Unable to steady herself, she ploughed into Eli's body. With an oomph, they both crashed to the ground, Julia landing on top of him. The ice melted under their bodies. Mortified, Julia shifted, trying to stand. Her foot slipped in the water, and she slammed back into him – hard.

"For Danu's sake, stop," Eli moaned.

Julia stilled. Theo and Valera started laughing, making her even more self-conscious. Julia rolled off him and covered her face. Eli grabbed his ribs where she'd crushed him.

Theo took Valera's arm. "Um, we're going to go look around at the other artifacts."

They bolted out of the room. Julia's cheeks could have melted the sun. She couldn't look at Eli, so she lay on her back, trying to hide her embarrassment.

"I'm sorry. I didn't mean to hurt you," she murmured.

He turned on his side and brushed hair from her face. She turned to face him. His smirk was radiant. Julia didn't know if she should crawl away, or stay. She couldn't look away. His finger traced the line of her cheek.

"I know," he whispered.

Pulling away, she stood up.

"I... uh, I... maybe I should..." she stammered.

He sighed. "You're right. We're here to practice. Not play."

He winked at her and got up. Relieved and reeling, she closed her eyes and soaked in aether. The energy felt like a shield around her. With a deep breath, she reformed the icicle in her mind. This time she felt the power flowing through her arms and out her hands. A pillar of ice rose at her feet. It grew until it reached the ceiling.

"Ahem!" Professor Scrod stood at the door, tapping her foot on the floor.

Julia jumped. She suddenly felt like a naughty child caught playing in in her mom's armoire. Even Eli wilted. Professor Scrod entered the room and dug through the pockets of her house robe.

"I don't even have my notebook! How am I going to record this?" She tsked at the two of them. "You should have woken me. Amazing... just amazing. How did you form the pillar? Did the Sword activate your power? Was the ice created from the moisture in the air? Hold on a second, I need to write this down."

Professor Scrod left the room and proceeded to tear apart a desk. Pens, books, and a large stapler went flying. Theo and Valera returned to the room. They grabbed Julia and hugged her. She'd finally done something on her own.

"That was awesome!" Theo squealed.

"Ah, ha!" Professor Scrod shouted.

The lab doors burst open and a light shone into the room. Eli dropped to the ground and the girls followed his lead.

Professor Scrod walked back into the glass room and blocked the door. Someone approached the professor. Julia held her breath.

"Rowan, is that you?" A male voice rumbled.

"Yes, yes, I forgot my notebook down here and had an epiphany and needed to write it down right away before I forgot and I came down here to find it so no need to worry nothing strange going on down here. . ." Professor Scrod's disjointed explanation drifted off into silence.

Julia cringed. The professor's rambling would raise suspicion for sure. The guard shone his light into the glass wall, but Professor Scrod stood in front of him. Julia heard the man grumble.

"Any reason the relic room is open? Is that ice?"

"Well, you see after I found my notebook I remembered a marking I saw on the Sword and decided to make a note of it because it was important and that is what I do and it couldn't wait so I opened the door. It gets very cold down here at night... I saw a water leak in the ceiling yesterday. It must have frozen. I'll get it looked at right away."

"If you say so, Rowan. Just lock up when you leave," the guard chuckled at the woman.

"Of course, I am the lead director of archeology. I do know how to lock things up..." she continued on even after the man walked away.

The lab door closed, and Professor Scrod popped into the room. A huge crooked-toothed grin appeared on her face.

"You can come out now. I have so many questions to ask you..."

CHAPTER SEVEN

V*alera*

Midway through Professor Scrod's babbling, Valera dozed off. It was wonderful that Julia had finally managed to use aether, but the cold exhausted her. Valera had stepped into the lab, found a quiet corner, and surrounded herself in warmth. She hadn't had a good night sleep in ages. However, her nap was short lived.

"I thought I'd find you down here," Dr. Lawless stated, hovering over her.

Forming a small flame in her hand, she examined his face for any sign of crazy. Lately, she never knew which personality would present itself – Dr. Lawless or Mr. Dubious. Tonight, he seemed normal.

She yawned, "We came to practice."

"I see. Why was I not consulted?"

He appeared hurt, but a flash of anger flickered in his eyes. Valera frowned. He needed a reminder of who he was dealing with. She smiled politely, but the fireball in her hand flickered and grew. Whatever hold he thought he had was in his head.

"We weren't sure how you'd react after your little repartee this afternoon," she shrugged.

He scoffed, "I thought I made my position clear. I'm on your side." Sighing, he rubbed his chin. "Well, we should join the others. I have something I need to discuss with you girls."

Valera took her time in standing up. She was still miffed at being awaken. Inside the relic room, Julia worked with the sword. Swirling patterns of ice covered the blade and a pale blue light shone from the metal. She touched the tip of the blade to an ice pillar. The sword vibrated in her hand. A musical chime filled the room. The ice expanded. Tentacles spread across the ceiling and down the walls. The glass froze over. Before the entire room became a giant block, Julia released aether. In an instant the ice dissipated, raining down on them in a fine mist.

"Julia! I can't believe it," Dr. Lawless said, surprising everyone in the room.

"What are you doing here," Julia snapped.

"I came to speak with you three. You're in danger. The True Followers are unhappy with the progress you've made. I was hoping they'd give me more time to find another way, but..."

"Another way for what?" Theo asked.

"They've decided to perform the ritual earlier than I expected." He looked at Professor Scrod, whose face shriveled.

"What ritual?" Julia spat.

Dr. Lawless' Adam's apple bobbed in his neck. "There's a codex that suggests that the suffering of the Trinity will release Danu. Professor Scrod and I disagree, but the leadership is impatient. I was working on another way, but we're out of time."

"What do you mean our suffering?" Julia shrieked.

"The plan to sacrifice you, but I won't let that happen. However, we don't have much time..."

"Are you kidding? Sacrifice? Danu's Ass," Julia growled.

"Like Dr. Lawless said, we won't let that happen. We believe that Aeda's Sextant is the key to finding the tomb," Professor Scrod said, scrambling around the room. "Valera, it's up to you."

Professor Scrod held the sextant out to Valera, but Valera didn't take it. Taking a step back, she shook her head. She didn't like being the object of everyone's curiosity. They all looked at her expectantly. She didn't know how to use the Sextant. Professor Scrod had to be mistaken. Valera's insides twisted. Even though the room was freezing, she felt beads of sweat forming on her forehead. Aether teased her, and the smell of salt burned her nose.

"I can't..."

Theo took the Sextant from Scrod's hand and approached Valera. "You have to try. We can't stay here any longer. This is the only way. We'll be right here with you."

Valera took the instrument. Professor Scrod picked up her notebook and prepared to make notes. Everyone else stood back. Valera felt like throwing up. She held the Sextant in her hands, turning it slowly before bringing it up to her eye. She channeled aether into it. The metal warmed in her hands. She pushed herself harder. A faint light flickered in the eyepiece.

"All I see is a small light," she stammered. "It isn't working."

Julia and Theo stood next to her. She felt their hands on her shoulders as they added their power to hers. An intense blast of aether flowed through her. The instrument hummed and shook in her hands. She focused on aether and chanted "Danu" over and over again in her mind. The light became stronger and poured from the eyepiece, blinding Valera. She pulled the Sextant away from her eyes.

"Look, on the far wall!" Eli pointed out shapes forming on the wall. "It's a projection of...."

Professor Scrod squealed, "A map!"

An image of the world shone on the wall. The Arctic Ocean appeared, and, just north of Iceland, a small spot of light twinkled. Valera knew what the dot represented – the Sextant was showing them the location of Danu's tomb.

All three girls said in unison, "She's there."

The professor marched up to the wall and squinted at the dot. "Are you sure? Perhaps it's a piece of dust on the mirror."

"I'm sure. Hurry." Valera's voice shook, and her strength weakened.

Professor Scrod scribbled the map in her book. Valera couldn't hold aether any longer. The map faded in and out on the wall. She had to release aether or risk passing out. Theo and Julia let go of her, and all three collapsed to the floor. The map disappeared.

"We know where to go now," Valera breathed.

Relief flooded her. She hoped that the nightmares would end, and life would return to normal. They were so close.

"I knew you were conspiring against us! I've known all along," a man shouted from the lab doors. "I want them arrested. All of them."

Slammy stormed into the room with a platoon of white robes. His men moved forward, charging at the relics room. Valera struggled to her feet, leaning on Theo and Julia. Professor Scrod handed her the notebook.

"Keep it safe," she whispered before leaving.

She closed the door to the relics room, locking them inside. Turning on Slammy's men, she held her hands in the air.

"Stop, I... order you to stop... these people are here on my request... they are —

"Enough Scrod! You have no authority," Slammy screamed.

The professor turned to face the relics room. She looked at Dr. Lawless and mouthed the word, "Go." Grabbing a copper-coiled pistol from the table, she aimed it at the approaching guards. She pulled a trigger and an electric bolt shot from the muzzle. It hit two of the men, and they fell to the ground twitching. Eli dragged a large table to blockade the door, holding off anyone who tried to get in. The lab erupted into chaos. More men stormed Professor Scrod. She shot one more time before she was disarmed. Mercy wasn't a word in Slammy's vocabulary. Valera felt helpless as she watched Slammy's men beat the professor.

"We have to help her," Valera shouted, banging on the door. "We're trapped in here!"

Eli pulled her away. "There's nothing we can do right now."

Dr. Lawless opened a drawer and removed the Trinity Key, stuffing it into a duffle bag along with the three relics of Danu.

"This way." Dr. Lawless cranked a lever and a hidden doorway opened. "Hurry."

Dr. Lawless went through first, followed by Theo, Julia, and Valera. Eli snapped off the gear that opened the secret door and squeezed through before it closed. He lit a torch and whispered to the doctor.

"I know a place we can hide until we figure this out," Eli informed them. "Follow me."

The tunnels curved and zigzagged for what felt like forever. Valera wondered if they'd ever find their way out the labyrinth. Everyone stopped in front of her. They'd arrived at a welded metal grate. Aether and anxiety slipped through her, creating a wave of heat in the cramped space. Theo touched her arm.

"Everything will be okay," she whispered.

The grate screeched open, and they emerged into an alley in the dirty part of the city. Instead of the glorious glass buildings, dilapidated wood structures surrounded them. The air smelled like rotten eggs, which made Valera gag. She wrapped her collar around her face, but it only dampened the odor.

Julia wretched. "What is that?"

Eli turned to her and handed her a handkerchief. "Welcome to the Lows of Pacifica City. Put this over your nose. You'll get used to the smell." He pointed to a fissure in the ground. "It comes from the sulfuric gases. Pacifica uses the volcanic vents to heat the city. The air recyclers don't always work in this part of town."

Eli led them through the seedier part of town as if he'd frequented the place in the past. The simple boards that formed a sidewalk sank into the wet sandy ground. Crabs skittered in the alleyways, picking at the muck. Loud music and boisterous voices emanated from the series of gambling and drinking establishments. Greenish slime grew on the rotted wood planks of the buildings.

"Where are we going?" Julia asked Eli.

He took her hand and helped her step over a drunken man lying across the walkway. Valera followed along behind, but the drunkard grabbed her ankle.

She shrieked, "Get away from me!"

"Hey, yer a purdy lil thing, ain'tcha," the man slurred. "Be nice to an ole' man."

She kicked him as hard as she could. He yelped, pulling his hand away and coddling it.

"Ya don't hafta be so sore bout it," he huffed.

He struggled to stand, smacked his filthy brown cowboy hat on his leg, and stumbled back into *The Crooked Crab Tavern*.

Valera felt the urge to scrub the spot where the man had touched her.

"Are you all right?" Theo asked.

Valera nodded, but stayed close to the others.

"Keep moving. We're almost there," Eli said from the front of the pack.

They wound through a few busy streets and came to a quieter neighborhood. The buildings were brick, but they still lacked the grandeur of the Elders' tower. They stopped in front of *Madame Blackbird's Hostelry*, a crumbling, two-story place.

Two lace curtains cracked open and a dark figure appeared. Eli walked up the steps and pulled on a cord. A bell rang inside the building, and the figure disappeared from the window. The door swung open, and a robust woman with a massive pile of blonde hair on her head filled the frame.

"Eli, mon beau oiseau! We've missed you," the woman squealed.

When she moved, her ample breasts threatened to leap out of her low-cropped chemise and cinched purple corset. The woman grabbed Eli and buried him between her cleavage. Julia gasped. He came up for air and turned to his friends. His face was visibly redder than before the woman's hug. He looked at Julia and grimaced an apology. Valera stifled a laugh. If Eli wasn't careful, Julia would skin him alive.

"Madame Blackbird, my friends and I need a place to stay."

"Of course, bien venue. Come in, please."

She opened the door wide and smiled at everyone. When they were all inside, she looked up and down the street before shutting her door. She clapped her hands and a teenage girl rushed into the room. The girl smiled coyly at Eli, wrapping her hands around his bicep and giggling. Valera peeked over at Julia, and saw pure venom.

Don't do anything rash, Julia. Valera said. *We're guests here.*

Theo looked between Eli and Julia and added, *We don't know that there's anything between them.*

Julia scoffed, *Why would I care. He can do as he likes. I don't care... I can't stand him.*

Valera sighed. Julia was always so hard even when her heart must be breaking. If it had been Gideon, Valera would have turned the girl to ashes... or at least singed her eyelashes off her fluttering eyelids. Madame Blackbird cleared her throat, and the teen girl released Eli.

"This is Alouette, my daughter. She'll show you to your rooms, where you can freshen up."

Alouette twisted the end of her braided blonde hair that hung like a fishtail over her shoulder. Perfect ringlets of hair framed her high cheekbones. Her violet colored eyes flicked back to Eli before she ushered the girls upstairs. Valera had the sudden urge to blacken those pretty purple-tinted eyes. Even if Julia denied her feelings for Eli, Valera couldn't take Alouette's utterly flirtatious behavior.

"You are friends with Eli?" She asked in a thick French accent.

"Yes, he's our friend," Valera snapped at Alouette.

The way she purred Eli's name irked Valera. The girl was clearly trying to size them up. Valera noticed Julia ball up her fists. She touched Julia's shoulder. It was ice cold. Julia grit her teeth and shrugged Valera's hand away. Alouette stopped and turned with her hands on her curvy hips. Her violet eyes flickered over the girls one at a time. With her nose upturned, her pouty lips grinned.

"Humph, I too am his... *bonne* amie," she simpered. She continued down the hall muttering, "Mais, je ne savais pas qu'il aimait les chiennes hideux ausi."

Even though Valera had a French tutor, she'd never picked up the language. However, she knew enough to know that Alouette was insulting them – something about Eli liking dogs. She felt Julia draw on aether.

Easy, Julia. She's not worth it, Theo said.

Julia huffed, *Why not? The tramp deserves a good beating.*

She does, but now's not the right time, Valera said, scowling at Alouette's back.

Theo moved to Julia's other side and linked arms with her. The gesture seemed casual to an ordinary onlooker, but Valera knew Theo was holding Julia back. Valera felt Julia release aether, but saw that she kept her fists in tight balls. Alouette opened a room with three small cots in it. A small cracked washbasin sat on a square table, and a dingy lace curtain hid a view of the alley. Valera stepped onto a damp spot on the threadbare rug and cringed.

"Désolé, we had a small incident in here a few days ago… blood stains are quite difficult to clean." Alouette feigned a frown. She shrugged, and her smirk returned. "This is our finest room. Nice and cozy, oui?"

Valera doubted that this was anywhere near their finest room. She was about to complain, but Alouette slammed the door on her way out. Valera approached one of the cots and lifted a corner of the blanket, expecting to see stained sheets covered in creepy crawlies. The clean white sheets covering the beds were a surprise.

"Well at least the beds are clean."

Julia scoffed, "I guarantee a black light would prove otherwise."

Julia threw herself on a cot and crossed her boots on the footboard. Valera didn't understand what Julia meant, but she didn't want to know either. Valera slumped onto the mattress.

She could feel one of the springs poking through the blankets. She didn't care if it were a bed of nails. She was exhausted.

"How do they know each other?" Julia blurted. "I mean, of course, I don't really care. I'm just making conversation. I just didn't think this is the kind of place Eli would frequent. You know?"

"Maybe they're just acquaintances. I wouldn't worry about it. I'm sure Eli has way better taste than a wispy, innkeeper's daughter." Valera closed her eyes and yawned.

"What kind of acquaintances giggle and bat their eyes. Did you see her? She was practically drooling," Julia hissed. "It's not that I care."

Valera rolled her eyes behind her eyelids. If Julia said she didn't care one more time, Valera would scream. She obviously cared a great deal. Eli and Julia were perfect for each other – they were both arrogant and stubborn.

Theo sat next to a Julia and sighed, "You should ask him about it. Don't torture yourself with speculation. Trust me."

"Why should I... I don't ca—

"For Danu's sake, you *DO* care, Julia. Just admit it. Go talk to him and get his side of the story," Valera groaned.

Julia's eyes grew wide. The room grew colder, but Valera countered it with heat.

"Will you two stop it! Enough, Julia, Valera's right. Go talk to him," Theo said opening the window for some air.

"Fine, I will. But not because I care—

Both Valera and Theo screeched, "Just go!"

Julia stood up and marched to the door. The knob turned before she could grasp it, and Eli's face appeared in the crack. His smirk had transformed into a sheepish sulk. Julia faced him, murmuring under her breath. She stepped out, leaving the door open. Theo and Valera moved closer to the door just out of sight, but within earshot.

"Before you say anything, let me explain," Eli pleaded.

Julia scoffed, "What is there to explain?"

Eli let out a long exasperated breath, "Just hear me out. In the past, Madame Blackbird has done favors for certain members of the Elders. She... attains items, which can't be obtained otherwise. The leadership is pretty strict and forbids various human made goods. A certain professor has a penchant for whisky. On occasion, she asked me to run orders. That's how I know Madame Blackbird and Alouette."

"You're talking about Professor Scrod? You expect me to believe that she drinks whiskey?" Julia gritted.

Professor Scrod didn't seem the type to drink hard liquor, but then again she was muddle-headed. Valera giggled behind her hand, eliciting a jab from Theo. Theo put her finger over her lips. Valera shrugged.

"She does. I swear it," Eli muttered.

Julia pretended to be disinterested. She picked at her fingernails and yawned. "Well, I don't care how you know *these* people. I mean, it's clear that Alouette is quite... smitten with you. If you're into *that* kind of girl, then who am I to judge." Julia's voice became more strained as she spoke.

"No, it's not like that. I mean... Yes, Madame Blackbird kind of has her eyes on having me as her son-in-law. But only because there aren't many *options* around this part of the city and, well, the Blackbirds aren't exactly welcome in the nicer parts of the city." Eli sounded tired. "BUT, I've turned her down every time."

Valera wondered how long Julia would deny her real feelings. It was obvious to her that Eli liked her... a lot. Out of the corner of her eye, she saw a blonde head pop up near the stairs. She pointed it out to Theo, and they both slunk closer to the door. Julia was too busy arguing with Eli to notice, so they waved to Julia. When Julia saw them, Valera nodded toward the stairs and mouthed the name "Alouette." Julia grinned and grabbed Eli's face, planting a kiss on his lips. He jumped at first, then wrapped his arms around her. Valera and Theo burst into a silent fit of giggles.

A loud gasp interrupted the couple.

Alouette growled, "So this is why you don't want me. Humph, you have such cheap tastes, mon chère."

"Cheap? I'm cheap?"

Valera felt Julia soak herself in aether. Before she started an indoor blizzard, Valera and Theo burst from the room and grabbed Julia's arm. Julia struggled against her friends' grasp. Alouette's eyes formed slits. She crossed her arms under her chest and tapped her foot on the ground.

"Oui. Cheap," Alouette chirped.

Julia's skin turned to ice in Valera's hands. If they didn't ease the tension soon, she'd get up with frostbite and Alouette might end up a human snow girl. Valera tugged Julia's arm toward the bedroom door. She tried to pull in aether to warm the hall up, not wanting to raise suspicions. They didn't need anyone inquiring about their real identities or why they were hiding at a boarding house in the Lows.

"Julia, we have something to show you... in the room..." Valera muttered.

"Yeah, in the room," Theo mimicked, giving Julia a shove.

With a lot of effort and a bunch of coaxing, the girls moved Julia safely into their room. Eli shrugged at Alouette and followed Julia. Valera slammed the door. Outside, she heard an ungodly shriek and a string of what she assumed were French curses. Just in case Alouette tried to make good on her threats,

Valera locked the door and leaned against it. Julia sat on the bed huffing.

"She's so... so... so... GAH! I've never been so insulted in my life," Julia griped and pointed to Eli. "This is all your fault! Coming here was your idea."

"The Hostelry was the only place we could hide," Eli said, staying far away from the fuming Julia. "Madame Blackbird is good at keeping secrets and helping... fugitives."

Valera grinned behind her hand. He was trying so hard not to make things worse. Julia scowled at him. She wasn't going to fall for it. Valera shook her head, wrapped herself in warm aether, and waited for the inevitable mini-blizzard.

"Fugitives? Is that what we are? Ha! Slammy Magee wants to murder us in some ridiculous attempt to bring back a dead woman and that makes *us* fugitives."

As predicted, the room temperature dropped. Valera could see steam rising from the other people's breath. She smiled nice and cozy in her aether cocoon.

"And just how long are we meant to suffer that... that... guttersnipe hussy?" Julia ranted.

"Julia... Alouette isn't at fau..." Eli stopped midsentence.

Valera bit her tongue. Eli was about to cause the next ice age, and the poor fool didn't even have a parka. She noticed Theo wrapped in her blanket, watching the exchange with trepidation. Valera saw icy fingers crawl across the window.

"Look. Madame Blackbird's spies are posted all over Pacifica. If the True Followers come for you girls, we'll know. We'll stay until morning, and then find a way out of the city. Okay?"

Valera thought overnight was too long. Keeping Julia from killing Alouette would be difficult – not that she could actually stop Julia from turning the blonde into a popsicle. Valera felt aether slip away from Julia. The room returned to normal, and Julia wilted on her bed.

"Okay, just one night," Julia bit out.

"Perhaps, you three should stay in here." Eli suggested. "I'll ask Madame Blackbird to keep Alouette busy." He turned to leave, but then added, "There are some less than reputable men staying at the inn, so don't wander around alone. I, uh... I'll see you later."

Julia sighed, "Whatever."

The girls remained in their room the rest of the day. Thankfully, Alouette kept her distance. Madame Blackbird brought them a simple, but satisfying meal. Although the woman was friendly and accommodating to Theo and Valera, she seemed reserved towards Julia. Valera suspected that Alouette had informed her of Eli's predilections and their confrontation in the hall- no doubt with a few exaggerated details.

"I hope you enjoyed the crab stew. It's a family recipe," Madame Blackbird clucked as she gathered up the dinner dishes. "It will be dark soon. The Lows electricity shuts off early. You should get some rest."

"Do you have an extra pillow?" Julia asked.

Madame Blackbird harrumphed, "Non." Then, she smiled sweetly at Theo and Valera. "If you need anything just ask. À demain, mes petite chouchous."

The woman left with one final grimace at Julia. Julia rolled her eyes and beat her flat pillow into submission. Valera could only imagine whose face Julia was envisioning on that poor defenseless sack of fluff.

"Like mother, like daughter," Julia huffed and dropped her head on the thoroughly thrashed pillow. "Tomorrow can't come soon enough."

Less than an hour later, just as Madame Blackbird had warned, the lights in the district blacked out. The dim glow of candle light shone under their door. Valera yawned and laid in the dark, listening to every sound the old building and its occupants made. Apparently, the residents in the Lows didn't need lights to keep their festivities going long into the night. She couldn't sleep. The bed was uncomfortable, the blankets were thin, and anxiety troubled her mind. It seemed that the world was against them. She tossed and turned and ended up staring at the peeling wallpaper.

Every few minutes, elephants stampeded down the halls. On Valera's thousandth position change, heavy footsteps tromped down the hall and stopped at their door. She waited, thinking it was just a confused patron. The door creaked open, and the faint smell of liquor touched her nose. A large shadow crossed their room. Before she could scream, a hand covered her mouth. Another figure slipped into the room and pounced on Theo's bed. Theo's muffled screams woke Julia.

"What are you—

Julia was cut off by a third man, who grabbed her. The man holding Valera leaned over her face. He stank of sweat and rotten seaweed. His bristly whiskers rubbed against her cheek.

"I'd 'ave paid double 'ad I known 'ow pretty you be," he leered.

CHAPTER EIGHT

*T*heo

The crushing weight of the man on top of her made Theo scream, but the taste of dirt and grease cut off her voice. His hand covered her mouth and nose, and she couldn't get air into her lungs. Her confusion turned to anger. Aether coursed through her. A flash of fire appeared on the other side of the room, and a man shrieked as his beard burned. The air crackled around Theo, and a purple flash lit up the room. The intruder twitched and rolled off the bed. Theo gasped for air.

"Get off of me," Julia screeched.

A third man screamed. Two white handprints were welts on his cheeks. Dr. Lawless and Eli charged into the room. The three intruders were already retreating toward the exit, wild-eyed and whimpering.

"What is going on in here?" Madame Blackbird shouted from the hall. She yelled at the three retreating men, "You three, what are you doing in this room?"

One of them stammered, "We was told them doxies were fer hire. We paid our coins."

"WHAT?" Valera shrieked. "How dare you!"

"Who told you that?" Eli growled.

One of the men pointed to the hallway. Alouette shrunk behind her mother's bulk. Everyone glared at the girl.

"She dun it. We paid the wench ten pence apiece," the man slurred.

"I want me coin back!" Another one of the men shuddered. "I didna pay to be hexed by a witch!"

"Out, now. All three of you!" Madame Blackbird swatted the men as they left, then she turned on the girls. "I apologize for this. I'll deal with them before they cause a problem." She grabbed Alouette by the hair. "And I'll deal with this one."

The girl struggled in her mother's grip and squealed. "Maman, ce n'est pas ma faute!"

"Are you girls hurt?" Dr. Lawless asked.

Theo shook her head. She wasn't hurt, but she was furious. They all were. Tiny sparks crossed between her fingers, frost covered Julia's bedframe, and the air rippled around Valera. Madame Blackbird was smart taking Alouette away, otherwise she'd be electrocuted, barbequed, and frostbitten. Eli dragged a wooden chair from the hall into the room.

"I'll stay here for the night," Eli said, sitting in the chair and facing the door. "In case, any more *patrons* come knocking."

Dr. Lawless wrung his hands and frowned. "Perhaps, I, too, should stick around."

"We're perfectly capable of handling ourselves," Julia snapped.

Dr. Lawless sighed, "Very well. I will speak with Madame Blackbird to ensure this debacle doesn't reoccur."

Dr. Lawless left, and Eli locked the door behind him. After all that had transpired, there was no way Theo was sleeping. She lay in bed, eyes wide open. All of them still held aether, so she knew they were all awake – all but Eli, who was snoring peacefully in the chair.

I've never been so humiliated in my life, Valera said. *I can't believe Alouette would do such a thing.*

I can, Julia hissed. *She's a jealous...*

We know, Julia. Theo said. *So, what's going on with you and Eli?*

Theo turned to look at Julia and caught her starring at their sleeping bodyguard. Julia flipped over right away.

I don't know what you're eluding to, but absolutely nothing *is going on with Eli.*

Theo laughed. *Uh huh, we saw you kissing him in the hall. Why won't you admit that you like him.*

It is pretty obvious, Julia, Valera added.

Julia scoffed, *As if... He snores... he's arrogant... and... I only kissed him to get under Alouette's skin.*

You like him. Admit it, Theo needled.

Okay, I don't not like him. Happy now? Can we just go to sleep?

They didn't say another word about it. Julia saying that she didn't hate someone was as good as declaring her undying love. Theo sighed. Thinking about Julia and Eli made her lonely for Victor. She worried that he'd never speak to her again after the way they had left things. Hopefully, he'd forgive her. She imagined life beyond all this craziness. She and her parents would live on Aetherland with Victor. Life would be happy. Julia and Eli would be there, and of course, Valera.

Before she knew it, light seeped through the window. She groaned and sat up. Glass shattered in the hallway, and Eli snorted, leapt off the chair with his fists in the air. Boots clomped down the hall and someone downstairs screeched. Something was wrong. Theo shook Julia and Valera awake.

Julia yawned. "What?"

"There's something going on," Theo whispered.

Someone banged on their door. Theo gathered aether and waited. Eli put a finger to his lips and gestured for the girls to stand to the side. The door swung open, Eli grabbed the person by his collar, and sparks shot from Theo's hands.

Dr. Lawless shrieked, "Whoa, Theo. Careful. Eli let me go!"

Eli released him, and Dr. Lawless straightened his jacket. He harrumphed and frowned. Theo released aether.

"We don't have much time. The True Followers are raiding the city," Dr. Lawless warbled. "The men from last night disappeared before Madame Blackbird could deal with them. She believes they've informed the True Followers to your location. It won't be long before they show up. Hurry! Change into these."

He tossed a pile of clothes onto the bed. The dresses were much like the frocks that the Madame wore herself – colorful and cringe-worthy. They reminded Theo of Harmony's Circus costumes. She held up a garish blue and red dress, whose petticoats were a thousand layers thick. She shook her head. They were worse than the circus outfits... much worse.

"Dibs on the yellow and green one," Valera chirped.

"Here take it," Theo threw it at her. "These are horrendous."

The last dress was two shades of pink. Before Julia could argue, Theo threw the pink dress at her.

"I'm not putting this on," Julia grumbled.

Theo slipped out of the white robe and pulled on the petticoats and dress. It was loose, but it covered most everything. She felt like a mound of frosting on a cupcake. Valera changed and twirled around the room.

"They're not so bad," she grinned.

Julia held hers in the air as if it were dirty dishrag. Madame Blackbird popped into the room.

"You don't like the dress?"

"Dresses aren't my thing," Julia muttered.

Madame Blackbird scoffed, "Is going to jail your thing? You won't make it out of the city looking like that. Suit yourself. I'm here to put your hair up. You sit."

Theo sat in the chair, and Madame Blackbird got to work. She was none too gentle, yanking and pinning Theo's hair into a scalp numbing coif. Valera went next. In the end, Julia gave in and donned the dress. After Madame Blackbird was finished, Julia looked like a miserable pink flamingo. Grabbing Professor Scrod's book, they went downstairs.

"Where is everyone?" Theo asked the Madame.

"I sent them away. We can't have prying eyes and ears around, while we get you out." Madame Blackbird ushered them into a parlor.

Dr. Lawless held the bag of relics and waited by the window. He peered through the lace curtains, shaking his head. He sighed.

"There you are. We're heading to another safe house."

Eli stumbled into the room and choked when he saw the girls. He erupted in a fit of laughter. Julia glared at him, and the air cooled.

"Not now. There's no time," Dr. Lawless grumbled.

Madame Blackbird opened the front door. She waved them out, but as soon as they stepped into the street, a whistle sounded. Slammy Magee was at the end of the road and heading right for the girls with an army. Another group of men charged from the other side of the street. They were surrounded. They fumbled back into Madame Blackbird's, and the woman barred the door.

"Zut, I thought we had more time," she growled.

Slammy's voice sounded over a blow horn. "Give me the girls, and the rest of you can go free."

Madame Blackbird placed her hands on her hips and walked in a circle. Her face drained of color. She stopped next to Dr. Lawless who peeked through the curtains.

"There's no way out," he whispered.

Alouette stormed out of the kitchen, "Maman, just give them to him. They are not worth it!"

Madame Blackbird scowled at her daughter. "Go back in the kitchen, Bête Fou."

Alouette huffed and stomped her foot, but one growl from her mother, and she ran into the back room. Theo had a bad feeling in her gut, and she followed Alouette through the corridor. In the front hall, she heard Dr. Lawless and Madame Blackbird speaking.

"I'll stall him for as long as I can. You go out the back," the Madame said.

With one eye on Alouette and the other on the front hall, Theo waited. She heard the front door open and Madame Blackbird stepping onto the front walkway. Dr. Lawless and Eli barricaded the door behind her. Madame Blackbird muttered something, and then shouted. When Theo turned her attention back to Alouette, the girl was gone.

"Dr. Lawless, we have a problem," she shouted and went to the back door.

Alouette was in the back alley talking to a white robe. The man called for more men, and they ran toward the kitchen. Theo locked the door and stared at the men through the glass. The men leered back at her.

"Watch out," Eli shouted, overturning a table and blocking the exit.

Behind it, Theo heard banging. Glass broke in the front room. Someone yelped. Julia covered the window in an ice wall, but the men tried to break through it.

"They're everywhere," Theo stammered.

Theo peeked out a small side window and saw Madame Blackbird fighting with Slammy. A white robe chained her up. Slammy turned and grinned at Theo. They were trapped.

We should turn ourselves in, Valera said.

We can't. You heard Dr. Lawless, they're going to kill us, Julia spat.

Theo racked her brain to formulate a plan. *We don't have much choice. We can't let him hurt Madame Blackbird.*

"Fine, we can go outside and face Slammy. But I won't go down without a fight," Julia said aloud.

"What do you mean? You aren't going out there," Dr. Lawless fumed.

Theo pushed a chair away from the door and unlocked it. "We don't have a choice. We'll try to talk to him. If that doesn't work, we'll... use a different method."

Eli grabbed Julia's forearm. "Don't do this."

"We have to do something. I'll be okay," she said, gently removing his hand.

"Then let me go first," Dr. Lawless said. "I'll act like I'm turning you over. Maybe you can make a run for it."

Theo nodded, and Dr. Lawless slipped onto the porch with his hands in the air. The white robes came for him and dragged him down to Slammy. Theo heard him muttering, and then the guards backed off. Theo took the cue to step onto the walkway with the bag of relics held tight against her body. Julia and Valera followed close behind. Slammy's smile grew. He dropped the blow horn. The men behind him inched forward. He shot his hand in the air and the men paused.

"You've seen reason... excellent. I need you girls to come down slowly."

"I'm sorry, but we can't do that. We're not going to let you sacrifice us, Slammy," Julia yelled.

"We'll find a different way to do what you want, but we need assurances," Theo added.

The man shook in anger. "Do you think you can dupe me? There will be no assurances or sacrifices. No one makes a fool of me."

Theo frowned. He was crazy. He fumbled for something at his belt, pulled a pistol, and aimed it at the girls. Without another word, he pulled the trigger. He didn't anticipate the ricochet from the gun and was thrown to the ground. The rogue bullet missed the girls and flew off the protective dome above. A loud ping echoed through Pacifica as the bullet hit the glass. The sound of cracks forming along the worn barrier intermingled with the screams of people. The pressure of the Pacific Ocean pushed against the dome and water sprayed into the city. Slammy stared at the hole in shock. The gun fell on the ground beside him, and the mass of white robes stood in stunned silence.

More fissures formed every second, and the water flowed inside faster and faster. Slammy's men fled in fear. Slammy sat on his haunches, looking between the girls and the gun sitting on the sand.

"What have you done?" He muttered.

A wave of people stampeded down the streets in order to escape the rising water in the Lows. A woman stumbled over Slammy, knocking him on his back. She got up and kept running. Slammy struggled to get up, but the stampeding herd didn't stop to help. Dr. Lawless grabbed Theo's arm.

"We have to get to the docks. It's the only way out of the city," he shouted over the screams.

"What about the people?"

"We don't have time to worry about them," Dr. Lawless hissed.

Theo knew there wouldn't be time to get everyone out of Pacifica. The dome was failing. The city was flooding. People were dying. She wouldn't stand by and watch another part of Aether crumble. She searched the bag for Maera's Scepter. Holding it out, she slammed it on the ground and channeled aether through it. Valera and Julia both gripped the staff, and Theo felt a surge of power flowing through all three of them. In waves of radiant light, the power of the scepter struck out over the city.

Theo felt as if her spirit left her body, and she flew over the city. She was a soaring bird. Below her the cracks in the dome sealed closed. People swept up by the flood were lifted free, and the water receded. Pacifica glowed with Maera's healing light. The power of the scepter flowed through every living creature in the city. The screaming stopped.

Theo saw everyone and everything. She felt every heartbeat quicken, even as hers slowed. Her strength dwindled. She was yanked back into her body by force. Eli held the staff in his hands, twitching. The light of the staff flickered and blew out like a candle. Theo teetered on her feet until her legs gave out.

Theo blacked out as a new uproar echoed through the city as people rejoiced in wonder.

CHAPTER NINE

Valera

Valera woke up inside a white room. The bed beneath her was soft and warm. She definitely wasn't at Madame Blackbird's anymore. She remembered Slammy shooting at them, and the Scepter shining. After that, her memory fuzzed out. A woman wearing a crisp blue uniform walked past the end of her bed. She looked at Valera and smiled.

"We were worried about you." The woman's voice was comforting. "How are you feeling?"

"I'm..." Valera's mouth was parched. "Water?"

The woman helped Valera sit up and held a plastic cup to her lips. The water was pure bliss. Theo and Julia were asleep in the beds next to her. She frowned, but the woman patted her hands.

"Don't worry. They'll be fine. You girls over-exerted yourself."

"Where are we?" Valera choked.

"Pacifica City Dispensary. You were brought here after... the miracle. You've all been laid out for several days." The nurse fluffed her pillow, checked on the other two girls, and headed for the door. "Oh, your mother is here. Would you like me to fetch her?"

"Maybe later. I feel woozy," Valera lied.

"Of course, dear. You rest."

The nurse left the room. Valera flopped back on her bed and put an arm across her forehead. The thought of facing her mother was enough to make her ill. Although, if her mother were here, that had to mean that Slammy's short reign was over. She looked out the window. The world outside seemed brighter somehow. She reached out for Theo and Julia.

Are you there?

Julia groaned, but both of them remained asleep. Valera sighed. They'd really exhausted themselves. Valera still felt an ache in her head. It got worse, when her mother's shrill voice shouted outside her room.

"I demand to see my daughter at once!"

Dr. Lawless interjected, "You must calm yourself, Victoria. The girls have been under an immense stress."

Valera closed her eyes and played dead. Their door opened, and she heard a pair of high heeled shoes walk across the room. She knew her mother's perfume. She stopped at Valera's bedside and placed a cool hand on her forehead. Valera stayed as still as she could.

"What's wrong with them?" Victoria whispered too loudly.

"The intensity of the... event... depleted their vitality," the nurse's voice returned. "With rest and care, they should recuperate."

"I want them transferred to Aetherland Isle immediately," Valera's mother didn't even pretend to whisper.

"That's quite out of the question. Any exertion could cause a relapse," the nurse raised her voice.

Dr. Lawless sighed, "Ladies, please. The girls need quiet."

One of the woman harrumphed and left. Valera could still smell her mother's perfume. Her skirts swished on a hard floor. The other person in the room, whom Valera assumed was Dr. Lawless, moved closer to the side of her bed.

"Victoria, dear, I apologize for my presumption, but the girls do need their rest. Why don't we go speak with Parmelia? The rebels will face judgment soon, and Valera needs you to be her advocate."

Her mother sighed. "Very well."

Victoria's lips touched Valera's cheek. The room grew quiet again. Valera relaxed.

"Faker," Julia chuckled.

Valera's eyes shot open, and she sat up. "You're awake!"

"That sickly-sweet, flowery fragrance that your mom wears is like a dose of smelling salts. How can she stand that stuff?"

Valera laughed. Julia stood on wobbly legs for a second before making her way to the window. Along the way, her hospital gown fell open in the back. Valera coughed.

"Cover up, sheesh. No one wants to see that."

Julia looked around behind her and grinned. "I'm proud of my assets. Nothing to be ashamed of here." Still, she pulled her gown around her body. "You should come see this."

Valera slipped out of bed, making sure to wrap a blanket around her shoulders. She preferred to keep her assets private. The muscles in her legs seemed to have forgotten how to work. She toddled over to the window and leaned on the sill. A mass of people crowded the front of the hospital. From the second floor, the girls could see that the people wound all the way around the building. None of them looked sick that Valera could see, although many of them held flowers and gifts.

"What's all that about?" Julia asked.

"The flooding must have done more damage than I thought. Maybe they're visiting the injured?" Valera shrugged. "Do you remember anything after Theo got the scepter?"

"I know that we helped her. I remember a bright white light. But that's about it. Why is she still out?"

Valera looked toward the sleeping mass that was Theo. "I think she got most of the blast."

The nurse peeked into the room. "Ah ha! You are awake," she chuckled. "I don't blame you for pretending."

"Sorry about my mother... she can be... headstrong." Valera wilted.

The nurse waved away Valera's concern and entered the room. Three young girls followed her in, carrying massive bouquets of flowers. The nurse directed the girls to place the flowers on a side table. The little girls kept their wide-eyed gaze on Julia and Valera. Two of them giggled and whispered to one another. The other approached Julia and curtsied.

"You're my favorite," the third girl blurted and ran from the room.

"Uh, Thanks," Julia murmured, and then turned to Valera. "Her favorite what?"

Valera shrugged.

"Sorry for the disruption. They are the daughters of some of the staff. They were quite eager to deliver the flowers themselves. It's good to see you up and moving around. Just don't overdo it," the nurse said.

"What's with all the people outside?" Julia asked. "And why were the girls acting so strangely?"

The nurse seemed surprised. "They're here for you, of course."

She left Valera and Julia more confused than ever. Valera pulled one of the roses out of the vase and sat on her bed. The delicate pink petals felt like velvet between her fingers. The effort of walking had worn her out. She laid the rose next to her and put her head on the pillow.

"Why do I feel like the sacrificial lamb? Are they here to bolster our ego, fatten us up, and then slaughter us?" Julia mused.

"Don't be silly. I don't think those little girls were planning on murdering us, Julia." Valera yawned, "I'm so tired."

"Go ahead and sleep. I'm going to stay up… and keep watch… just in case."

Valera drifted off, and visions of Danu swept through her mind. Although, Danu had no voice in the nightmare, she saw Danu being squeezed to death. The only sound was of bones snapping and crunching. Valera tried to force the image from her head, but Danu continued to infiltrate ever subconscious thought. Valera woke up in a cold sweat.

Julia and Theo spoke to Dr. Lawless. Flowers and gifts covered every surface in the room. One table glistened with jewels. Valera heard singing and chanting outside the window. She shook her head, trying to wake from the strange dream.

"She's alive!" Theo quipped.

"How long was I napping?"

"An hour or so. As you can hear, they know we're awake now. Dr. Lawless says the whole city is here," Julia said. "And the word is spreading."

"What word?" Valera stretched.

Dr. Lawless spread his arms wide and proclaimed, "You three are the saviors of Pacifica, of course. It was magnificent until Eli yanked the staff from your hands, but by then you'd healed everyone and everything in the city."

"Eli did what? Is he okay?" Julia asked. "Why didn't you tell me?"

So much for Julia not caring. Valera smiled.

"You needed to heal." Dr. Lawless seemed to grow annoyed. "He received quite a shock... but he's fine."

Valera could tell by the frown on Julia's face that she was still worried, so she sat next to her and changed the subject.

"How are you, Theo?" Valera asked. "You seemed pretty out of it before."

"I'm okay. This is pretty insane, though. Oh, my mom came by. Apparently, she came in from Aetherland yesterday along with Parmelia and your mother."

"I know that Mother came earlier." Valera shuddered.

"I have good news. I was just telling Theo and Julia that the proper Elders have been reinstated. The True Followers and their cohorts are being dealt with as we speak. They won't be free for a very long time." Dr. Lawless clasped his fingers together.

"What about Slammy Magee?" Julia snarked.

Theo rubbed the back of her neck. "The last I saw of him; he was being trampled in the Lows."

"When you girls healed the city, you healed him as well. He's been charged with the rest of them." Dr. Lawless grinned.

Valera squeezed her eyes shut, trying to crush a headache that burrowed in between her eyes. She couldn't shake the image of Danu.

"Are you all right? Should I call the nurse?" Dr. Lawless asked.

"No... no... it's just... I had another Danu vision. This time it was... different. She died."

Dr. Lawless' tongue moved slowly over his lips. His fingers squeezed together, cutting off the blood supply to his knuckles. He muttered something under his breath, and then blurted, "I'm afraid we are running out of time. Danu's spirit must be freed."

"We're not going to let you sacrifice us," Julia snapped.

"Of course not, don't be ridiculous. The True Followers wanted to sacrifice you, not I. We'll simply go to the place on the map, and you three will free her," he grumbled.

"Shouldn't we confer with Parmelia and the Elders?" Valera asked.

"NO!" Dr. Lawless' face contorted into a brief angry mask. He composed himself and continued in a normal voice. "Forgive my outburst. The truth is – I'm concerned for your safety."

"Why? The True Followers are gone, right?" Valera asked.

"Yes, but... your destiny lies with Danu. She must be released, and I'm afraid the Elders won't allow that. They believe that if her tomb were opened, Danu herself would return to Aether."

"But Danu's dead. The visions just come from the aether, right? There's no way she could still be alive," Valera stammered. "She's been entombed for millennia."

"Maybe, maybe not..." Dr. Lawless leaned forward as if sharing a forbidden secret. "There is a legend that conflicts with the beliefs of the Elders. It suggests that Danu didn't die, but was deceived..." Lawless gritted through his teeth, "By her own daughters!"

"That's ridiculous. Why would her own children turn on her?" Julia spat.

"They were jealous of their mother's power and wanted it for themselves, so they ensnared Danu in a trap and destroyed the key."

Theo scoffed, "If that were the case, then wouldn't the Elders want to release her?"

Dr. Lawless grinned. "Ah, but that's the real question isn't it. The Elders have reigned for over a hundred years. With Danu freed, they'd lose the power they have over Aether. When you three united the key, you threatened their hold. You left them no choice but to control you."

Valera rubbed her eyes. None of this made any sense. The Order of the Azure Serpents wanted to steal her powers. The Elders wanted to control her powers. The True Followers wanted to sacrifice her for her powers. What was Dr. Lawless' game? She just wanted the schemes and the nightmares to stop. She wanted to see Gideon, Victor, and little Vivi. The only thing she didn't want was to face her mother again, but that was inevitable. Her mother's voice echoed through the halls of the clinic.

"I'm going to see my daughter," she yelled.

Their door swung open, and Victoria swept into the room, her skirts sweeping across the tiles like a great black broom. Victoria took in the scene with squinted eyes. Dr. Lawless smiled and greeted her with a bow.

"Madame Corvus-Stein, it's lovely to see you again." He kissed her hand.

His eager attention to her mother made Valera cringe, and the way Victoria blushed and fanned her face was nauseating. Theo's mother scooted past the pair and went straight to her daughter. A twinge of jealousy stabbed Valera. The reunion between Theo and her mom was loving and sweet. Her own mother didn't even notice her because of Dr. Lawless' attention.

"I've missed you, Honey," Marjorie murmured to Theo, as she embraced her.

"I've missed you too."

Julia seemed surprised when Theo's mom turned to her and gave her a hug as well. Marjorie smiled at Valera and touched her cheek, but it felt awkward. Theo, Julia, and Marjorie chatted to each other, while Valera sat on the outskirts – alone. Valera moved to the window and looked out over the gathered crowd. Only when Dr. Lawless finished fawning over her mother, did Victoria deign to join her daughter. She removed her long black gloves and pinched Valera's cheeks between her fingers and thumbs. Valera didn't dare pull away. She knew better than to incur the wrath of Victoria Stein... again.

"You seem to be doing better," her mother said with as much warmth as a glacier.

Valera exhaled, "Thank you, *Mother*."

"I see your attitude hasn't changed." Victoria turned to face the entire room. "You should know I've commandeered passage on the *Manta Ray* for all of you. We depart tomorrow morning for Aetherland Isle."

Valera didn't have the energy to argue, and part of her was happy to be headed home. She was tired of running. She was tired of insanity. She was tired of everything. Home sounded like heaven. Julia, however, grew rigid in her seat.

What are we going to do? She exclaimed.

I don't know about you, but I'm going home. I need to see Gideon and the rest of my family, Valera murmured.

Theo sighed, *I'd like to see my father before we open Danu's tomb. If we open Danu's tomb, that is... I don't know anymore.*

What do you mean, you don't know? We have to finish this. I can't have these nightmares in my head any longer. Julia panicked.

Julia, we'll finish it. But at least let us do this first. It's important, Valera said.

Okay, we'll go. But promise me we'll open the tomb. Promise me we'll finish this.

Valera and Theo nodded. Victoria shivered. Valera had forgotten that her mother could sense their telepathic communication. In order to appear meek, she stared at the floor and clasped her hands together. Dr. Lawless stared at Victoria with a frown on his face. He looked at each girl in turn and muttered under his breath. He approached Victoria and pulled her aside.

"My dear, is it safe to move the girls quite so soon? They've been through a great deal," he stammered.

"I've spoken with the doctors. They are all in agreement. The girls will leave tomorrow."

Dr. Lawless flinched. Valera couldn't figure out why he acted so oddly. Running his hands over his crazy hair, he touched Victoria's arm. She startled at the gesture. He released her at once, but clenched his fists several times. He didn't want them to leave, and Valera wanted to know why.

He softened his voice to a low rumble. "I just think it isn't in their best interest. I mean there is still so much we don't know... that they don't know about their powers. The girls can't leave yet. Their training—"

Victoria huffed, "This isn't up for discussion, Ellwood." With that, Victoria moved toward the doors. "I will see you in the morning, Valera. Marjorie, Ellwood, we should let the girls rest."

Marjorie seemed reluctant to leave Theo alone, but finally followed Victoria out of the room, waving one last time at Theo. Dr. Lawless held his hand up.

"I'll be there shortly," he muttered.

After the mothers' exit, he turned to the girls. His lips turned down in an angry sneer, and his eyes seemed wild. A shiver went through Valera's spine. She moved closer to Theo and Julia. Dr. Lawless leaned on the table, gripping the sides as if he were going to pick it up and throw it across the room.

"We can't waste any more time. Danu needs our help. We must free her."

"We will, but first we *are* going to Aetherland. We need to regroup," Julia said.

Dr. Lawless shot her an annoyed glare. He lifted the table legs in the air and slammed it back to the ground. Valera reached out for aether. Julia already had a mist forming in her hands. But then his sneer faded, and he composed himself.

"Forgive me. You're right. You should see your families before we go to the tomb. Arrangements need to be made. Professor Scrod is a few rooms down. She received quite a beating because of us." He paused and looked each girl in the eye as if to accuse them.

His tactic worked. Guilt niggled at the back of Valera's neck. She'd wondered how Professor Scrod was, but never asked. And it was their fault that she was hurt.

Dr. Lawless continued, "I'll speak with her before we go."

He spun around on his heel and slipped out of the room. Valera didn't like his strange mood swings. From the confused looks on Theo and Julia's faces, they didn't like it either. There was something more going on with him, and no matter how he claimed otherwise, she was beginning to think he was like all the others. She plopped on her bed without a word. Her mother's visit had been more than she could deal with in a day.

The chatter and singing from the people outside drifted up to their room throughout the day. The nurses came and went. Most of the time they brought in armfuls of flowers. The endless day turned into a quiet, but restless night. Valera's mind churned with worries. Tomorrow, she'd be returning to her gilded cage, but she wasn't a canary anymore. She was a hawk - strong and dangerous. She'd get to see Gideon soon, but wondered what state he was in and if he still cared for her. Victor would be on the island, but would he ever forgive her? After hours of tossing, she slumbered, and, thankfully, Danu stayed away until light filtered through the windows.

"Good morning, ladies," a nurse chirped, waking the girls. "I've brought you a wardrobe change. They're brand-new and made specially for you - a gift from a Madame Blackbird. She brought them in early this morning. She claimed she owed you for some... shenanigans while in her care?"

The nurse's eyebrow shot up, but none of the girls answered her question. Valera found their night in the hostelry too embarrassing to share. The nurse dropped the clothes on the bed and left. Valera was happy to see ordinary Aetherian leathers and simple shirts. Even she couldn't handle Madame Blackbird's froufrou taste in dresses. The leathers felt like a second skin now, and she wouldn't give them up - no matter how much her mother protested.

"I hope you girls are up and ready." Victoria burst into the room with Dr. Lawless and Marjorie. Victoria assessed the room and almost smiled. "Good. There's no time for delay. We're going."

Before leaving, Julia stuffed a pillowcase with the more luxurious gifts of gems and jewelry. Valera tilted her head and cleared her throat. Julia raised an eyebrow and scoffed.

"What? They were *presents*. It would be rude to just leave them behind."

"We'll have everything delivered to the docks," Dr. Lawless said, eyeing a ruby. "Although perhaps it's for the best that you carry the valuables aboard. You never know who might have sticky fingers."

Valera noticed the ruby didn't make it back to the table, and Dr. Lawless had an extra lump in his shirt pocket. She also noticed the duffel bag in his hand, the same one that held the relics. She suddenly didn't feel so at ease with him in control of them.

Victoria gave Valera a nudge toward the door, and they walked out of their room into a barrage of clapping nurses, patients, and doctors. Victoria and Marjorie stood on either side of the girls, acting as the protective mothers. Dr. Lawless took the lead, joined by a grinning and bandaged Eli. Julia's smile grew so large, Valera wondered if her cheeks would tear.

When they stepped outside the building, the whole of Pacifica City was there. Dr. Lawless had to push people aside to clear a path for the party to move. Valera felt like she was wading through an ocean. The crowd cheered and tossed flowers at them. Banners and signs claimed the Trinity as the saviors of Pacifica City. A few Elder-loyal white robes appeared behind them to keep the crowd from flanking them.

They reached the main gates where a battery of guards held the crowd at bay. Parmelia awaited the girls from behind the safety of the guard, and Julia ran to her grandmother. The Elder kissed her granddaughter's forehead and whispered in her ear.

"I'm so happy to see you girls alive and well." Parmelia's voice shook. "The transport is waiting. We should go before the city riots past the guards. You've made quite the impression on the people of Pacifica." She smiled.

Outside the docking tubes, Valera saw an elegant submersible. Two wings spread wide on either side of the submarine, and two massive propellers rotated in the rear of the ship. The outside surface was covered in an iridescent blue substance. The submarine was much fancier than old Rusty's Blowfish. But then again, anything was better than his leaky deathtrap.

"Stay here, and don't move." Victoria turned to Dr. Lawless. "Don't take your eyes off them."

He nodded. Valera rolled her eyes. Did her mother seriously think she would run away... or even could run away? People were swarming the main gates, and guards surrounded the group. There was nowhere to go.

A voice came over the loud speaker. "The *Manta Ray* is now boarding."

Valera stood near the glass, staring at the shimmering blue ship. She stopped a spindly man wearing a green uniform and asked, "What is that stuff covering the ship?"

"Well young lady, that *stuff* is a patented blend of aether-grown blue algae. It protects the hull from the corrosive nature of salt water, as well as adds camouflage. I could park her under any fancy upperworlder ship, and they wouldn't even detect her." He stood straighter and looped a thumb inside his coat pocket. "There is no finer ship than the *Manta Ray*. I should know – I designed her myself. Captain Thatcher Stoddlemeyer, at your service."

"I'm Valera. It's good to meet you. She's a lovely vessel, sir."

The man's grin spread. "Yes, yes, she is."

A familiar face appeared out of nowhere. Nessie's fiery red hair bobbed toward them from the crowd. Nessie slapped Valera on the back and squeezed her in a shoulder-crushing bear hug. When she faced the captain of the *Manta Ray*, he flinched.

"STODDY!" Nessie's voice bellowed.

Captain Stoddlemeyer cringed. "Nessie, how... nice to have you aboard."

"Just like old times, eh, Stoddy?" Nessie winked. "Valera! How are you feeling, girl? You threw us for quite a loop." She ruffled Valera's hair, gave her a bump with her hip, and turned back to the captain. "Stoddy, I see you've met my niece. You gotta keep these three under a watchful eye. They're wily."

Heat crept into Valera's cheeks. "Nessie, stop. We are not."

Captain Stoddlemeyer's eyes widened, and he blustered. Nessie elbowed him in the ribs and hooted.

"She's being modest. She's one of the Trinity. You're hauling precious cargo, Stoddy, old boy. All of Pacifica is in love with these girls. Muck it up, and you'll have a mutiny on your hands."

"Yes, well, I'm honored. I knew we had important guests, but... why are they under guard?" He eyed the entourage.

"Like I said... wily. And she's got a temper on her. Could make the ocean boil if she wanted. And that one." Nessie pointed to Theo. "She's a sneaky little devil."

Theo's head popped up. She winked at Nessie and smiled at Captain Stoddlemeyer. Valera exhaled. Theo didn't seem to be troubled by the fact that Nessie was blabbering on about them. Parmelia, on the other hand, wasn't smiling. Nessie nodded toward Julia.

"And watch out for the blonde one. She's as cold as..."

"Nessie, that's quite enough. Captain Stoddlemeyer has already been properly informed about his passengers. There is no need to elaborate," Parmelia scolded. "I suggest you get aboard, find your stateroom, and stay there. You are not out of the woods yet."

"Yes, ma'am," Nessie saluted to Parmelia, and then turned to Valera, Theo, and Julia. "Hang in there, girls. And try not to sink the ship."

Parmelia swatted Nessie away. Nessie skipped down the docking tube. Captain Stoddlemeyer's eyes looked as if they'd pop out of their sockets. Parmelia sighed and pulled him aside.

Victoria returned as stern as ever. She pushed Valera forward, and they boarded the *Manta Ray*. Exquisite tin tiles glimmered above her, and luxurious purple carpets lined the floors. Men in crisp red uniforms welcomed them inside and offered to help them find their rooms. Valera breathed in the faint scent of ocean water and violets.

They were escorted to a cabin near the rear of the ship. Although it was small, it held two ornate brass beds, an armoire, and a tiny bathroom. Victoria's trunks sat on the bed, opened and ready to be unpacked. She hung each dress on a cushioned hanger and placed them in the armoire. Since her mother refused to speak to her, Valera kicked off her boots and lay down.

Captain Stoddlemeyer's voice blasted over the ship's speakers. "Welcome aboard the *Manta Ray*. I'll be your captain for the length of this voyage. We're due to arrive at the Atlantic Island Aerodrome in approximately seven days, so please settle in and enjoy the trip."

"Seven days? Ugh." Valera threw her head onto the pillow.

Victoria paused her unpacking. "I wouldn't be so ungrateful, if I were you. The *Manta Ray* is the finest submarine in all of Aether. I would have thought your time in the Elder's dungeons would have made you more appreciative."

"Airships are faster," Valera whined.

Her mother huffed, "And after all the chaos you've caused? You still don't understand. Do you have any idea how many people your stunts have affected? Those horrid True Followers exiled all of us from Pacifica City. Poor Nessie and Joe are still in trouble from the *rightful* Elders for their part in this mess."

"Nessie and Joe?"

"You didn't think they would have immunity from your crimes, did you? Adora and Benji went back to Harmony. Apparently, she has some sway with the remaining Elders. Nessie and Joe didn't have that luxury. Your aunt almost lost *the Cornelius*, and Joe was nearly exiled to the human world. You're just lucky that Parmelia is Julia's grandmother and sympathetic to the three of you."

Valera swallowed a hard knot. "But that's not fair. They didn't do anything. We're the ones who caused this."

Victoria threw her hands in the air. "You think any of this is fair to anyone? Did you consider for one second the implications that your actions would have on your family? The embarrassment you've caused the Stein name? I can't even look at you."

Her mother's accusations stung. Valera flopped around on the bed and faced the wall. Wiping her hand across her face, she closed her eyes. The events of the past weeks drifted through her mind. Leaving Aetherland, reuniting the key, being imprisoned by the True Followers – it all happened because of lies, deceptions, and secrets. Had Theo, Valera, and Julia known the truth about themselves, maybe none of it would have taken place. Yet, they were being blamed for everything.

Valera resisted the temptation to toy around with aether – sensing it all around her, but not touching it. Her mother would have felt it, and she had no desire to deal with Victoria. Still, knowing aether was there comforted her. Like a wave of molten steel, a peace and resolve washed over Valera. She didn't regret bonding herself with Theo and Julia. Had they not united the Trinity Key, she would never have known the truth. She also didn't regret meeting Gideon, nor did she regret having been free.

Victoria answered a knock at the door. Valera heard Parmelia speaking in the hall.

"I see you've settled in. May I speak with your daughter? If you like, you can go explore the ship."

Valera smiled to herself. Parmelia wasn't asking her mother to leave, she was telling her. She wished that she could brush her mother off so easily. Victoria huffed, but left. Sitting up in bed, Valera faced the old lady. Parmelia fascinated her.

"Ah, Valera, descendent of Aeda. You know, she was considered the weakest of the sisters, but I always thought she had a quiet courage about her. Ealga was the leader, proud and strong. Maera was the spiritual of the three, a healer. And Aeda, the mindful navigator, thoughtful and true. You're very lucky." Parmelia pointed to the spot beside Valera. "May I?"

"Of course."

Valera scooted over, so the woman could sit. Parmelia slowly lowered herself to the mattress.

"Much better. My old legs tire quickly. So, I haven't had the opportunity to speak with you as I have the other two."

Valera reached out to Theo and Julia, but she couldn't get through. She was cut off. Parmelia chuckled and waved her hand.

"The blue algae disrupt telepathy. It's what Professor Scrod used in the cells to block aether, although a different recipe I presume. Strange, I know. It's quite disconcerting at times to be cut off from what is natural to us."

Valera bit her lip. "So you're telepathic too? Theo said you were."

"Yes, dear. I know all your tricks." The woman smiled and tapped her forehead. "My generation studied the three sisters and practiced their ways. We never reunited the key of course, but we learned to use what we could. That all ended after the death of my daughter. We thought the Trinity was lost forever. We had no idea."

"I didn't know about your daughter. I'm sorry."

"No, you didn't know. We failed the three of you. It was up to us to teach you and guide you. Instead, we let you down. Faced with the danger of the Order, we cowardly stayed away, leaving you girls to defend yourselves." Parmelia sighed. "What's done is done. We must go forward, and do our best with the situation." Parmelia stood and walked to the door. "Some legends come out of necessity rather than truth. I'm sorry we weren't there for you."

CHAPTER TEN

*T*heo

"The pressure outside this ship would crush you like tin foil," Captain Stoddlemeyer said, making squishing gestures with his hands.

In the six days she'd been aboard, Theo hadn't made it through a single meal without feeling queasy. She dropped her forkful of mashed potatoes and pushed her plate away. The Captain's constant explanation of the marvels of the *Manta Ray*'s engineering made her nauseous.

"Faulty hulls have been the death of many a sailor. Of course, my *Manta Ray* can withstand twice the oceanic pressure than the average vessel, so have no fear girls. The *Manta Ray* is one fine ship."

Theo hated submarines. Fancy décor didn't change the fact that the *Manta Ray* was a metal tube at the bottom of the ocean. The Captain sat with them at every meal, otherwise, she would have avoided him all together. Unfortunately, meals were the only time she was allowed out of her room, and, although, she and her mom's relationship improved daily, she wanted to interact with other people. She couldn't even speak with Valera and Julia in her head because of the damned blue algae – another favorite topic of Captain Stoddlemeyer. At least, Valera, Julia, and Nessie were at the meals, although Eli was strangely absent.

Theo had been disappointed when she'd learned that Benji and Adora were gone. She hadn't seen them since the Order in Pacifica City and worried about how they fared in the fighting. Her mother said that they were back with Harmony and doing well, but Theo missed them nonetheless.

"Sit up," Victoria barked at Valera.

Valera shifted in her chair, but minutes later was slouching again. Lately, Victoria had resorted to pinching her daughter into submission. Valera seemed tired. Theo wanted to zap Victoria into oblivion for treating Valera so badly. Instead, Theo crossed her eyes at Valera and made her giggle.

"Is there a problem, Theo? Perhaps it would be best if you kept your eyes on your plate," Victoria hissed.

Her venom seemed to be aimed at everyone but Dr. Lawless. Marjorie stopped chewing. With squinted eyes, she glared at Victoria.

"If you have a problem with my daughter, I would appreciate it if you would address me," Marjorie said.

Theo kept score.

Marjorie 1 – Victoria 0

"If you'd taught your child manners in the first place then maybe I wouldn't have a problem with her."

Victoria 1 – Marjorie 1

Marjorie gripped her fork tight enough to turn her knuckles white. Theo worried that there would be a brawl... although it would be intriguing to watch. Marjorie could totally take on the stuffy Victoria. However, Theo doubted that Victoria would fight fair. Julia smiled at the exchange. Valera kept her eyes glued to the table.

"Ahem," Parmelia interrupted. "I believe Captain Stoddlemeyer has something to say."

And the winner is: Parmelia by a landslide.

The Captain stood at the head of the table and raised his glass of wine. "Our voyage is almost at an end, so I'd like to take this time to thank you all for entrusting me with your safe passage." He cleared his throat, covering his mouth with his hand. Theo thought she saw a hint of a smile. He seemed happy to see them go. "Of course... ah..." He eyed the room as if determining what he wanted to say next. "Yes, well... You are all welcome on the *Manta Ray* any time."

The passengers gave him a round of applause, which he received with gracious bows and no-no-it-was-nothing-but-keep-clapping head shakes. After a significant amount of time, he popped back into his seat and ordered another round of drinks. The repartee between adults continued, minus the bickering under Parmelia's watchful eye. Then, at the usual time, the adults condemned the girls to an evening of staring at stateroom walls.

Inside the boring blue box, Theo sank onto the bed with an exaggerated sigh. One more night and she was free – of the submarine at least. She couldn't wait to get off the ship. Much of Aetherland Isle remained an unknown. Victoria still seemed to believe she had control over them, which she didn't. They could play-pretend for a little while, but once it was time to go, they'd go with or without Victoria's permission.

"You want to play checkers?" Theo's mom asked.

"No thanks. I think I'm just going to go to bed."

Her mom sat beside her. "I'm sorry about dinner. I don't know what's gotten into Victoria. She's been so... awful lately."

"When has she ever been nice?"

Theo's mom frowned. "Now that's not fair. She's done a lot for us. Your father would be dead without her help. She's just under a lot of pressure." Marjorie kissed Theo's forehead and stood up.

"I guess."

Theo flopped backward on her bunk. Her mom sat at the small desk in their room and opened a book. Theo watched as her mom read and scribbled notes in the margins. The simple ritual of watching her mom intently devour a book was soothing and nostalgic.

"Why do you do that?" She asked.

"Do what, honey?"

Her mom didn't even lift her head from the pages. Theo smiled. All she needed was the smell of peppermint tea and stacks of worn books, and they'd be back in her mother's office in their old Victorian home in Boulder.

"Write all over the books that you're read. I still have your copy of Frankenstein back in Aetherland. It's almost unreadable."

Her mom laughed. "Old habit, I suppose. I don't just read the books. I study them. There is a lot of truth behind fiction." Her mom nibbled on the back of her pen. "By the way, I'd like that book back if you don't mind."

"I love you, Mom."

Her mom's head popped up. Her eyes were moist, and her smile was soft.

"I love you, too."

Theo grinned, rolled over, and gave into her sleepiness.

*

Theo woke up the next morning to people lumbering down the hallway with luggage banging against the walls. The *Manta*

Ray had reached the Atlantic Island Aerodrome and was surfacing. Her ears popped, making her head ache. She covered her head with a blanket and moaned.

"Get up, Lazy Bones. We're here. I swear you could sleep through the end of the world," her mother chirped.

Theo rubbed her eyes and groaned, "I'm up... I'm up."

They packed and joined the fray in the hall. On the balcony of the grand lobby, Theo watched chaos erupting below. Most of the passengers waited patiently for the doors to open, but one grumbled and complained. Victoria pushed her way through the crowd to the gangway doors. Two uniformed stewards were holding the crowd at bay, until the crew completed the proper docking procedures. The poor men tried to tell Victoria to wait, but her new companion, Dr. Lawless, rudely knocked them aside.

Ever since the hospital, Dr. Lawless had weaseled his way into Victoria's esteem, and, over course of the voyage, he had become her faithful lap dog, sucking up to her at every occasion. The whole relationship made Theo uneasy. His games were growing tiresome. Any trust she had in him was gone by the time they docked.

"Open this door immediately," Victoria shouted.

"Ma'am we can't, The —

"Out of the way," Dr. Lawless demanded. He took the handle and cranked it. The gears churned. With each bolt loosening, a strange gurgle and hiss filled the room.

The two stewards shrunk back away from the door, and Victoria's eyes grew wide. She tried to step back, but the lobby was crowded with passengers. With a loud slurp, the door flew inward, knocking Dr. Lawless onto the floor. A film bubbled into the room and popped like a giant blue pimple. Blue sludge exploded into the lobby. Passengers screamed. Victoria got the worst of the blast and looked like a shimmering smurf. She shrieked and spat the blue algae onto the floor.

"What's the meaning of this?" She wiped slime from her face.

"Ma'am, we warned you not to open the door before the bio film extraction," one uniformed man yelled back.

A long bellow erupted at the back of the room. Captain Stoddlemeyer rushed to the door, picked up handfuls of the algae, and held them as if they were babies. "Do you realize what you've done? It takes months to cultivate a proper layer of aether-grown blue algae over the hull. You've created a gap in it. It's dying!"

Victoria pulled a stringy chunk of goo from her head. "How dare you! I've never! This is unacceptable."

Victoria huffed and puffed, and left the ship with Dr. Lawless in tow. Julia and Valera were on the lower level, safely tucked away behind a mass of people, laughing. Theo waved to them and started laughing too. Her mother nudged her in the back and frowned.

"Now's not the time," she whispered, but smiled.

Passengers filed off the ship in a single line, stepping over blobs of algae. Theo and Marjorie were two of the last people to leave. On the way out, Theo passed Captain Stoddlemeyer examining the damage done to the *Manta Ray*. His face was red from grief. Theo couldn't understand how a person could love something so much. Still, she felt bad for him. Dried up algae covered the inside walls and floor of the lobby. The algae around gaping hole in the side of the ship shriveled and dried. Theo picked up a piece of it and held it in her hand.

"Captain, how exactly is this grown using aether? And how does it stick to the ship?"

"Huh? Oh, Theo..." He sighed. "The plant is submerged in salt water tanks and aether gas is pumped through the saline. The aether gives it the iridescent quality, which helps camouflage and stabilize the hull of the ship. It's applied to a thin layer of breathable film over the ship. That's why the extraction process is so important. It moves the film layer from the doors without killing the algae and allows for pressure differentiation." He held out a piece of clear plastic. "The pressure ruptured the membrane and killed the algae."

Theo stared at the blue flecks in her hand and had an idea. "Can you fix it?"

"We can fix the film, but growing the algae takes time and can't be done without the proper equipment."

"I think I can help with that. Have someone fix the door. I just need you to trust me."

The Captain's eyebrows shot up. "I suppose you can't cause any more damage. I'll have them work on the door right away."

Theo turned to her mother. "Mom, can you get me some ocean water in a vase or something."

"Sure, honey."

Theo gathered an armload of the algae from the lobby and took it outside. Captain Stoddlemeyer watched her work, wringing his hands. Some of the passengers, who waited for the transport ship, turned to see what she was doing. Her mom brought a jug full of briny water.

I need your help, Theo sent out to Julia and Valera. It felt good to be able to talk to them again.

Julia whispered in Parmelia's ear. The old woman nodded, and Julia joined Theo on the dock. Valera pulled away from her mother. Before Victoria could throw a fit, Parmelia stepped in.

"Let them work."

Theo put the dried algae in the jug. Together they each put a hand in the water.

Let aether pass through the water. Imagine the algae growing in your mind, Theo said.

The other two nodded. The crowd stood by, barely breathing. Theo called on aether and the smell of rain filled her nose. Closing her eyes, she let it flow through her into the jug and algae. She sensed Julia and Valera doing the same, and after a few minutes, the crowd gasped. Theo opened her eyes and watched slimy blue algae creeping over the sides of the bucket.

"Oh, by Danu's light! It's a miracle," Captain Stoddlemeyer shouted.

"We need more water," Julia said, pulling her hand out of the algae and shaking it off. "I hope this stuff doesn't stain."

Captain Stoddlemeyer ushered his men to get every bucket, jug, and vase in the ship. The ship's engineer took the overflowing bucket and gingerly plastered the algae on the new film. Captain Stoddlemeyer gathered the dried algae from inside the ship. The girls regrew algae over and over again until the door was covered and their hands were dark blue. By the time they were done, the transport was waiting. None of the passengers had boarded it. They all chattered about the girls, clapping and cheering. Captain Stoddlemeyer grabbed Theo, Valera, and Julia in his arms and squeezed them.

"I won't forget this, you wondrous creatures. In fact, I will tell everyone I know of this marvel. You will all be hailed as heroes," he gushed.

"Please don't," Theo squeaked. She'd had enough of that in Pacifica City.

Parmelia came forward and urged the Captain to release the girls. Then she pulled him aside and talked to him. He nodded enthusiastically to everything she said. When they returned, he was all smiles.

"You are welcome aboard my ship any time. No charge... ever! Goodbye, girls."

He and his men returned to the *Manta Ray*. The ship submerged, creating massive bubbles on the surface. Parmelia patted Theo's back.

"Well done, my dear."

Parmelia took Julia's and Theo's arms and took the winding stairs to the upper deck where the aerial vessels docked. They moved to the front of the group of passengers waiting to board the transport ship. The small aerial vessel filled with people and scuttled up to the floating island of Aetherland. Once it docked, people filed off the transport and integrated into the villagers. Alongside the transport, Nessie's dry-docked ship, the *Cornelius*, appeared lonely and empty of people.

Upon arrival, the girls' reception was less than friendly – not that Theo expected a fanfare. But after their departure from Pacifica, Aetherland felt... ordinary.

"I've got business to attend to here in the village. You will return home with Parmelia," Victoria ordered them. She turned to Dr. Lawless and softened. "Ellwood, would you mind joining me?"

Theo gagged. The two of them were growing more insufferable every second. Dr. Lawless followed Victoria down the street, carrying the bag of relics.

Shouldn't those be with us? Julia hissed.

Theo grumbled, *Yes.*

"Girls, please speak aloud. Keeping track of your chatter in my head gives me a headache," Parmelia scolded. "The relics will be kept in a safe place. Now, shall we?"

She gestured toward the fountain where the mechanical horse and carriage were parked. Theo had forgotten that Parmelia could hear them if they didn't block her. The old woman ushered the girls forward.

The closer they moved to the carriage, the more Theo's stomach fluttered. Her dad was here. Vivi was here. Victor was here. She couldn't wait to see them, especially Victor. Their last departure went horribly bad, and she wanted to fix things. Perhaps, if she could explain herself better, he'd forgive her for leaving him.

"Pssst, come here."

Theo looked around for the voice. Jesse, Vivi's young friend, was hiding between buildings, waving at Theo. As usual he looked mischievous.

"I'll be right back," she said to her mother and pointed to the little boy.

Marjorie smiled and nodded. "Don't take too long."

Theo snuck between the buildings and dropped to one knee. "Hey, Jesse! How are you doing?" She ruffled his hair. "Thanks for helping me escape before. I hope you didn't get into too much trouble."

"Naw, they didn't even know I was fakin' it. I'm not supposed to talk to you, but I'm hopin' you can give Vivi a note." He held up a small slip of paper with blocky handwriting on it. "She can't come play with me anymore, and the mean people won't let me near her house. Can you give it to her?"

Theo smiled, "Of course, I will."

"But don't read it!" Jesse's plopped his tartan cap on his head and added, "It ain't mushy or nothin', just secret."

"I promise not to read it." She crossed her fingers over her heart. "Take care, kid."

He gave her a gap-toothed smile and ran off. His prosthetic leg squeaking. Theo slipped the note in her pocket and returned to the others, who were already getting into the carriage.

"Thanks," she said to Parmelia. "He's a good friend."

"Yes, as I recall he's quite the little actor."

Theo's face felt like fire. Parmelia seemed to know the truth about everything. Thankfully, Julia's grandmother was on their side. Theo reached out to Valera and Julia, making sure to block out Parmelia.

I can't wait to see my dad, she mused.

Julia shifted on the crimson velvet chair. *As long as we don't stay long. I don't want to escape one prison just to get stuck in another.*

Theo groaned. *We won't.*

I hope Gideon is doing better. Mother wouldn't say much about him. When I asked, she kept telling me that I'm not to see "that boy." All she would say was that Victor's watching over him.

Theo sighed. *I hope Victor will forgive me. We didn't exactly see eye to eye when it came to helping you.*

Sorry about that... but, I say you're better off. He's such a bore, Julia quipped, then added, *No offense, Valera.*

Offense taken. Geez, he is my twin.

Julia smirked. *Like I said, he's a bore.*

Valera scowled. *Ha, ha, ha. Funny. I know Victor can be stubborn, but he's a good guy.*

I know. I know. I'm kidding... kind of. Anyway, what do you think of my —

"If you girls are finished gabbing. We've arrived at the mansion," Parmelia said with a hint of a smile. "Don't look so shocked. You may have blocked me, but I've never met teenage girls who sat silently and stared at nothing while in the presence of friends."

Marjorie laughed in agreement. Theo cringed. She'd have to watch out for Parmelia. The carriage stopped at the base of the marble stairs. The mansion was as impressive as ever, and oddly it felt like home to Theo. The Stein family automaton butler, CHAD-4, stood in the doorway, waiting for them to enter. Victor was nowhere to be seen.

"It is a pleasure to see you again, M...m...m...Miss Valera, Miss Theodora, Mistress Marjorie, Mistress Par... par... par...Parmelia." CHAD-4 looked at Julia and blinked. "Pardon me, we have not been properly introduced. I am CHAD-4, and you... you... you are?"

"This is Julia, my granddaughter."

"Thank you, Mistress Parmelia. Nice... n... n... nice to meet you Miss Julia, granddaughter to Mistress Parmelia. Welcome to the Stein Family est... est...estate."

Julia leaned toward Theo and whispered, "What's wrong with him?"

"Marcus," Theo replied.

"Enough said."

Her first visit to the mansion felt like a different lifetime. She remembered the horrible sound of CHAD-4 ripping apart after Valera's step-uncle Marcus pushed him down the stairs. Now, she was back, Marcus was dead, and the sound of him falling into the volcanic vent echoed in her mind. It was karmic really. Just like CHAD-4, she'd never be the same.

Parmelia dismissed the automaton with a wave of her hand. "Yes, yes, that's all very nice Thank you, CHAD-4." She turned to the girls and put her hands on her hips. "You girls should freshen up in your rooms. I'll see you at dinner," Parmelia said in her most this-isn't-a-request-but-an-order tone.

Marjorie gave Theo a quick kiss before leaving to find her dad. Theo retreated up the stairs, picking at the blue stuff that

SAVE AETHER | 133

still clung to her hand. On the way to her room, Theo saw Victor on the second floor. She smiled and waved at him.

"Victor!"

His door closed. He must not have seen her. He didn't even turn to look at her. Theo felt as if she'd swallowed glass. She took a few steps toward his room, but paused. If he had just snubbed her, she wasn't sure she could face him without breaking down. Instead, she went to her own room. She scrubbed the gunk from her hand until her skin was more purple than blue, and then she flopped into her bed.

"Why so glum?" Joe's voice made Theo jump.

Joe, a Stein family friend and Auntie Grace's new beau, stood in her doorway, holding three boxes in his arms. Dropping them on the floor, he sat down and put his boots up on the hearth.

"Geez, you scared me." She eyed the boxes. "What are you doing here?"

"Hi, Joe! How are you doing?" Joe chided. "Danu's light, Theo. I came to see how you're doing."

"Hi, Joe. How are you doing?" Theo deadpanned.

She was glad to see him, but it was more likely that he was sent to keep an eye on her. She sat on the edge of the mattress. A smidge of guilt seeped into her. He'd helped her, and she was being ungrateful, but she had to know.

"Did Parmelia send you… or maybe Victoria?"

Joe cut her off and grinned. "I came all the way back from Colorado, just to say hi to you. And all I get is accusations?"

She raised an eyebrow, and he chuckled.

"I'm not at liberty to divulge any information. Besides, I've already gotten in enough trouble for helping you girls."

"Really? Why would you get in trouble? You didn't do anything wrong."

He shrugged. "It doesn't matter. Nessie and I knew the risks. We helped you fight the Order in Pacifica and we defied the Elders. What's done is done."

"I didn't know. I'm sorry," Theo muttered.

Had she known he'd get in trouble, she would never have asked for help.

"Don't get me wrong. I don't regret a thing, except making your auntie Grace angry. Once she found out how... messy things got, she lost it."

Theo flopped onto the edge of the bed. "She's pretty mad, huh?"

Joe scoffed. "That's an understatement. Just wait till she gets a hold of you."

"Ugh, can't wait."

"Well, you've got a little time. She has to finish up in Colorado, which reminds me. She sent some of your stuff." He pointed to the three boxes piled up near the door. "I'll leave you to it."

After he left, Theo hopped up and dug into the first box. All of her old clothes were folded neatly inside. She squealed as if she were reunited with old friends. Graphic tees and jeans flitted around the room like snowflakes. At the very bottom of the box she found gold – two pairs of Converse sneakers. She hugged them to her chest, kicking off her boots and slipping one of the sneakers on her foot. It was heaven. Aetherian clothes were fun and all, but nothing compared to the comfy goodness of a tee shirt, jeans, and a pair of Converse sneakers.

The next box held old memorabilia. A few ancient report cards – no need to revisit those. Her "Best Camper" award from summer camp – a decade ago. She didn't even like camp that year. An elementary school spelling bee championship trophy. A stumble off the stage after winning left a big crack in the plastic cup. At the bottom, she found several photos of past friendships. She couldn't even remember the names of the kids. Most of the pictures in the box felt foreign to her as if she was going through a stranger's past and not her own. She sealed the box and set it aside.

The last box made her smile. She pulled out her table lamp, her old diary, and the framed picture of her father that used to be on her nightstand. Leaving the rest of it in the box, she set the three items near her bed.

Her two worlds meshed together. It felt... right.

CHAPTER ELEVEN

Julia

After one of the weird Stein robots showed Julia to her hideously frilly room, she didn't know what to do with herself. She paced the length of the space. As far as she was concerned, this detour was a waste of time. It was nice to spend time with her grandmother without being in a cell. Still, she didn't want to hang around any longer than they had to.

"Julia?" Eli's voice came through her door.

Her nerves shot up into her throat. She hadn't seen Eli since their brief encounter on the way to the *Manta Ray*. Her emotions wreaked havoc inside her belly. She wasn't sure if she wanted to speak with him. Part of her was miffed at the whole Alouette thing, and he hadn't even visited her at the clinic. Sure, he was a patient there too, but he could have come to say, "Hi." Furthermore, they'd had a whole week on the submarine, and she hadn't seen him once.

"Julia, can I come in?" he asked.

"Fine," she huffed and unlatched the door.

He slipped in and shut the door behind him. Julia avoided looking him directly in the eyes for fear of losing her nerve. She stormed away from him and continued pacing. *Why am I so nervous?* She tried to play cool.

"Could you stop stalking around like a tiger for one second?" he grumbled.

She paused and crossed her arms, keeping her eyes on the far wall. She heard him move around behind her. When he got close enough that she could feel him, she stepped away.

"I wish you'd look at me." He sighed, "At least talk to me."

"I really don't think we have anything to talk about," she squeaked. Her eyes caught a glimpse of the thick white bandages wrapped around his hands. She pointed to them and murmured, "Is that from the scepter?"

"Yeah, that'll teach me to get in the way," he chuckled.

She loved the sound of his laugh. A strange sound escaped her throat. A sound she'd never made before – a ridiculous girly giggle. She coughed to cover it up. Thankfully, a knock disrupted them and gave her a reason to get away. CHAD-4 bowed outside her door. The creepy mechanical man was her best friend at the moment.

"Pardon me, Miss Julia. Dinner will be served in five… five… five… minutes," CHAD-4 reported.

Julia smiled at the robot. "Thank you, CHAD-4."

She took a step out the door, but Eli trotted forward and stopped her. He held his arm out as if escorting her to a royal ball or something. Feeling silly, she rolled her eyes and left without touching him. Her snub didn't stop him from following close behind. She walked to the dining room in a fog. He confused her more than anyone ever had. Eli pulled a chair out for her.

When she sat down, he leaned forward and whispered, "You look beautiful."

Her heart pumped fire through her veins. No one had ever said that to her, and she didn't know if he was being sarcastic. She assumed the latter. She spun around ready to rip his face off, but others were arriving and she didn't want an audience when she murdered him. Much to her dissatisfaction, he sat next to her. Parmelia and a small entourage entered the room. Eli stood up right away and bowed.

"Madame Elder."

"Ah, Eli. No need for formalities. I do hope you're feeling better. I heard you took quite a shock when you saved the girls in Pacifica, and that you had a mild relapse aboard the submarine."

Saved us in Pacifica? What? He hadn't saved them. He grabbed the scepter like a dolt. Julia frowned. Julia felt a twinge of guilt. She thought that he was better when she saw him escort them to the ship. Julia glanced at him out of the corner of her eye. His eyes were glued to her.

"Yes, Ma'am, much better." He bowed.

"So, how have you and my lovely granddaughter been getting along?"

He sat down with his mouth hanging open. It seemed Julia had never mentioned that Parmelia was her grandmother. *Oops.* Julia grinned. She remembered the first time they'd met, and he'd made such a huge deal about Parmelia asking for him directly. Parmelia held her arms open for Julia.

Julia gave her grandmother a quick hug and muttered, "Hi Grandma."

Parmelia took her seat with a smile. Eli gulped a long drink of water. Julia turned to him and smirked. He mouthed the words, "Grandma?" She nodded and mouthed the word back.

She leaned back in her chair victorious. He looked good in the color of confusion.

Valera and Victor slunk into the room and plopped onto their seats. Victor looked like he had a mouthful of War Head candies. Theo sat across from them and gave him a longing look, but he didn't even acknowledge her. Julia scowled. Theo didn't deserve to be treated like this, especially for helping a friend.

"What a jerk," she mumbled.

"What did I do this time?" Eli leaned in and whispered.

Julia rolled her eyes at him. "Not you, him." She nodded at Victor. Then, she thought about it for a second. "Come to think of it... you too."

Eli looked at Victor and lifted an eyebrow. "I like him already."

"Ugh, just mind your own business." She couldn't help the smile that crossed her face.

CHAD-4 and the other automaton servants brought in a huge meal. Everyone seemed to pick at their plate, not eating or talking.

I think someone sent Joe to spy on me, Theo burst into Julia's brain.

Valera eyed her brother out of the corner of her eye, *I think you're right. Victor's been following me around.*

Julia scoffed, *Well, I'm stuck with Eli.*

We're not back to this are we? I thought you liked him. Valera griped.

Well... I mean... I don't know. He can be such an annoying bastard —

Julia! For shame, Parmelia's rasp slipped into the conversation. *Eli is a good boy, and vulgarity is not a desirable trait in a girl, especially in Ealga's heir.*

Julia jumped at the sound of her grandmother in her head, bumping her legs on the edge of the table. Everyone quieted and stared at her. After a few seconds of silent judgement, the room returned to its miserable dinner. Julia's body flamed with embarrassment, then she saw Eli's grin and couldn't take it anymore.

"Excuse me, but I'm feeling ill. I need to go," she muttered and stood up.

She scuttled from the room, eager to get fresh air. Finding the closest exit, she escaped into the gardens. The night air was crisp and cooled her skin. Happy to finally be alone, she walked along the path. Her thoughts splintered into a million directions, but one face popped up over and over again. She hated him for it. When the gravel crunched behind her, she didn't need to turn around to see who it was.

"What do you want?" she hissed.

"Geez, kid. I came to check on you," Eli responded.

"Spy on me is more like it, and I'm not a kid."

Julia stormed away. Although Eli maintained a safe distance, he kept pace with her. He hummed an annoying tune. His footsteps increased until he was beside her.

"Just hear me out." When she didn't respond, he continued, "I don't know what you think happened with Alouette, but nothing *ever* happened between her and me. In fact, I don't even like her."

Julia's heart bumped and stuttered in her chest. She hated to admit it, but hearing him speak made her jelly-kneed. She closed her eyes – still unwilling to look at his eyes – and turned around to face him. The gravel crunched, and she felt his slightly rough bandages on her cheeks. Her eyes flew open, but it was too late. His lips brushed against hers. Molten lava pulsed through her veins. She wrapped her arms around his waist and kissed him back. In the back of her mind, she knew he was smirking the same irritating, egomaniacal, wonderful smirk.

CHAPTER TWELVE

Valera

Valera envied the way Julia could get away with storming out of dinner. If Valera tried that, she'd be roasted alive by her mother. She also envied the way Eli went after her. At least Julia had someone new to talk to. Valera was stuck with her cantankerous brother. She eyed Victor and scowled. He was too busy sulking over Theo to notice. That's all he ever did – brood. If Valera even said Theo's name, he threw a fit. Across the table, Theo tried to make eye contact with him, but he kept his eyes on his fork.

Valera focused on blocking Parmelia and said, *He'll get over it.*

Theo looked at her. *I hope so. I miss him.*

He misses you, too. He's just too dumb to know it yet.

Have you seen Gideon?

No.

Valera hadn't been allowed to see Gideon. Victoria refused to let her visit him. Then again, in the few hours that they'd been home, her mother refused to let her do anything. The attention that Dr. Lawless lavished on her was the only reason Victoria wasn't yelling at her now.

Valera moved the potatoes around on her plate, mushing them into mash. The walls of the mansion shrunk in on her. She missed the open air of the human world. It seemed as if every city in Aether was closed in, and it was making Valera claustrophobic.

"May I be excused?" she asked her mother.

Victoria was too enthralled with Dr. Lawless to hear her daughter's request. Valera was about to try again, but Victor stopped her.

"Don't bother. Mother is obsessed with *him*," Victor murmured.

"What's going on? He wasn't like this before. He actually helped us in Pacifica, but now he's... he's creepy."

Dr. Lawless had barely spoken to the girls during the stay on the *Manta Ray*. He flattered Valera's mother every chance he got, and Victoria touched his arm and giggled at everything he said. Valera gagged. She glowered at the man. Dr. Lawless met Valera's eyes, and she quickly turned away. When she looked up, his eyes were planted on Theo. He continued the conversation with her mother, but kept his eyes on the two girls. Victoria was too enraptured to notice. He'd become exactly her mother's type – cold and calculating.

"She hasn't wasted any time, has she?" Valera spat.

Victor stabbed the chicken on his plate. "Titus is locked up. She's lonely."

"More like desperate. She's making a fool of herself... and she thinks I'm a disgrace."

"Don't be so hard on her."

Valera ignored her brother. She watched Vivi get up and walk over to Dr. Lawless. Valera's little sister said something to him, but he patted her brown curls as if she were a puppy and dismissed her. Vivi's face crumpled, and she left the room. Victoria did nothing. His casual dismissal of her sister and her mother's neglect made Valera want to lash out. She felt aether all around her.

"Let's go before I do something stupid."

"*Before* you do something stupid?" Victor muttered.

Valera glared at him and stood up. He threw his napkin on the table and pushed his chair back. Victor's eyes flickered toward Theo on the way out, but then he looked away and scoffed. Valera wanted to smack some sense into him.

I give up. Theo's voice popped up in Valera's head.

I'm sorry —

"Where are you going?" Victoria shrill caw interrupted Valera's thoughts. "I didn't give you permission to leave."

Bitterness gripped Valera's spine. She turned on her heel and faced her mother and the doctor. "Forgive my discourtesy, Mother, but I did ask to be excused. Perhaps I mistook your captivation with Dr. Lawless' company as consent. I didn't want to disrupt your repartee to double check."

Victoria's mouth opened slightly, and her brow dropped. Her pale skin turned bright red. Valera knew she'd pushed too far, and she didn't care. The doctor, on the other hand, grinned at the mounting tensions. He dabbed the corner of his lips with his napkin.

"Valera," he trumpeted. "You mustn't be too upset with your mother. I've been monopolizing all of her attention tonight. You're free to go."

Victoria's eyes widened. Surely, now she'd let Dr. Lawless know his place. Valera anticipated an epic outburst. But, one look from Lawless, and Victoria cleared her throat and waved

Valera away. Valera couldn't take it. She blurted the first thing that came into her head.

"You should have that cough looked at, Mother. It could be pneumonia," Valera sneered.

She knew it was a pathetic slight, but it was enough. Mother and daughter glared at each other in a silent battle of pertinacity. Valera refused to give in. Victor touched her shoulder.

"Let it go," he whispered.

Finally, her mother's control snapped. "Valera, go straight to your room, and you're not to come out unless you are summoned," she shrieked.

The doctor went silent. Victor tugged on Valera's arm. She wouldn't budge. Her hands balled in fists, and aether tickled her senses. She met Theo's eyes.

Valera, don't.

"I said go to your room!" If her mother's voice rose any higher, she'd break the glassware.

"Gladly," Valera spat and stormed from the room.

She stomped up the stairs so hard that the soles of her feet ached. Victor ambled behind her. Once in her room, she let loose. She stalked across the carpet and swiped her arms across her desk, sending papers flying onto the floor. Next, she attacked her chair, toppling it over and throwing the cushion at the canopy of her bed. Her brother leaned against the corner wall and watched his sister's rage with straight-lipped grimace.

"She's terrible. I hate her. Did you see how she ignored poor Vivi? Do you know how she treated me all the way home? Here, look at my arms." She pulled on her sleeves revealing a mosaic of bruises. "See? I can't take it anymore, Victor. I'm going to... I don't know what I'm going to do, but I won't let her do this anymore. She's gone mad!"

Victor crossed his arms and shrugged. "I'm beginning to think all of the women in this house have."

Valera turned on her brother. "What's that supposed to mean?"

"Mother, Theo... you. You're all insane."

"What did I do?"

He scoffed. "Really? For one, you left. You left Vivi and me behind as if we meant nothing to you. And with *her* of all people." His voice grew louder with each word until he was yelling. "Not to mention you three have basically turned all of Aether upside down. You betrayed us, Valera."

Valera had never seen her brother so angry. He rubbed his face, threw his hands up in the air, and turned away from her. She knew he would never understand why she left, but she couldn't stand to see him suffering.

"Victor, I didn't mean to hurt you. I had to go. I was suffocating here. And then, the Trinity key fell into the Order's hands, and I couldn't let Marcus destroy it. We had to go after it."

She could tell by the frown on his face that he wasn't listening. She tried to touch his shoulder, but he pushed her hand away. He faced her and poked her arm with his finger.

"No, you don't get to just gloss over this. You tossed us aside out of selfishness and greed. You didn't *have* to reunite the Trinity Key. You didn't *have* to help Julia. You did it because you wanted the power of Danu as much as Lazarus did. You're no better than the Order." He poked her again. She flinched from the sting of his words. "Did you think about the consequences at all? Did you wonder what might happen to your family for even a second? Were we even a blip on your radar?"

"Of course I did," she murmured, uncertain of the truth.

Had she thought about them? She had missed them, but she'd never thought about their feelings, or what might happen to them because of her actions. All she'd cared about was her own freedom. She plopped onto the sofa and put her head between her hands.

"I'm sorry," she whispered.

A chill blew in from the window, and Valera wrapped her arms around herself. Without thinking, she lit the fireplace with a simple waggle of her fingers. Victor's eyes grew wide.

"How can you be so absentminded? Danu's power isn't a toy you can just throw around."

She sighed. She was tired of being beat up by everyone around her. She closed her eyes and muttered, "I don't need your admonishment, Victor. Please, just leave me alone."

She heard his footsteps stamp across the floor, and the door slam. She opened her eyes to an empty room. Sobbing, she curled up on the seat. Her world crumbled. Mother resented her, Victor hated her, and Vivi... she hadn't even talked to Vivi since she left in the first place. If she'd just been stronger, then none of this would have happened. If she'd just—

Help me, daughter. Free me from my torment...

She sat up and looked around the room. It was as if the voice were right next to her, but she was alone. Danu. She couldn't take anymore. Danu already tormented her nights, and now the goddess was stalking her days.

"Leave me alone," she yelled.

A knock made her jump. Wiping her face off on her sleeve, she marched to the door and flung it open.

Expecting her brother, she yelled, "Here to apologize?

Kind grey eyes blinked at her.

"I'm sorry?" Gideon laughed.

A cast stabilized his arm, and a bandage bound his head, but he looked better than ever to her. She threw her arms around him, forcing him to grunt in pain. Still he didn't pull away. After releasing him, she ushered him into the room, checking the hall and shutting the door.

"Sorry about yelling. My brother and I, well he isn't very happy right now. Here, sit down. How are you feeling? Are you in pain? Your poor arm."

Gideon chuckled. "I'm fine. Actually, I don't have much time."

"What? Why? You just said you were fine." Valera began to tear up again.

"No, no, that's not what I mean. In fact, I've got some exciting news. Parmelia is allowing me to study the relics of Danu. Dr. Lawless brought them to the Aetherland town hall for further examination, and they think my work in the Order may be useful. I'll be staying at the inn."

"Oh."

She tried to smile even though she felt like a hot iron pierced her heart. No doubt this was her mother's scheme to keep Valera and Gideon apart. He seemed so excited that she didn't have the heart to mention the deception. The number of friendly faces around the Stein mansion was dwindling. Besides Theo and Julia, he was all she had. She sucked back more tears and pretended to be happy for him. His smile faded, and he put his good arm around her shoulders.

"I'm just staying in the village. I'll be minutes away. This is a good thing. Don't look so sad, please."

Valera wiped her hand across her face. "I'm happy for you Gideon. I've missed you is all."

"I've missed you too."

He pulled her into him and kissed her. Burying his head in her neck, he sighed. His breath was warm and soft against her skin. She didn't want to let him go, but she didn't stop him from leaving. His good hand touched her cheek.

"We'll be together again soon."

And then he left.

CHAPTER THIRTEEN

Theo

After the disaster that was dinner, Theo decided to pay Vivi a visit. The square of paper in her pocket piqued her interest. Dr. Lawless' casual dismissal at dinner had clearly hurt the little girl, which made Theo even more distrustful of the man. Theo hoped that the letter might cheer her up. Vivi was curled up on her bed, sucking her thumb. Theo sat down next to her and brushed the brown curls from her face.

"Guess what I have in my pocket?" she teased.

The little girl's big green eyes looked up at her. Vivi sighed.

"I dunno," Vivi voice was garbled by her thumb.

"Well, I ran into a friend of yours in the village, and he gave me a letter for you. But you don't want to read, so I'll just—

"I do too want to read it!"

Vivi sat up and held her hand out. Theo removed the paper from her jeans. Vivi's name was written in blocky handwriting across the front of it. Vivi carefully untied the blue ribbon Jesse had tied around it, and unfolded it as if she were unwrapping a precious gem. She stared at the words for a minute and scrunched her nose.

"I can't read his writing," Vivi said.

"Let me try." Theo took the letter and squinted at the chaotic script. "Dearest Vivi (Mama told me that letters always start with dearest, but I don't know why. I think it's silly.) I wish we could play. I try to come see you but no one lets me in. Please come out and play again. From, Jesse. PS." The last bit was one big squiggle. "I miss you."

"I wish I could go play too, but Mother won't let me out anymore."

"Since when do you call your mom Mother?" Theo chuckled.

Vivi put her hands on her hips. "Since she stopped letting me go outside."

Made sense to Theo. Vivi plucked the letter from Theo's hand and tucked it under her pillow. Taking the blue ribbon, she wrapped it around her wrist a couple of times.

"Can you tie a knot in it?" She asked, holding her arm out.

Theo secured the ribbon. "There. It makes a perfect bracelet." And then she hugged Vivi. "I'll come back and see you soon."

Vivi smiled for the first time in a long time. "Thank you, Theo."

Theo got up and headed to her mother's Pepto Bismol-colored suite. Before she called it a night, she wanted to see her parents. She knocked, but no one answered. Poking her head inside, she found the room empty as if no one had been there in a while. None of her mother's clutter sat on the desk. The bed was perfectly made. The fireplace was cold. Her stomach clenched. She felt as if she were standing back in her foyer in Colorado on her sixteenth birthday. This room, like the old

Victorian vestibule, was lifeless. She found CHAD-4 dusting a table lamp in the hall. She headed toward him, and, at the last second, he turned. She collided into him. His metal exterior remained in place, whereas Theo's much squishier body flew to the floor.

A pair of metal hands gripped her shoulders. "Pardon m... m... my clumsiness, Miss Theodora."

"No, it was my fault." Theo stood and brushed off her clothes. Her pride stung more than the fall. "Sorry, I was just in a bit of a hurry. I was looking for my parents, but their room is empty."

"Master Nathaniel and Mistress Marjorie are... are... are..." The butler tapped his metallic head with the handle of the duster. His brass moustache twitched. "Your parents moved to the p... p...peacock suite."

"Oh, um." She almost hated to ask any more questions. Even if it was a ridiculous thought, his stutter seemed to bother him. "Where might that be?"

"Down... down... down stairs."

"Thanks." Theo smiled.

He bowed and continued dusting. She started down the hall and realized she had no clue where the room was downstairs. She turned to ask CHAD-4, but he was already gone. The front door slammed, catching her attention. Sneaking to the third floor landing, she peered over the rail. The tapestries hanging in the foyer fluttered against the walls.

"You sent him away!" Valera's voice reverberated up the stairwell.

"I don't think I like your tone, young lady," Victoria hissed.

"You can't keep me trapped like a leashed dog, *Mother*."

"Nothing is good enough for you, is it? You have everything you could ever want, but you want more. You're a selfish, ungrateful... I've given you everything... and I lost everything because of you and your spoiled little trio," Victoria snapped. "You should all be locked up."

Victoria's floor-length, black gown whooshed across the red floral rugs. She grabbed Valera's shoulders and shook her. Valera screamed. Victor came in between them and pulled his mother away from his twin.

"I hate you!" Valera shrieked at her mother.

"Stop it," Victor said. "Both of you."

Dark circles lined his eyes, and a layer of scruff covered his chin. His clothes were wrinkled and splotchy. His mother smoothed and straightened her dress, scowling at Valera.

"Don't let her set one foot outside this house," she told Victor and left the foyer.

Valera crumpled to her knees and broke down into tears. Theo wanted to go comfort her friend, but felt as if she would be interfering in family matters. Victor put his hand on his sister's back, whispered in her ear, and helped her up. They disappeared, going in the opposite direction from their mother.

Theo leaned against the railing and stared at her sneakers. Victoria thought they'd ruined her life. That was interesting. Victoria was the one who married a member of the Order of the Azure Serpent sent to betray her. Victoria was the one who lied to her daughter for years. Victoria was the one who made her children hate her. But, somehow everything was always the girls' fault.

"Pffft, serves her right," she muttered.

"Hello, Theo."

Her heart jumped in her chest. Dr. Lawless stood a little too close in front of her. She took a step to the side to create some distance. He followed. The scent of jasmine soap and cigars filled her nose. No matter how hard she tried, she couldn't shake the eerie feeling he gave her. He had changed overnight. He no longer looked like the man who'd helped them escape the cells in Pacifica City. He used to be their advocate, but now a strange desperation seemed to creep up in everything he said. If his interest in Victoria was unnatural, so was his behavior toward Theo. His eyes darted around the hall as if someone were watching them.

"Uh, hi," she stammered, trying to inch away.

"Isn't she a vision?" He looked over the railing.

Theo followed his eyes down to the foyer. Victoria had returned and stood alone, staring at Danu's tapestry. After what Theo had witnessed, Victoria was a vision – of contempt. Theo shrugged. She wasn't going to share her thoughts with the doctor, so she lied.

"Uh, Mrs. *Corvus-Stein* is okay I guess."

"Who? Oh, yes of course. Victoria is very pretty as well."

Theo shook her head. *As well?* There was only one person in the foyer – the man was clearly going insane. She made a move to leave, but he gripped her forearm. His long thin fingers dug into her flesh. The more she struggled the bigger his grin got. He pulled her close and inhaled. She cringed.

"Have you had any more dreams of Danu? Is she still calling to you? Our time is waning. We must act soon," he whispered.

Theo pulled on aether, hoping to force the man away. Instead, his smile grew, revealing his glistening teeth. He leaned closer to Theo's face, sniffed her hair and her go. With a bow, he spun on his heel and strolled away. Theo watched him go, holding onto aether in case he returned. She released the energy, her hands still shaking from the experience. Disturbed, she stumbled downstairs on trembling legs, nearly plowing into Victoria.

Victoria was still glaring at Danu's tapestry and didn't notice Theo's arrival. Theo was about to speak, when she heard Victoria whisper to the image.

"Why? Why didn't you choose me? Why her? I could have been the one..."

Victoria whirled around with a scowl on her face. Theo had never seen the terrifying glint in the woman's green eyes before. The anger faded, and Victoria's face returned to normal, but Theo felt an underlying hostility in her.

"May I help you, Theodora?"

She spastically straightened her dress again. If she tugged on her sleeves any harder, she'd rip them off. Theo tugged on the hem of her own shirt.

"Um, well, yes. I, uh, were you just talking to yourself?"

"Don't be ridiculous. I was simply admiring the craftsmanship of the tapestries. They were hand stitched by my great grandmother. The artistry is perfection."

Victoria caressed the cloth. The woman was losing it. Big time. It was as if there was a plague of insanity spreading through the house, and Theo wasn't going to be its next victim. She covered her mouth and nose with her hands to ward off infection, eliciting a frown from Victoria.

"Is there a problem Theodora?"

"Uh, no," Theo muttered, feeling silly. "I was just searching for the peacock suite?"

"I assume you're looking for your parents. I moved them to the peacock room to be closer to me – in case your father has any problems with the upgrades," Victoria stated.

"Upgrades?"

"They're on the second floor next to my room," Victoria waved Theo away. "I'm very busy, so if you'll excuse me."

With that, Victoria strolled away toward the library. Theo was left standing under the tapestry of Danu. The fabric swayed, and for a split second, it looked as if Danu's wavy brown hair blew in the wind and her green dress sparkled. Her piercing amber eyes peered down at Theo. In the back of her mind, she heard Danu's voice.

Release me, and I shall make the world whole again.

Theo shivered. She couldn't get away from the tapestry fast enough. She took the stairs two at a time and headed straight to the peacock room. The door opened before she had a chance to knock, and her mother stood in the doorframe in a silk bathrobe, laughing. Theo winced.

"Oh, Theo! Hi," her mother tittered. "Your father and I were—

"Ew, Mom, I don't want to know what you two were doing," Theo shrieked.

Her mother put her hands on her hips and frowned. "I was going to say – we were just talking about you. Come in. I'll get dressed."

Theo inched into the room. Her dad was in a sitting room, reading a book. Thankfully, he was fully dressed. Theo sighed in relief. There was nothing worse than walking in on your parents... Theo couldn't even finish the thought without gagging.

Her dad put the book down and waved her over. He was no longer pale and ashy. His skin shone with a pink healthy glow. The sparkle had returned to his hazel eyes.

"Hi, honey. I'm glad you came by."

Theo wrapped her arms around her dad's shoulders. "You seem so much... better."

"Victoria gave me a few upgrades." He tapped on his chest. "I'm as good as new. Wanna see?"

Theo didn't want to see – the mechanics in his chest always creeped her out – but she didn't want to disappoint him either. He unbuttoned the top of his shirt and pulled the two halves of his artificial chest apart. Her cheeks stretched into what she hoped was a suitable smile. He pointed at various gears and pumps explaining the new parts with excitement. Theo nodded and swallowed her disgust.

"The upgraded heart has a biventricular resynchronization system... are you okay Theo? You look a little green." He paused and touched Theo's cheek.

"Yeah I'm okay. Sorry, it's just that the whole Robo-Dad thing still weirds me out." She pointed to his ticking chest.

Her dad grinned and re-buttoned his shirt. "I know this is strange. I'm just glad I've gotten to spend more time with you."

"Me too, Dad."

Theo sat on the couch. Her mom joined her and took her hand. With all the dysfunctional family problems in the mansion, Theo's parents seemed to be better than ever. She almost felt like they were a normal human family back in Colorado.

Her mother smiled and sighed, "We want to let you know how proud of you we are."

"Proud?" The word rang in her ears. Everyone else seemed to think she'd committed some heinous sin, but her parents were *proud*. She felt the threat of tears in her eyes. "According to the Elders, I'm a criminal. How can you be proud of that?"

Her mother laughed – a genuinely happy laugh that Theo hadn't heard since before her father's "funeral." With a wave of her hand, Marjorie dismissed Theo's worries.

"You're not a criminal. Besides, prison-jumpsuit orange is not your color," her mother joked. "And you're not built for hard labor."

Theo wondered if her mom had been hit by the insanity bug as well. Her dad chuckled, but then grew serious.

"Theo, we should have talked to you a long time ago about our family history. As far as we're concerned, you've done the best you can. We're proud of you. Not all Aetherians hold to the Elder's view on things."

Tears trickled from Theo's eyes. She hugged her mom and felt her dad's arms wrap around both of them. A loud rap on the door interrupted their family utopia. Without waiting for an invitation, Victoria and Dr. Lawless strolled in. Theo groaned. Even Marjorie seemed to blanch at the pair. Her mom squeezed her hand.

"Sorry to intrude. Dr. Lawless was eager to see my handiwork," Victoria said. "I've told him all about the advancements I've implemented in my patients."

Something about her tone bothered Theo – the way she called her dad "handiwork," as if he were a broken clock instead of a human being. Aether tickled her senses, but she held it at bay, remembering the way Dr. Lawless reacted the last time.

"I, uh, I think I should find Julia," Theo stammered, trying to find an excuse to leave. "I promised her we would talk," she lied.

"That's a shame," the doctor said. "I was hoping you'd join our conversation. I'm sure your parents would like you to stay."

Dr. Lawless looked at her mom and dad with anticipation. Her mother must have sensed Theo's unease, for she took Theo's hand and walked her to the door. Kissing her cheek and hugging her, she gave Theo a nudge out the door. Theo hesitated. She looked at the discomfort in her mom's eyes.

"Is everything okay?" Theo whispered.

Her mother nodded and spoke loud enough for the room to hear, "I know you're busy, sweetheart. Go find Julia and tell her hello for us."

Dr. Lawless' eyes turned to slits, and his smile disappeared. Victoria pulled at her sleeves and wrung her hands. Theo didn't waste the opportunity to leave. She had no desire to watch the storm brewing. She whispered a quick, "Thanks."

Skittering away from her parent's room, she decided to go for a short walk. She needed fresh air and to be alone with her thoughts. On her way out, she heard Joe's voice in the library.

"You can't hold that against them," he said. "Theo was put in a difficult situation."

At the mention of her name, she slunk over to the door. Joe sat in a chair, and a second person stood in front of the fireplace.

"She made her choice," the second person grumbled.

Victor. He'd never forgive her. His arrogance and stubbornness wouldn't allow it. She was sick of his evasiveness. This time he was going to listen to her, like it or not. She steeled herself to face him. A thousand confident and witty thoughts went through her mind, but the closer she got to opening the door, the faster she lost her nerve. Her hand stopped just short of the knob. Victor ran his hands through his disheveled hair and frowned. He paced back and forth, muttering. Joe tried to console him, but Victor's frustration was impenetrable.

Theo wanted to hold Victor and tell him everything would be all right. She wanted to confess how she felt about him and apologize. She wanted to have a normal teen romance with him and be a normal teen girl. But the ever present tingle of aether reminded her that none of that could happen. He turned toward the door and spied her. Their eyes held contact for a brief and beautiful few seconds, and then he turned away.

"I can't."

With two simple words, he ruptured any hope she had. He didn't want her. Heart broken, she escaped to her room. Stripping down, she crawled under her blankets and cried herself to sleep.

CHAPTER FOURTEEN

Julia

After her rendezvous with Eli in the gardens, Julia felt as if she were floating. He walked her to her room and kissed her goodnight. Everything was perfect. She slipped into bed and wished for sweet dreams of Eli.

As soon as she drifted off, her subconscious replayed her wonderful night with him. He held her, kissed her, and whispered in her ear. The air smelled like hot chocolate. The garden around them lit up like a million twinkling stars. She basked in their beauty.

Suddenly a cool breeze blew in, bringing with it the overwhelming stench of decay. She covered her mouth and nose, but Eli didn't seem to notice. The twinkling lights blinked out one by one until they were masked in darkness. She lost hold of Eli. Stumbling around, she tried to find him. She felt a breath on her neck.

"Eli? Is that you?"

Arms wrapped around her waist, and she ran her hands along their length. Instead of skin, her fingers touched soft leathery scales. The breath came back, this time tickling her ear. It wasn't a voice, but a long, slow hiss. She screamed. The snakes around her waist squeezed. The smell of damp earth swallowed her. More snakes entangled her legs, and she fell forward. Her face hit a hard cold surface.

Come to me, daughter.

Danu's voice interrupted the hissing snakes, or maybe Danu was one of the snakes. Julia couldn't tell. The serpents tightened, crushing her chest.

Help me! Julia reached out to Theo and Valera.

Snakes, so many snakes, Valera shrieked in return.

Theo added, panting, *I can't breathe.*

Julia woke inside a layer of ice that covered the entire room. She couldn't feel the cold, but steam poured from her lips. Eli banged in the hall and yelled.

"Julia, is everything okay in there?"

He pushed his way through the ice-sealed door. When he saw the room, he shivered and wrapped his arms around himself.

"I must have done it in my sleep," she muttered.

"Seems like a reasonable thing to do... sure," he quipped and grew serious. "You were screaming."

"Bad dreams."

"I'll get a fire started," he offered.

She crawled out of bed, shuffled her way to the bathroom, and got dressed before joining Eli by the fireplace. They curled up in a chair together. He was all smirks. She'd grown used to his annoying grin, and if nothing else, he provided attractive scenery.

Valera's head popped into the room. "Can I speak with you for a second?"

Julia nodded. The ice melted under Valera's feet. She looked around the room, and didn't look surprised. Julia looked at her quizzically.

Valera shrugged, "I woke up in a sauna, so who am I to judge."

Eli shook his head and stood up. "I'll never get used to you girls. I'll be in the hall."

"So, you two made up?" Valera quipped, sitting near the fire.

Julia felt her face grow warm, but scoffed. "I guess he's all right."

Valera laughed, "Uh, huh."

Julia changed the topic before Valera needled her again. It was none of Valera's business what she and Eli were doing.

"So, that dream last night felt... stronger than last time."

"Yeah, it did. And lately, I've been having waking dreams. I think we're running out of time," Valera said. "We need to talk. All of us."

Theo, are you awake? Julia asked.

Theo appeared in the doorway. Her hair stood on end as if she'd been rubbing a balloon on her head. Julia stifled a chuckle. Theo frowned.

"Yes, I'm awake," she droned.

Valera snorted, "Rough night?"

"It must have been electrifying," Julia laughed.

Theo raised her brows and looked around Julia's thawing room and at Valera's sweat ridden pajamas. They both shrugged. Theo smoothed down her hair.

"You two are hi-la-rious. Now, can we please get serious. We need to find the Trinity Key and the Relics of Danu."

Valera bounced up and down. "The relics are in the village town hall. Gideon is studying them. I bet the key is there too."

"Maybe he can help us." Julia stretched her neck. "Before we do anything, we need to find a way off of —

"Off of what?" Victor growled.

All three girls spun around. Victor, Joe, and Eli stood in the doorway. Victor's arms were folded over his chest, and he looked ready to slaughter them all. Julia scowled at Eli. He just smirked like always. He plopped down beside her, and she elbowed him in the side.

"What? The man was determined. Who am I to stop him?"

Julia grumbled inaudibly, and then looked at Victor. "Off of the island, duh."

"Julia," Theo hissed.

"What? We need to know which side they're on - ours, or the Elders."

"I didn't realize there were any sides." Eli smirked.

Julia sighed. "You know what I mean. We need to know if we can trust you. Really trust you."

Eli's smirk faded. He rubbed the stubble on his chin. His brown eyes softened, and he looked directly at her.

"You know you can trust me."

Joe sighed, "If you can't trust me now, after all the trouble I've gotten into because of you three, then you'll never trust me."

Theo smiled, "We trust you, Joe."

All eyes turned to Victor. He was a wildcard, but Julia knew he cared for Valera. He just needed to know the whole truth.

"Tell him about the dream, Valera."

Victor scoffed, but leaned against the wall and listened.

Valera took a deep breath. "Every night, and some times during the day, we all have visions of Danu. It never stops. I hear her screaming and begging for help. Victor, I can't live like this anymore. It's torture."

After a few minutes of scowling, he ran his fingers through his hair and sighed, "You're going to go through with this no matter what I say, aren't you?"

Valera nodded. "We have to."

Julia expected him to yell, and then run to the Elders to tattle. Instead, he shut the door and joined them.

"So be it. I'm in."

"What about Dr. Lawless?" Eli asked.

All three girls flinched. Julia certainly didn't trust him. As far as she was concerned, they were going to leave him behind. His strange behavior hadn't escaped her notice.

"I don't trust him," she blurted.

Theo and Valera visibly relaxed.

"Me neither," Theo said. "But I'm pretty sure he has Professor Scrod's notebook, which shows the location of the tomb."

"Then we leave him out of it," Victor muttered. "Probably for the best. I don't like the way he's been looking at you."

"I'll speak with Gideon. He'll get us the Trinity Key and the relics," Valera offered. "And maybe Nessie can help us find a way off the island."

"I need to say goodbye to my parents," Theo said.

Joe nodded. "I've a few things to take care of before we go as well… Grace is going to kill me."

"And I should say something to Parmelia. Don't worry, I won't tell her our plan." Julia took a deep breath. "Leave Scrod's notebook up to me. We'll leave as soon as we have everything in place."

Everyone except Eli and Julia left the room. She was a big tangle of excitement and fear, and she had to gather her thoughts before facing her grandmother. Eli sat up and ran his hands along his long lean legs. Julia was acutely aware of his proximity.

"Uh, thanks for helping," she murmured.

"Someone's gotta keep you safe," he whispered.

Julia could feel her face burning. The sun broke through the curtains, illuminating Eli's eyes. Julia's stomach twisted in knots. She stood up. Eli stood at the same time. Neither one took a step to leave. Their eyes met, and she swallowed a lump that appeared in her throat. He leaned forward. She closed her eyes.

Then, he murmured, "We should go find your grandmother."

"I think she's downstairs," she sighed.

Her mind raced. Had she overthought their time together last night? Did he not feel anything for her? Why didn't he kiss her? The last thing she wanted was for Eli to see her disappointment and uncertainty. She had no clue where her grandmother was, but other people would be downstairs, and right now, she needed to be around other people. She left the room and darted down the steps, two at a time. Sure enough, she heard Victoria's voice in the library. Without knocking, Julia opened the door to find Dr. Lawless kissing Valera's mom. Julia gasped, alerting them to her presence.

At first, she wanted to puke. The thought of kissing that man grossed her out. Eli let out a whooping cough and covered his mouth with a fist. Julia wasn't sure whether to say something or try to disappear quietly.

"Oh, um, sorry, uh, I, well..." she stammered.

Eli stepped forward. "Do you know where Parmelia is?"

Victoria's face turned crimson, and she fidgeted with the bun on her head. Dr. Lawless looked as if he were ready to commit murder. He adjusted his suit jacket.

"She's most certainly not in here," he seethed.

"We'll, uh, try the gardens," Julia blustered.

She shut the door and backed away laughing. She heard Victoria bemoaning the intrusion inside the room. Eli doubled over and guffawed. Julia wondered if Victor or Valera knew about their mother's new "friend" – Daddy Lawless. She shivered.

"Well that was… fun. How about we check the gardens?" Eli snorted.

"Agreed."

They were still chuckling as they emerged into the roses. Sure enough, Parmelia sat on a seat under a gazebo with Vivi dancing around her. Julia hadn't thought much of the little girl, but seeing her with Parmelia made her smile. Parmelia clapped at the little girl's performance.

"Bravo, you are the very image of a prima ballerina," the old woman gushed.

Vivi's green eyes lit up. "Really?"

"Absolutely," Julia said, startling Vivi.

The little girl's curls bounced. Eli held a hand out to her and bowed.

"May I have the next dance?"

Vivi giggled and took his hand. The two of them danced to non-existent music, circling the rose garden. His ease with the kid made Julia smile. He was amazing, which made her even more confused than ever. She sat next to Parmelia, who took her hand.

"How are you and Eli getting along?" Parmelia asked with a sparkle in her eye.

Julia tried to act nonchalant. "He's okay. A little bit dopey, but he's okay. I just…"

The smile on Parmelia's face made Julia's palms sweat. It was as if her grandmother could see her every thought. The old woman patted her hand.

"He reminds me of your grandfather, Declan. That man was a scoundrel with a romantic heart."

"I wish I had known him."

"He would have loved you." Parmelia took a long breath and closed her eyes. Her translucent, wrinkled eyelids rippled over her eyes. After a minute, she turned to Julia. "I'm glad you came. There's something I needed to discuss with you. I've been called back to Pacifica City. I think it would be best if you stayed here until everything is settled."

Her grandmother's timing couldn't be better. She'd be happy to know Parmelia was safe in Pacifica City. She hugged the old woman's shoulders and kissed her cheek.

"I'll miss you, Grandma."

"And I you," Parmelia chuckled. "Oh, and Julia… Eli likes you very much. Don't doubt that." Julia's grandmother winked.

She did know everything.

CHAPTER FIFTEEN

*V*alera

Valera needed to get to the village. With Victor acting as her mother's pigheaded watchdog, she doubted she'd make it far. And he certainly wouldn't renege on his duties. He may have gone along with their impromptu meeting, but that didn't mean he wouldn't turn on her as some kind of payback. She had to get a feel for where his head was at – without him knowing it.

She strolled down the hall outside of Julia's room, examining the old family portraits that hung on the walls. One of them caught her eye – a young woman in her early twenties with the same brown hair and green eyes. The girl's smile was radiant. She stopped to look at it. Victor came up beside her and scratched his chin.

"Do you know who that is?" he asked.

"No, but she's very pretty."

Victor chuckled, "That's Mother."

Valera raised a brow. "I can't imagine her ever being that happy."

"I don't think she was happy for long," he murmured.

"Why?"

"She'd just had us. A month or so later, Juliet died. Mother lost her connection to aether. It's been hard on her... you have what she never did."

Valera felt tears form in her eyes. She'd never thought of her mother's past, or how hard it must have been to lose the Trinity, not to mention losing a close friend. When Valera left, Victor must have felt like he'd lost her.

She turned to her twin and blurted, "I'm so sorry."

He hugged her and patted her hair. "I know. Me too."

After a few minutes, he released her and wiped her face with his hand. She smiled at him. He looked older than he had before she'd gone away. He looked tired.

"We should go find Nessie. I think she's at the pub," he said to her surprise. She'd been wrong about him. "We'll stop by the town hall as well and collect the relics... and Gideon."

"But what about Mother?"

Victor sighed, "I think I'm beginning to understand why you *need* to do what you're doing. I thought you were corrupt like the Order, but it's not that... It's Danu. We have to end this, and if that means releasing her, so be it."

Valera hugged her brother one more time before heading downstairs. Keeping an eye out for their mother, they snuck into the foyer. Out of the corner of her eye, Valera caught a glimpse into the library. Dr. Lawless and her mother were sitting close – too close – and whispering to each other. She'd already been through one evil step-father. She didn't want another. Valera swallowed the urge to cause a scene. Victor harrumphed beside her, shaking his head. He nudged her toward the front door. Victor called for the mechanical horse, which clip-clopped out of the carriage house.

"I should warn you, Nessie's in a bad state since the *Cornelius* has been dry docked," Victor said on the way into the village.

"I really messed her up," Valera muttered.

Victor shook his head. "I've been blaming you for a lot lately, and I was wrong. It wasn't your fault. Besides, Nessie hardly needs your help getting into trouble. She is trouble." He grinned.

Sure enough, they found their aunt in the pub – full up the knocker. She had a pint in one hand, a pitcher in the other, and her head on the bar. Her eyes popped open when they walked in.

"Hello, my little twinsisssies," Nessie hooted.

"Hey, Auntie Nessie," Valera began, but was promptly slapped on the back by her aunt so hard, she lost her breath.

"This one's a fire ball. Go 'head, Vlara, you show 'um," Nessie slurred to the other drunken patrons.

The men at the bar ignored her. Victor wrestled the pitcher out of her hand, during which Nessie spilled the contents of the pint all over Valera. A long string of nonsensical curse words poured out of Nessie's lips. Finally, Victor won. He placed the pitcher on the other side of the bar and grabbed his aunt under her shoulder. Valera grabbed her other side, and together, they dragged her into the light of day. She screeched and cowered away as if she were allergic to sunlight. She slipped back under the protection of the awning.

"Why you draggin' me away. I was 'avin fun," she blubbered.

"We need your help," Victor grumbled. "Pull yourself together."

Nessie's bloodshot eyes took on a mischievous glint. "Whatcha planning?"

"First let's get some tea into you. Then we'll talk," Valera suggested.

They went into the bakery. Valera ordered four cups of strong tea, while Victor took Nessie to a quiet table near the back of the room. Nessie downed the tea one right after the other. The caffeine perked her up and returned some of her wits. She leaned across the table, burped, and grinned.

"So, what trouble are we causing this time?"

Valera shook her head. Victor had been right. Nessie created plenty of her own problems even without Valera pulling her into dangerous situations. Victor put his fingers to his lips.

"We're leaving," Victor whispered.

Nessie guffawed. "Well it's about darn time. Where are we going?"

"Shhh," Valera hissed.

Nessie ducked her head and said with quiet but equal gusto, "Where are we going?"

"Danu's tomb," Valera said. "It's in on an island in the far north Atlantic Ocean."

"The *Cornelius* can't take the winds up there. We'll have to go by sea. I bet Ole' Rust Bucket will help us." Nessie grinned. "I'll just tell him Adora's going with us. He's had a crush on her since our first trip in the *Blowfish*."

Valera didn't need to be on the *Blowfish* to already feel seasick. Their first voyage to Pacifica City had been a nightmare. She wanted to protest, but there was no other way to get to Danu's Tomb.

She sighed, "Just don't let anyone know what you're up to. We need to speak with Gideon in the town hall."

"Mum's the word, gotcha! I'll use the telecom on *the Cornelius*. No one will question me there. I'll meet you back home when the deed is done."

Nessie slunk off to the *Cornelius*, while Valera and Victor went on to find Gideon in the town hall, which seemed strangely quiet. Valera expected guards and officials with the precious objects that were inside, but apparently, her mother didn't think the security was necessary.

The receptionist squinted at them. "Can I help you?"

"We're looking for Gideon," Valera stated.

The pinched-faced woman looked them up and down. She hitched her thumb to the right hall.

"Down there," she said with a thin-lipped frown.

"Thanks," Valera said, scampering down the hall.

She heard Gideon's voice before she saw his face. He was in a back room, bent over the relics with a group of white robes. She recognized a few of them from Pacifica City. They recognized her as well. They bowed as she walked in. The Trinity's *miracle* nonsense came in handy. Victor frowned at them in confusion. Valera just took his arm and pulled him into the room, giving him a don't-ask look.

"Valera!" Gideon beamed. "Come in. Please."

"I'm honored to have one of the saviors of Pacifica in my presence. If there is any way I can be of service, you have but to ask," one of the white robes said.

"I'm fine thank you... but you've done excellent work here," Valera said.

The man smiled and bobbed his head. His face turned five shades redder, and for a second, Valera thought he might pass out. Instead, he scuttled off to the side of the room with the other scientists. Victor grunted.

"What's that all about?"

Gideon chuckled, "You haven't heard about Pacifica, have you?"

"No, and I'm not sure I want to," Victor grumbled.

"Forget about all of that. We're here on important business." Valera kissed Gideon's cheek and whispered in his ear, "We need the relics and the key, Gideon. We're leaving for Danu's tomb."

"What about Dr. Lawless? Does he know?" Gideon asked, taking his cue from Valera and keeping his voice low.

"No," Victor rumbled. "He doesn't know anything, and it's going to stay that way."

"Yes, of course. I won't say anything." Gideon replied. "Although, I have to ask why? I thought he was helping the girls. What changed?"

Valera shuddered. "*He* did. He's… not stable."

Gideon nodded. "It will be difficult to get the artifacts out of here with the archivists around, but I can bring them to the mansion tonight, if that works."

"I knew you'd help!"

Valera wrapped her arms around him, noting that Victor's frown grew exponentially. She released Gideon, whose face was now bright red. He straightened his coat and cleared his throat.

Valera smiled. "I'll meet you at the garden pond at midnight."

Gideon nodded. Everything was coming together, and Valera felt as if she were flying.

Victor touched his sister's shoulder to get her attention. "We should return before anyone notices we're gone."

Bidding Gideon farewell, they quickly climbed into the waiting carriage and went back home.

Valera couldn't believe they had gotten away with leaving. She had expected her mother to send out a platoon, or be waiting at the door for their return, but it seemed she hadn't even noticed their departure. She was still in the library when they walked through the front door.

Valera and Victor went straight up to Julia's room to share their success. Julia and Eli were on her bed reading Professor Scrod's notebook and laughing.

"Who knew the Professor lives a secret life as a romance writer... *The fisherman's tight muscular arms wrapped around Marina's trim waist and pulled her against him.*

'No, I won't, she cried.

'Face it, Marina you are mine," Julia read aloud, falling into a fit of laughter.

"Are you sure you stole the right book," Valera quipped.

"Positive. The map is the last entry," Eli chuckled.

"Did you have any trouble?" Victor asked.

Julia grinned. "It wasn't hard. Your mother kept Lawly busy in the library. Seems you might have a new daddy."

Victor growled, "Watch it, Julia."

Eli got off the bed and went face to face with Victor. *Boys.* Valera rolled her eyes and got in between them. They didn't need a brawl to ruin their plans. They couldn't risk drawing attention to themselves. Valera scowled at Julia.

A little help here?

Why? This is amusing. Who do you think would win?

"Come on, guys. Victor, it isn't worth it," Valera pleaded.

Julia finally sat up on the bed and droned, "I'm sorry, Victor."

Sorry that Dr. Lawless might be your dad, Julia added telepathically, drawing a glare from Valera. *Kidding... sheesh.*

Although Victor eased off, Valera knew he was still fuming. Eli plopped back down on the bed as if nothing had happened. She was beginning to understand why his ever-present smirk annoyed Julia. He picked up the book and tossed it to Valera, who flipped through the pages and found the map.

"Here's where we're going, Victor. I discovered it with Aeda's Sextant. You should have seen me," she said, trying to diffuse the situation.

A brief smile touched Victor's lips. He took the book and examined the pages. "I've got some nautical maps in my room. We may be able to pinpoint an exact location. Do you mind if I take this for a while?"

Julia stiffened up, but Eli patted her leg. "I'll go with him."

"I can handle it on my own," Victor groaned.

"I grew up in Pacifica. I know nautical maps... besides have you ever been alone in a room with these two? You either freeze or boil... sometimes both at the same time."

Julia threw him a nasty look, and he skipped out of the room, laughing.

"Men..." Valera bemoaned.

"Oh, well. What can you do?" Julia smiled. "You might want to go pack a few things."

"Hmm, good idea. I wouldn't want to leave with only the clothes on my back... again," Valera sneered.

"Hey, I apologized for that kidnapping-you business."

"Well, I don't recall it, but *okay*. See you later."

Valera left Julia alone and went back to her room. It didn't take long to toss some clothes into a satchel. Afterward, she sat on her bed, unsure of what to do next. She picked up a book from her nightstand – a fairytale she'd started before everything had changed. The story seemed so childish now. She was living her own crazy fairytale, and it was nothing like she ever imagined. The final chapter started at nightfall and still felt like a million hours away. She watched the hour hands slowly tick around the clock face until dinnertime.

She considered feigning sickness to avoid the inevitably uncomfortable meal to come, but didn't want to raise suspicion. Taking her time, she walked to the dining room. Her mother didn't notice her arrival. Marjorie and Nathaniel chose to eat in their room. Parmelia had left earlier in the day. The rest ate in silence except for Dr. Lawless and Victoria. Their sickening interaction repulsed Valera… and it seemed everyone else at the table as well. After an appropriate amount of time spent pushing food around on their plates, they left one by one. Valera was the last, and her mother didn't notice her departure.

Valera met up with Theo and Julia, and together they waited in Julia's room. Valera was too nervous to talk, so she sat in a chair and created small flames in her hands. Victor and Eli came later, maps in hand and ready to travel. Joe meandered in a few minutes later. Lastly, Nessie burst into the room.

"I've contacted Rusty. We're in luck. He's doing business with some humans nearby. He'll meet us at the aerodrome at dawn. We just need to borrow a transport." Nessie's wicked grin gave Valera the chills.

"We've located the region where the tomb should be. The maps don't specify any islands in the area, but according to Professor Scrod's notes, it should be there," Victor said, pointing to a blank spot in the north Atlantic.

"Gideon is bringing the relics and the key to the pond. If we're ready, we should go meet him there." Valera's nerves rattled in her voice.

They moved through the quiet mansion and out into the gardens. Valera's stomach was tangled in so many knots, she thought she might pass out. Theo wiped a hand across her face and looked back.

"I hope my parents will understand. I feel like we're just now getting back to normal," she murmured.

Valera put a hand on her shoulder. "They'll be fine. Once this is done, we can all go back to normal."

Even as the words came out of her mouth, she questioned the truth of them. In reality, they didn't know what they were doing. Seeing Gideon under the willow with a duffle bag made her feel a bit better. At least, she had him with her. She waved to him.

"I brought everything you asked for," he said.

Nessie slapped his back. "Good Lad, did anyone follow you?"

Gideon shook his head.

"Well then, let's get out of here," the captain barked.

They couldn't risk taking the carriage this late at night, so they walked along the fields all the way into the village. The docks were empty except for a few of Nessie's crewmembers. With a simple word, they stood watch while the rest of the group climbed aboard the small transport ship. Nessie started the engines and pulled away from the dock. Once they were far enough in flight that Aetherland disappeared in the clouds, Valera took a deep breath. They were free.

The ship floated through the skies, landing at the aerodrome with a splash. Eli and Victor tied the mooring lines to the pegs. Valera rushed across the gangplank to the floating wharf. The Atlantic Island Aerodrome custodian fumbled out of the tiny lighthouse, rubbing his bloodshot eyes and grumbling.

"Captain Stein, is that you?" He looked at a clipboard in his hands confused. "I don't have a notice of your arrival."

Nessie clasped the man on the shoulder. "Bernie, it's good to see you." She plucked the clipboard form his hands. "No need to worry about logs and such. This visit's... top secret."

The docks shook as if there were an earthquake right below them. The caretaker's eyes bulged. Valera fought to remain standing. The ocean bubbled and two glass eyes rose out of the deep.

"Rusty's early," Nessie shouted over the noise of the *Blowfish*'s engines. "How about we keep this between us?"

The caretaker named Bernie nodded. "I'm too tired to mess with your shenanigans. Just get going before I change my mind."

"That-a-boy, Bernie. Just go back to bed and forget we were ever here," Nessie urged.

Rusty popped out of the main hatch. "Well, ya got me 'ere. There ain't no time for lollygagging. The *Blowfish*'s burnin' fuel."

Rusty held a hand out to help Valera and the others aboard the submarine of her nightmares. Gideon was right behind her. The submersible still smelled like oil and seaweed, which brought back a torrent of memories from the last trip.

She leaned over to Gideon and whispered, "I wonder what this will cost us?"

Gideon shrugged. "This is my first time aboard this... ship." He lowered his voice, "Are you sure it's seaworthy."

Valera shook her head. "Not in the slightest."

With everyone inside, Rusty latched the hatch. He peered around the cabin and frowned.

Rusty snorted. "I dunna see Adora. Nessie said she'd be 'ere."

"Sorry, Rusty. Last minute change of plans," Nessie quipped.

She pulled a bauble from her pocket. Valera recognized the ring as a gift her mother had given her aunt. Rusty took the ring and held it up to a squinted eye. Valera frowned – it wasn't a fake this time. The ring had real diamonds and emeralds embedded in real gold. It was a high price to pay for a ride. Nessie nudged her side.

"It was too gaudy for my style anyway," her aunt chuckled.

Rusty spat in his palm. "Deal done."

Nessie did the same, and they shook hands. Valera rubbed her hand against her shirt. She'd never understand the intricacies and rituals of salty sea captains or their airborne counterparts.

Victor told Rusty where they were headed. The old man groaned and grumbled, but started up the *Blowfish's* engines. With all eight passengers and Rusty, the submarine was filled to capacity. The pistons spit and sputtered.

Bang... bang... bang...

"What in tarnation!" Rusty growled.

The sound was outside the hatch. Valera looked through a porthole and saw a blurry face. Rusty unhinged the latch and got out. After a few minutes of muddled voices, Rusty returned.

"There's a man outside who's sayin' he hasta come along. He says ya know 'im."

Rusty tried to hold the hatch closed, but a hand appeared and pulled it open. Then, a familiar face popped inside.

"No way, forget it!" Julia shouted.

"Now wait one second, just hear me out!" Dr. Lawless pleaded.

Valera crossed her arms over her chest. "How did you find us?"

"I knew you would make a move. It was just a matter of time. Earlier, I accidentally overheard a conversation, and well, I stowed away in the transport ship. It's important I go with you."

"No, it's not. Rusty, kick him out and let's go," Julia hissed.

Dr. Lawless pushed his lanky way inside and planted himself firmly in the way. "I insist on going. I've waited my whole life to see Danu's tomb, and I won't relent now. If you turn me away, I will tell the council everything."

"Is he comin' or goin'?" Rusty asked.

Victor stepped forward. "We don't have time to argue. You can come, but you stay away from the girls."

"I'll keep an eye on him," Joe growled.

Dr. Lawless nodded and sat at the back of the submarine, keeping his mouth shut. Rusty slammed the hatch shut and returned to the helm. With a jerk, the submarine moved away from the dock. Valera kept one eye on Dr. Lawless.

"He can't do anything with everyone here. Relax," Gideon whispered and put his arm around her shoulder.

She leaned against him and yawned. The vibrations of the engines and the sway of the waves lulled her into a light sleep. A couple of hours later, a tingling sensation pulsed through her.

Daughter… I'm here…

Danu's voice was inside the vessel. Valera sat straight up. Theo and Julia were also wide-eyed and upright.

"We're almost there," Julia murmured.

The submarine surfaced in the ice-covered North Atlantic. The hatch opened with a loud slurp, a blast of glaring sunlight, and a gust of frigid air. Rusty poked his head outside, returning a few seconds later with snow and ice covering his stubbly face.

"There ain't nothin' out there, but 'bergs," she shivered.

Victor opened the map in Professor Scrod's book and debated with Rusty over their location. Eli got into the mix, and soon voices grew louder and more irritated. Valera couldn't take it. She retrieved the sextant and shimmied up through the hatch. She sat on the submarine's slick exterior, holding the sextant to her eye. Theo and Julia appeared beside her, and together they channeled aether into the instrument. A line of light shone across the ocean, leading to a glowing blue light in the distance.

"Well, color me a barnacle!" Rusty quipped. "What's that?"

"That's where Danu's tomb is," Julia said.

They made note of where the island was and set course. The scuttled along the surface of the water along the invisible line. When they reached the location of the glowing lights, they still hadn't found the island. The ship came to a stop, and Rusty checked over his navigation controls and compasses.

"I dunna get it. I dunna see nothin'" Rusty exclaimed, wiping the haze from the great glass eyes of the *Blowfish*.

Valera moved to the front of the ship. She frowned at the captain.

"Rusty, it's right there." She pointed to the unmistakable large rocky landmass only a few miles ahead of them.

Victor squinted his eyes. "I don't see anything either."

Theo pushed them out of the way. "It's right in front of us."

"Don't be ridiculous. There's nothing—

The submarine rocked to starboard, and something big slithered across the metal exterior. Valera fell into her brother against the side of the hull. The *Blowfish* groaned. Rivets popped and small trickles of water poured into the cabin. The rocking stopped.

"What was that?" Julia shrieked.

Rusty and Nessie worked to fill the leaks with putty, but the water pushed through. Julia soaked in aether and froze the streams, temporarily plugging the holes.

Bleep... bleep... bleep...

Rusty moved to the radar. "There's something moving around us. Could be a whale... a big un. Wouldna be the first time some dumb fish tried a make friends' wit' the vessel."

Rusty grabbed a harpoon and threw open the hatch. The radar bleeped louder and faster. The ship shook. The monster in the water rammed the side of the submarine, denting the side. Rusty nearly fell overboard, but Eli and Joe grabbed his legs.

"Keep me steady, boy," the old man yelled from above. "I got a shot."

Valera heard the whizzing of the harpoon flying in the air and an odd metallic ping as it struck its target. Rusty came back inside, shaking and soaking wet. The harpoon gun was missing.

"That ain't no whale... I ner' saw nothin' like it. The harpoon bounced right off." His voice shook. "We need to get outta here."

An unearthly shriek filled the air outside. Through the window, Valera saw a massive worm-like creature swim past the ship. The monster turned and smashed into the other side of the submarine. The hull buckled and water poured into the compartment. No matter how hard Julia tried to stop the influx of water, the compartment flooded. They had to abandon ship. Nessie scrambled to inflate two rafts outside on top of the hull. Joe leapt into the first one and helped the three girls and Eli get inside. They grabbed the oars and moved as far away as they could. Nessie and Gideon scrambled into the second raft, but the sea monster turned and charged at the vessel. Victor pushed Dr. Lawless overboard, and jumped into the frigid water. The monster rammed the front of the ship, smashing the two glass eyes. Rusty was thrown off the doomed *Blowfish*. Nessie and Gideon fished all three men out of the ocean, and the two lifeboats rowed away from the submarine.

The sea monster crested out of the water and crashed onto *the Blowfish*. The beast's shiny exterior glistened in the sun light as if it were made out of metal. Its body slid over the remains of the submarine making a horrible grating noise. The monster screeched as the *Blowfish* sank into the water.

"Where do we go?" Joe asked.

Theo pointed toward the landmass. "To the island."

"What island? There's no island!" Nessie shouted.

"Just trust us," Julia said.

The girls steered the raft toward the island, which only they seemed able to see. The creature writhed around the wreckage of the *Blowfish*. Just as Valera thought they'd escaped its clutches, it surfaced and shot through the ocean like a torpedo. Something about it didn't seem real, and as it grew closer, Valera saw gears turning behind its green glass eyes. Its scales were black metal plates. The monster's gaping jaw opened, and Valera saw spinning razor sharp blades.

"It's a machine!" Valera screamed.

Julia stood and aimed her hands at the mechanical monster. She blasted it with shards of ice. The creature slowed down, but didn't stop. Valera joined in, throwing fire at it, and Theo electrocuted it with bolts of lightning. Nothing seemed to faze it. The others rowed as fast as they could, but still the monster got closer.

"Are we almost there?" Joe huffed.

Valera turned to look. The island was close. Then, the air thickened around her. Valera felt her entire body tingle. Both Theo and Julia gasped at the same time. The sea creature shrieked and slammed into an invisible barrier. The monster shattered into a million pieces and disappeared. Everyone in the rafts cheered.

Rusty rubbed his eyes and shouted, "I'll be damned. There be an island."

CHAPTER SIXTEEN

Julia

Julia peered over the side of the raft at the calm and clear water below. No ice. No seaweed. No fish. The place was unnatural. She felt as if she could see right to the bottom of the ocean. Rusty muttered to himself on the other raft.

"This ain't right... none of it," he rambled.

The rest of them paddled toward the rocky shoreline in silence. They landed the boats on a sandy outcropping. Julia was the first one out, and she dropped to her knees on the shore. She hated the ocean. She hated submarines. She hated sea monsters. From now on, she wanted solid earth beneath her feet. Eli came and knelt beside her.

"Are you okay?" He asked.

She nodded.

"You did well out there," he whispered and nudged her.

"We didn't kill it." She murmured, "The barrier did."

"No, but you gave us time to escape. That's a win in my book." He winked. "And you looked sexy throwing all that ice around."

She laughed, "You're insane."

Julia leaned into him and curled up against the warmth of his body. His arm slipped around her. She was perfectly happy to stay on the beach and wait for rescue. After facing off with a robotic sea monster, the idea of freeing Danu had faded to the back her mind. She wasn't the only one who wanted to rest. Theo plopped onto a driftwood log. Valera and Gideon chatted near a large boulder. Everyone but Dr. Lawless looked tired. He scrambled off the lifeboat, falling into the water in the process. He waded to shore and sniffed the air like a rabid dog.

"Danu is close... I can feel her. She's here... oh, sweet goddess... guide me to you..."

His incessant ranting drove Julia crazy. "Sit down and shut up, Lawly."

"No... no time for rest. We must hurry. We must find Danu," Dr. Lawless raved.

"Oh shut yer flappin'," Rusty yelled at the man, then dropped to his knees near the shoreline and lamented, "Me poor *Blowfish*."

The tide inched up over Rusty's knees. Nessie put a hand on the man's back. Together, they looked out to sea where the *Blowfish* had sunk.

"She was a fine ship," Nessie cooed. "She went down in battle – a noble death for a noble lady."

Rusty nodded his head, sniffling loudly. Nessie urged the man to come on shore and out of the water. Theo walked over to Victor and Joe.

In a hushed voice, she asked, "What was that thing?"

"A warning." Victor scratched his cheek. "One we didn't heed. This place is bewitched."

"We must have passed through some kind of aether barrier. That would explain why you girls could see past it, and the rest of us couldn't." Gideon joined them, picking up a handful of sand and examining it through his fingers. "It's odd for sure. There's no wind here, and it should be several degrees below zero. But it feels more like a balmy summer night."

Valera took Gideon's hand, "If we are going to do this, we should move on. This place gives me the shivers."

"I'll be goin' no further. Just leave me here wit' the risin' tide," Rusty muttered.

Eli pulled Julia up off the sand. She felt sorry for Rusty. Although *the Blowfish* was a leaky hunk of junk, it got them where they needed to go. She placed a hand on Rusty's shoulder.

"Sorry for your loss."

He patted her hand, keeping his eyes cast on the spot where his livelihood went down.

"I'll stay with him," Nessie said, and added with a whisper, "He's not in the right state of mind to be alone."

Julia joined the others further ashore. Gideon opened the duffle bag and pulled out the Sword of Ealga. Dr. Lawless snuck into the group and reached out for the relic. Julia slapped his hands away and took the weapon.

"Back off, Lawly."

"I was just going to hand it to you… I wasn't going to touch it…"

"What is your problem?" Julia hissed.

He backed away slowly and grinned like a maniac. With a shriek, he ran down the beach. Julia moved to chase him, but Eli stopped her.

"Let him go. He's lost his mind."

Julia slipped the sword into her belt. Theo took the scepter and put the Trinity Key in her pocket. Valera kept the sextant in the bag and slung it over her shoulder. Julia led the way up the shore and over a field of stones, keeping watch for any other *warnings* that the island contained. Climbing on one of the boulders that littered the barren landscape, she could see the shoreline all around the tiny island. As far as she could tell, there was nothing there.

"Where's the tomb?" She hopped down.

Dr. Lawless came back to them, muttering, "No... this isn't right... it has to be here. You did something wrong!"

He charged at Valera. Before Valera could defend herself, Dr. Lawless had his hands around her throat. Joe and Victor ripped the man off her. He stumbled back, but changed course and came after Julia. Eli cracked the man's head, knocking him unconscious. Gideon checked Valera's neck.

"I'm fine." She shuddered. "What's wrong with him?" she asked.

Gideon shrugged. "I suppose his mind couldn't deal with the situation."

Julia scoffed, "Leave him. We need to find the tomb."

"What if he wakes up?" Valera stared at the unconscious man.

"I'll keep an eye on him."

Joe stayed behind with the unconscious doctor. Everyone else spread out and searched. Victor walked off to the far side of the island by himself. Valera and Gideon searched the western shore of the island, and Theo took the eastern shore. Julia and Eli took the middle ground.

Julia turned over rocks and picked up old pieces of driftwood, looking for any strange markings and finding none. All of the rocks began to look alike. Finding the tomb began to seem like an impossible task. Perhaps Lawly was right, and they had made a mistake in their navigation. In her frustration, she misstepped and fell forward onto the rocks.

"Julia, are you all right?" Eli called from behind her.

Her knees and palms stung, but she wasn't hurt. In between two grey stones, she saw a flash of blue. She crawled toward it for a closer look. The blue slithered away, and then she heard a hiss. Something slid across her ankles, and she froze.

Eli stood nearby. "Julia, don't move."

Azure colored snakes writhed all around her, hissing and spitting. Every muscle in her body shook, but she didn't dare move.

"I'm going to get help," Eli said, slowly backing away.

Julia held her breath the entire time he was gone. Before long, the others arrived, standing at a safe distance. Julia's arms and legs tired from sitting in the same position. She couldn't wait much longer. Gideon inched forward, examining one of the serpents. To Julia's surprise, he picked one up.

"You can get up now, Julia. These are simple blue corn snakes. They are completely nonvenomous. In fact, they make great pets. Strange to find them this far north," Gideon blathered.

"I don't need a zoology lesson," Julia snapped. She stood up, sulking. "Stupid rocks!"

She stared at the offending rock that had tripped her up. Something about the flat triangular surface caught her eye. The stone was different from those around it. Moss covered the top of it, and the sides were too sharp to be a natural formation.

"Do you see this?" She asked.

Julia picked at the moss. Beneath the green plant, she found three wavy lines carved into the rock.

"That could be a sign for air," Gideon said. "Or perhaps water?"

"Here's another one," Theo said from a few feet away.

The second stone had flames etched into it. Victor found a third triangular stone with three spirals.

Gideon studied them for a second. "The flames represent fire; the spirals are similar to the Celtic symbol for water."

"Water, fire, air... like the powers," Theo said.

"Three pillars, three symbols, three sisters," Julia mused. "But what does it mean? What do we do?"

"Well, since I cast fire, it makes sense that I do something with this one," Valera said standing over the fire symbol.

The stones formed a larger triangle. The spirals made the most sense to Julia – water and ice. She stood on top of it and touched the symbol. Nothing happened. She channeled aether and felt the stone move. Valera did the same. Her eyes widened as her stone shook.

"Theo stand on the last one," Julia said.

Finally, Theo took her place on air symbol. The guys moved away, giving them some room. Julia closed her eyes, letting instinct guide her. Together, the three girls soaked in aether and let it flow through them.

The ground shook, and the three pillars lifted them into the air. A wind rushed across the island, nearly knocking them over. The snakes scattered. From the center of the triangle, a stone arch grew from the earth. When the quakes stopped, the girls released aether. A marble slab filled the arch like a monolithic door.

"What is it?" Eli asked.

He took a step forward, but a piercing chime blared from the marble. He covered his ears and sunk to his knees. The marble slab vibrated and exploded in two, throwing the girls from the pillars.

Julia rolled on her side and peered at the arch. A swirling black mist formed between the posts. Finger-like tendrils reached out to each girl. A howl came out of the mist. One of the tendrils broke off from the haze, taking shape in front of Julia. Before her eyes, the mist morphed into a human form. She shrieked and backed away from it. Dripping wet, the phantom's skin bubbled and peeled over its skeletal frame. Its eyes were deep voids, dripping black tar.

Eli charged at it. The apparition didn't even turn to look at him, instead it flung its rotting hand out. A gust of vile wind knocked Eli back against a boulder.

Julia struggled to stand, but the bones in her legs dissolved into quivering masses. She reached for the sword at her belt. The weapon wasn't there. Retreating, she scrambled around searching the rocks for the blade. The specter's hand reached out to grab her. She slid aside, but the putrid fingers of the dead brushed her shoulder, searing into her skin. Her arm burned as if she'd been dipped in boiling oil. The appendage hung limp at her side.

"Help." Her voice was a whimper compared to the howling monster.

On the other side of the archway, Theo lay unconscious. Maera's Scepter sat on the ground beside her. A second tendril of the black fog moved toward Theo. Julia stumbled toward Theo, but the specter followed close behind her.

On the ground near the broken stone, she saw a glint of metal. She crawled on her knees and good arm for the sword. The specter growled. Her fingers brushed the blade seconds before the specter reached her. Channeling aether, she lifted the Ealga's Sword of Ice. The blade sank deep into the specter's chest. He shrieked and writhed as aether tore through the phantom in an icy blast. The mist froze solid. Julia stood. With her last once of strength, she pulled the blade free. The specter splintered into a million icy shards.

Julia fumbled to find Theo. The second tendril of mist mutated into a thick rippling liquid that moved over Theo's feet and legs, swallowing her inch by inch. Theo woke as the blob reached her chest. Gasping for air, she struggled to free herself.

Julia reached her, swinging the sword at the liquid. The mass sucked the sword into its dripping maw, pulling Julia closer to it. Theo's face turned blue. Her eyes begged Julia to help her. Maera's Scepter floated inside the blob.

"Use the scepter," Julia yelled, pointing at Maera's staff.

Theo couldn't move her arms to reach the weapon. The sludge moved halfway up the sword. Julia released the blade, and the mass consumed it.

I have to get the staff. She didn't want to touch the liquid, but she had little choice. Drenching herself in aether, she held her breath. She leapt at the blob. For a split second, she felt as if she was swimming in a jello mold. Then, the mass thickened around her. Aether kept the beast at bay long enough for her to reach the scepter. She forced the staff into Theo's hand. As soon as Theo's fingers wrapped around it, Julia felt the transfer of aether. A light exploded from the jewel. The mass disintegrated around them. Air rushed back into Julia's lungs. Theo panted on the ground, and the color returned to her face.

"What was that?" Theo rasped.

Julia shook her head. She had no clue to what was happening. Behind the mound, they heard screaming.

"Where's Valera?" Theo asked.

Julia pointed to where the last pillar stood. Another scream pierced the air. Julia and Theo got up and ran toward the noise. They found Victor unmoving on the ground with a bleeding wound on his neck. Theo dropped to her knees and covered the wound with her hands. Julia went in search of Valera.

SAVE AETHER | 197

Gideon and Valera had their backs up to a boulder. A giant snarling wolf stalked toward them. Gideon tried to protect Valera by waving a fiery branch at the animal. A swipe from the animal's massive paw threw Gideon to the side. Valera threw flames from her hands, hitting the animal. He growled but continued his approach.

Julia charged the rear of the animal with the sword, striking the flesh of the demon's legs. He roared and turned on her. His fangs dripped with blood. The animal's eyes were black coal. His breath stunk like festering meat. Julia stepped back, swinging the sword. Even though the blade sliced through the beast's skin, it didn't stop. A massive blast of flame shot from Valera's hands, setting the wolf on fire. The heat of it burned Julia's face. Valera lashed out over and over again. Julia hacked at the blazing body until nothing but his grinning fangs remained. With a final howl, the beast dissipated back into mist and disappeared back into the earth.

Julia left Valera to check on Gideon, and she ran back to Eli. He leaned against the boulder, holding his head. She knelt down beside him. He smirked.

"Don't worry about me. The boulder broke my fall."

"Very funny," she grumbled.

"Are you okay?"

Her arm stung from where the specter had touched her. Her chest ached from holding her breath inside the blob, and her skin felt as if she had the worst sunburn of her life. She wasn't okay. She pulled her shirt off her shoulder. Three blackish wounds slashed across her arm. Eli tore the sleeve of his shirt and wrapped her arm up. Then, he took her chin in his hands and kissed her.

CHAPTER SEVENTEEN

*T*heo

Theo bent over Victor, crying. The wound on his neck still bled. Blood bubbled from between her fingers. Nessie ran to help, wrapping Victor's neck in rags. Julia limped over with Eli.

"Is he... dead?" Julia muttered.

Theo looked up through blurry eyes. "No, but this is bad."

"We need to get help," Valera wailed. "We need to contact the Elders."

A bruised Gideon held Valera against his chest. Julia picked up the scepter and held it out to Theo.

"You can help him. Remember in Pacifica, you can use Maera's staff to heal him," Julia urged.

Julia placed the scepter in her hands, but Theo shook her head. Theo couldn't do it. Pacifica was a fluke. She didn't know what she was doing.

"What if I hurt him?"

"Just try."

"I... I can't," Theo wept. "I might kill him."

Julia sighed, "Then try on me first. I have faith in you."

Theo looked at Julia as if she were crazy. She couldn't be serious. Eli knelt beside Julia and shook his head.

"I don't think this is a good idea."

Julia smiled at him and gently pushed him away. "It's okay. I know she can do this."

Julia removed her bandages and revealed three deep, blackened cuts around her arm. Even though Julia was acting strong, Theo saw her wince, and knew she had to help. Her hands shook. Theo touched the scepter to Julia's arm and poured aether through it. Julia flinched.

Through gritted teeth, she urged Theo on. "You can do this."

The gem on the scepter glowed with a soft light. Julia went rigid and sucked in a breath as the light passed into her wounds. Theo watched as the skin stitched itself back together, and soon, Julia was sighing in relief.

"I did it!" Theo smiled behind her tears.

She crawled over to Victor and placed the staff on his neck. His body twitched. His wounds were deeper, but they had stopped bleeding. The gash knit together, but he didn't wake. Theo slumped over him.

"Victor, wake up. Please." Theo cried.

Nessie felt Victor's pulse and took a deep breath. "He's breathing. He lost a lot of blood, but he's alive."

Theo sat on the rocks. Exhaustion ripped her in half. Theo looked at the archway. It had to lead somewhere. They were so close. Then, she looked at her friends. Victor was still hurt. Valera couldn't stop crying. Julia, although better, looked like she was about to pass out. Battered and fearful, they couldn't go on. Perhaps, they should have heeded the warnings.

Since the sea monster had destroyed the *Blowfish*, they had no way of getting off the island. Theo searched Victor's pockets for his telecom and found it in several pieces. She tried to piece it back together and failed miserably. Gideon also tried, but the device was damaged beyond repair.

"There has to be something we can do," Theo groaned.

"If we concentrate, we may be able to send Parmelia a message," Julia suggested.

Valera sighed, "We're too far away. It won't work."

"Well, it's worth a try. Link arms, and we'll combine our strength," Julia held her hand out.

Theo figured it couldn't hurt, although she doubted linking or combining would make any difference. They weren't satellite dishes. She took Julia's hand, and Valera took hers. Theo focused on sending a message to Parmelia.

Parmelia, if you can hear us, we need your help. Please, come, she chanted.

Julia and Valera did the same.

Julia added an image of their location on a map. Theo projected the same image in her thoughts. They continued trying until they couldn't hold aether any longer. They waited for a reply, but got none.

"It was worth a try," Julia shrugged.

Theo rubbed her eyes. Ever since coming to the island, Danu's voice had quieted. Theo would do anything to get a little sleep, but she feared that the nightmares would still be there. Footsteps raced over the rocks behind her. Thinking it was another specter, Theo pulled in aether and spun around. Dr. Lawless stopped in his tracks. His eyes were swollen and red. A purple, fist-sized bruise covered half his jaw, and dried blood crusted on his lips. His hair stuck out everywhere. He fell on his knees and prostrated himself in front of the archway.

"You've done it! Oh, precious Danu. We're coming. Open it! Open it now!" He raved and laughed.

Theo shook her head at the man. He was out of his mind. Standing, he grabbed Theo's shoulders, digging his nails into her skin.

"Release her... release Danu..." He shook her.

Pain and frustration took hold of her, and she zapped his hands off her. He screeched and let go, but his glare became demonic. She backed away from him.

"We're leaving this cursed place. We should never have come," she yelled.

"NO, you can't do that!" Dr. Lawless moved toward her again.

Theo formed sparks in her hands, daring him to touch her. He retreated.

"Look around, Lawless. Victor's hurt. We're exhausted. We've already called for help," she lied. She threw her hands in the air and turned to the others. "Why do you think there are so many booby-traps? It doesn't make sense. First, the sea monster, then the mist? What next? Face it, Lawless, we're not supposed to open the tomb. There has to be a reason the sister's put so many wards to keep people out of the tomb."

Julia and Valera groaned their agreement, but Lawless wouldn't relent. He picked up a stone and held it up like a weapon. He backed up to the entrance of the archway. Glowering at all of them, he hissed like one of the blue snakes.

"You're just like the others! You are jealous of Danu's power. You want it all for yourselves. You don't deserve her!" He cackled, "But I know what to do... I know..."

The man whipped something out of his pocket. He held the Trinity Key above his head. Surprised, Theo searched her pockets.

"How did you get that?"

Theo moved to take it from him, but he stepped inside the arch. Julia ran at him, throwing shards of ice. Valera had her fireballs in hand, but he was too quick. He laughed like a maniac, slamming the key into the stone. The three girls reached him at the same time, grabbing his arm. They pulled on him, trying to remove the key from the arch. But it was too late, the key activated and melded with the stone. With a sudden jerk, Theo felt her muscles clench. Aether rushed through her, even though she attempted to release it.

"I can't stop," Julia yelled.

Theo felt the aether flow from the three of them, through Lawless, and into the key. Theo couldn't let go. Dr. Lawless trembled as the power flooded his system. His eyes rolled into the back of his sockets. The Trinity Key drained them all until the archway shimmered like a mirror. Then the key freed them, and they fell to the ground. Still twitching, Lawless clawed his way through the portal. Part of Theo wanted to remove the key and lock him inside, but Julia growled and leapt into the opening after Lawless. Theo had no choice but to follow Julia inside.

Theo stepped into a room made of glass. From within the tomb, she could see the outside world and a sparkling white energy that surrounded everything. Aether. A blue light floated around the inside of the burial chamber radiating from a crystal block in the center of the room.

"Get Lawless and let's get out of here," Theo whispered to Julia. "I don't think we should be in here."

The translucent white crystal encased the body of a beautiful woman. She appeared dead, but at the same time, the whole block seemed to breathe.

"It's pure, solidified aether."

Valera stepped up behind Theo, startling her. She gasped. "Is that her?"

"Valera, we need to get out of here. I have a bad feeling…"

Dr. Lawless reached out and touched the crystal. The second his skin connected with the smooth surface, his fingers sizzled and blistered. He screamed. The blistering spread across his hand, smoldering and shriveling. Theo grabbed the back of his shirt and yanked him away before the rest of him burned. He held his scorched stub and whimpered.

"Let's go—

Theo's voice was cut short. A voice boomed inside her mind, calling to her… begging her.

Touch the aether, Maera. Release me…

"No… I can't… This isn't right," Theo stammered.

The body inside the crystal turned to look at her. The eyes drew her in. An invisible tether reeled her in, and she moved closer to the block. The eyes inside bored through her. She had to touch the aether. The crystal glowed brighter and brighter. Her hand reached out in front of her. Just one more step, and she would be free.

Maera… come to me, daughter…

"Theo?"

Someone shouted her name from outside, but outside didn't matter. Nothing mattered. Theo had to feel the crystal under her fingers. She had to touch it. She longed for the sweet sensation that filled her when she held aether.

The light radiating off the crystal blinded her. Theo felt as if she were on a merry-go-round, spinning out of control. Exhilaration overtook her, and then it contorted into something dark. A wisp of aether left her hand, soaking into the block.

More… give me more… touch the aether…

Theo's senses returned. She tried to lower hand. She tried to keep away from crystal, but her body wasn't her own. Danu ripped aether from her. Her heart raced. Beads of sweat rippled down her body. She couldn't breathe.

CHAPTER EIGHTEEN

Valera

Valera's vitality drained out of her, and she couldn't stop it. She didn't know if she would survive her skin connecting with the block. The crystal hummed and vibrated as the threads of energy filtered out of her hands. Her knees buckled.

Two strong hands grabbed her around the waist and dragged her back. She felt a sudden sense of loss, but also relief. Fresh air and sunlight hit her face. Gideon held her in his arms on rocky ground. He was speaking to her. Her ears rang so loud that she couldn't hear him.

"Valera, come back to me." He tapped her cheek.

Her senses returned in a rush of pain and chaos. The voices deafened her. Joe dragged Theo out of the archway. Julia shook in Eli's arms. Dr. Lawless screamed profanities at Nessie and Rusty, who held him back from the portal. The shimmering light between the arch disappeared. No light, no sound, no movement.

"I'm sorry, Gideon. I'm so sorry. I don't know what happened," Valera wept.

Gideon rocked her. "I know. Don't worry, we pulled you out in time... I think."

Valera felt something pass over her leg. The blue snakes had returned, swarming around the archway. She shuddered. Their hissing grew louder and louder.

"We need to get the girls away from here," Rusty shouted.

Gideon nodded. As he helped Valera stand, she saw a flash of light from the arch. No one seemed to notice. She pulled away from Gideon. Dr. Lawless shrieked with glee, pushing over Rusty and Nessie. He ran to the arch, rubbing against it as if he were one of the snakes.

"No... please, no," Valera muttered.

The portal flickered. Then, an ear-piercing, high-pitched hum blared in Valera's mind. She screamed and grabbed her head. She heard Theo and Julia scream as well. The others looked at the girls with furrowed brows. Couldn't they hear it? Valera writhed on the ground. The earth rose and fell beneath them, knocking them off their feet. Gideon scrambled to his feet and faced the doorway. The chime stopped inside Valera's head. The portal opened, and fragments of solidified aether exploded from the rippling mirror.

A woman emerged from the tomb. Her flowing green dress spilled around her like puddles of water. Her bare feet didn't touch the ground. Fresh green grass sprouted with each step, but shriveled and died just as quickly. Her face outshone the sun, and her amber eyes cut sharper than razors. Her long silken brown hair blew in a non-existent wind.

The blue snakes slithered around her ankles. She picked one up and kissed its head. It wrapped itself around her arm.

"The Azure Serpents, how long you've awaited my return. Rise again, my faithful guardians," she sang.

The snakes at her feet writhed beneath her. Their bodies formed limbs and grew. Their scales transformed into leathery skin. The serpents stood on two feet as men. Blue tattoos covered their bodies. Disheveled hair and beards covered their faces.

"It's true," Julia muttered. "The ancient stories of the Order are true."

"Ealga, why do you appear surprised to see your brothers-in-arms?"

Danu moved to touch Julia's cheek, but Eli stepped in front of her. Danu tilted her head and smiled. Her pack of human-serpents growled and hissed behind her. Her finger brushed across Eli's jaw.

"This brave, stupid boy moves to protect you from me?"

Danu's face contorted into a scowl. With a wave of her hand, Eli fell to the ground. Danu's eyes passed over the others, and one by one they dropped. Nessie, Rusty, Gideon, and Joe crumpled like broken dolls. Only the trinity remained conscious. Valera crawled over to Gideon and touched his neck. His pulse beat strong under her fingers. Danu laughed.

"My beautiful daughters, fear not. The mortals merely sleep. I desire a word alone with you." Her voice was like music, however her perfect downturned lips defied her tranquil tone.

Danu was awake, and she wasn't happy.

CHAPTER NINETEEN

*J*ulia

Julia moved closer to Valera and Theo with her hand on the hilt of Ealga's sword. This wasn't how she imagined facing Danu. She'd grown up listening to the legends of the Order. The academy prided themselves on their lineage to Danu's guard, but the azure serpents were metaphorical – or so she thought. Aetherians praised Danu as a benevolent, loving goddess, but the creature in front of her felt twisted and wrong.

As Danu approached them, Julia's grip grew tighter. Theo's knuckles turned white around the scepter, and Valera held aether. Danu's pointy-nailed fingers rose to touch her, and Julia lifted the sword. The strange serpent-men inched forward, but Danu held her arm in the air, and they calmed and backed away. The goddess laughed. With a simple swipe of her hands, the weapons were thrown to the side.

"Those toys are not needed, my children. You need not fear me," Danu chimed.

Holding her arms out wide, she wrapped them around all three girls and kissed each on the forehead. A warm sensation filled Julia. . . a memory flashed through her mind of her own mother cradling her as a baby.

"My Ealga, Maera, and Aeda, I've missed you so." Danu looked down at their faces and frowned. She gripped Julia's chin between her fingers and stared into her eyes. "No, not Ealga. A daughter long past Ealga."

She released the girls and looked them up and down. She touched Julia's hair and the material of her shirt. Her amber eyes flickered over those on the ground.

"How long have I slumbered?"

Julia stammered, "A… a long… time."

Her answer didn't seem to please Danu. Julia felt a vibration in the air, and the serpents cowered away. Then, Danu calmed.

She sighed, "What may I call you, daughter of my daughter?"

Julia swallowed the lump in her throat. "I am Julia, descendent of Ealga. This is Theo, descendant of Maera, and Valera, descendant of Aeda."

"Strange names indeed," Danu mulled and nodded. "So it shall be. You heard my call and came to me, therefore you shall rule at my side. Come, my children."

In the middle of the sleeping bodies, Julia heard moaning. Danu stepped over the bodies and found Lawless, semi-awake and groaning. Her smile widened.

"Who is this man?"

"A mad man named Lawless," Julia hissed.

Danu frowned. "I can sense his adoration. Could one so loyal be mad?"

She woke him. He sat up and looked around frantically. When he saw the other unconscious forms on the ground, he grinned. Then, his eyes saw Danu. He bellowed and bowed before her. His stump of a hand reached to caress the hem of her dress. Danu touched his head.

"Rise, loyal servant."

He stayed on the ground before her. "I cannot, for your beauty paralyzes me."

"Oh, please," Julia lashed out. "He's a dangerous maniac. He nearly killed us."

Danu spun around and held a sharpened fingernail inches from Julia's nose. Her amber eyes turned black. Julia stumbled back and rubbed her eyes.

Danu sneered through fang-like teeth, "Hear me, child. All who revere me are my wards and shall serve. Those who do not, shall be punished." Danu turned back to Lawless. "Will you serve?"

Lawless stood and gripped his arm, moaning. "I will serve you for all eternity, my goddess."

She looked at his blackened hand. "Your sacrifice will be honored. You shall stand at the head of my devotees."

He stared at her in awe, and then held his injured hand in the air. Julia wasn't sure what he thought would happen, but Danu patted him on the head like a dog and turned away. His face crumpled in disappointment. Julia almost laughed. Danu looked around the island and tsked.

"This place is barren and lifeless. I desire to see this *modern* world. Together, we will make it our empire," Danu declared.

There was no way Julia would release Danu upon the unsuspecting people of the planet – Aetherian or otherwise. Julia could only imagine the destruction Danu would reap. With access to modern technology and weaponry, she'd be unstoppable. Then again, she may be unstoppable without it. Julia was beginning to understand why Danu's daughters put her in the tomb in the first place. They had to distract her until they could get help.

Julia stepped forward and tried to humble herself. "Mother, would you not like to rest? Your waking must have been taxing."

Her mind raced to think of a place to take the goddess. Julia grimaced. She sounded like such a fool. She was tired and drained from the day. Theo stepped up beside her and curtsied.

"We know a place where you can rejuvenate," Theo said.

"A place called Subterria," Julia added.

Theo and Valera nodded. Taking her into the broken city would give them time to figure out what to do.

"Where is this… Subterria?"

Danu didn't seem impressed with their suggestion. Julia had to convince her and fast.

"Subterria is an underground kingdom fit for a goddess," she lied.

"Very well," Danu sighed. "We will go to Subterria."

Eli moaned on the ground. Julia knelt beside him. She didn't want to leave him behind. Danu stood over them and caressed the top of Julia's head.

"Something troubles you?"

"Um, well, these people. We can't just leave them."

"As I've said they are not in danger, and they'll wake soon." Danu said. Julia didn't feel any better. "And, yet, you still look troubled. You are attached to them?"

"Some of them, yes," Julia said.

Danu knelt beside Julia, taking her shoulders and kissing her cheek. "You may each choose one to revive. They will accompany us to our palace."

Julia's heart clenched. Although her choice was easy, she didn't want to leave anyone behind. She didn't know what would happen after they left – if they could leave. Julia looked to Theo and Valera. Valera's eyes teared up, looking between her brother, Nessie, and Gideon.

Julia bit her lip. She stood up next to Eli.

"Him," she whispered.

Theo moved toward Victor. She was leaving Joe behind.

"Him."

Valera knelt beside Gideon. Theo had made her choice easier.

"I will bring Gideon."

Danu raised her arms and a light flowed to each man. Their eyes popped open right away, and they sat up. Even Victor was awake and aware. Theo squealed in happiness. She dropped down next to him and wrapped her arms around him. He jumped in surprise, but hugged her back.

"What's happening?" He whispered. "There was a wolf…"

"Danu's awake. She's dangerous, Victor."

He released her and got up. Valera ran to her twin in tears, with Gideon close behind her. Julia and Eli joined the group. Julia pretended to bring them all into a group hug.

In the middle of the huddle, she whispered, "We've made a terrible mistake."

CHAPTER TWENTY

Valera

Valera was terrified of what they'd done. Danu wasn't the earth mother she'd expected. In fact, the very ground she walked on shriveled and died beneath her. This woman was demanding and selfish. She scared Valera to her core.

What did we do? Valera reached out to Theo and Julia. *I'm scared.*

The second the thoughts left her mind, she knew she'd made a horrible error. Danu faced Valera with her terrible grimace. Valera's chest tightened.

"Do you regret your actions? Do you still fear me?" Danu growled. "I am your mother... your goddess. Do not question me, dear one."

Valera cast her eyes at the ground. Danu's hand slid down her cheek to her chin. The woman's nail left a trail of pain over Valera's skin. Then Danu lifted Valera's head and wrapped her other arm around Gideon's shoulder. A cold chill rippled through Valera's spine. Even though a smile touched Danu's face, Valera saw contempt in Danu's eyes. She couldn't let Gideon get hurt.

"Forgive me Mother, this is all so... overwhelming." Valera's voice trembled. "I'm in awe of your greatness."

She hoped that flattery and humility would satisfy the woman, but Danu held tight to Gideon's shoulder. He stood frozen in place, his eyes pleading with Valera.

"You have good taste, Valera. This one is intelligent and handsome." Danu caressed Gideon's face, then sighed, "You are forgiven."

She released Gideon and whistled to Lawless, who came running to her side. Valera fell into Gideon's arms, shaking.

"We'll get through this," he whispered into her ear, as he stroked her hair.

"It's time to go, children. Take me to... Subterria," Danu commanded.

Valera looked at the weathered lifeboats. They were the only way off the island, but they weren't seaworthy. Not to mention, she didn't want to be on the tiny craft with Danu or her strange blue-tattooed minions. The question was: who would explain to her that they were stuck?

Julia stepped forward, clearing her throat. "Mother, our transport was destroyed on the voyage."

Danu erupted in laughter. "I have so much to teach you. You are like babes. We do not need the contraptions of man. We need only to imagine our destination. Close your eyes."

Valera took Gideon's hand and closed her eyes. She felt like a worm was wriggling through her mind. Danu's voice sounded inside her head.

Visualize our destination.

Valera pictured Subterria from the last time she was there. The charred remains of a city in civil war. She imagined the barricades and the wealthy district in ruins. Someone else took her free hand. Her eyes flung open. One of the serpent-men crushed her hand in his. She tried to pull away, but he held firm. Danu stood in the middle of their circle.

Concentrate, Valera.

Even though she was sickened by the creature beside her, she refocused on Subterria. Theo, Julia, and Danu's thoughts entangled with her own. Her body felt weightless as if she were drifting in space. A brisk breeze fluttered around her, turning into an icy blast. The feeling stopped, and the man beast dropped her hand.

When she opened her eyes, they were standing in a circle near the remains of the park. Subterria was dim and empty. The smell of decay was unbearable. Valera threw a hand over her mouth in disgust. Danu's eyes went from amber to red as she eyed the city.

"What trickery is this?" Danu accused. "This will not do. You've brought me to a dungeon."

Julia jumped forward and lied, "Mother, this is an atrocity. I lived in this city for many years. I don't know what happened."

Valera was impressed with the added tears that sprang from Julia's eyes. Danu's face softened – though her eyes remained red.

"Do not fret, my child. The city will be great once again," Danu cooed.

She peered at the ceiling and aimed her hand at the aether orbs in the sky. A wisp of blue light floated up from her fingers. When the wisp touched the orbs, they flared to life. The city lit up brighter than it ever had before. Danu inhaled and blew a gust of crackling mist across the cavernous city. The decaying material fizzled away. The river waters ran clear again. The fountain reformed itself into Danu's image and flowed to life. The charred patchy grass sprouted.

Danu turned to the Order's headquarters. With palms extended, she lifted her hands. The cavern shifted and crumbled. Massive chunks of rock fell from the ceiling. Valera cowered away, but the rocks disintegrated just above their heads. All of the debris from the ruined buildings lifted and reshaped itself. The wealthy district merged into one massive underground palace. Next came a storm of flame that seared across every surface, melting the stone into a smooth, glossy finish.

"Come, daughters. Welcome to our new home."

Moving toward the restored palatial headquarters, Danu ascended the stairs and the double doors swung open. Julia, Theo, and Valera filed in after her, followed by the boys and snake-men. They entered into a large empty room with crystal columns that ran up to the ceiling. Danu peered around the room, tapping her chin.

"A goddess needs a throne," she snapped her fingers.

A polished rock throne grew from the ground at the end of the hall. She marched up to it as if she were in a royal procession. With all the grace of a queen, she sat upon her throne and looked out over the empty room. Once again she snapped her fingers, and Lawless sat on the floor beside her like a favored pet.

"I shall rest here, my children. On the hall to the left, you will find your rooms. My awakening was difficult for us all. Repose now, and we will speak later. Your companions may accompany you. Sleep well, my daughters."

With that, the girls were dismissed. They explored the left wing of the palace and found three huge suites full of fine furnishings. Valera wondered where the antiques came from, remembering similar furniture in the wealthy district during the battle. Their names were carved on the stone doors. Valera stopped at her suite, but couldn't bring herself to go in. She and Theo gathered in Julia's room at the end of the wing. Valera wanted nothing more than to be far away from Danu. Valera curled up with Gideon in a chair. He ran a hand up and down her back. A yawn cracked her jaw. She had never felt so tired. Julia flopped on the bed. Theo fell beside her. Valera tried to speak to them, but she felt so drained. Instead, she closed her eyes and slept.

CHAPTER TWENTY-ONE

*T*heo

Theo bolted awake. Julia snored beside her. Theo didn't even remember laying down. All of them were in the same room, asleep in odd places. Eli was curled up on the ground, shivering. Victor was also on the ground, leaning against the wall. Valera and Gideon were still on their chair. Embers glowed in the fireplace. Had there been a fire when they came into the room? She couldn't remember. With no clock, she had no idea what time it was or how long she'd been asleep. She shook Julia's arm.

Julia muttered and rolled away. A strange thickness hung in the air as if there wasn't enough oxygen. Her mind felt tipsy. She had to move. Slinking off the bed, she steadied herself and explored the suite. The walls and floor glistened. Danu's magic had created extravagant linens and rugs, or perhaps they were taken from the rest of Subterria. A tiger's pelt sat on the floor in front of the fireplace, and Theo almost screamed. The last tiger she saw was Moose from Harmony's circus, lying dead near the fountain. Theo didn't want to know if the fur on the floor had been his, but she had a sinking feeling that it was poor Moose. She picked it up and gently put it in a wardrobe. He didn't deserve to be stepped on.

Theo wanted to explore the entire palace, but not alone. Danu scared her. Although Danu looked similar to the tapestries and pictures that Theo had seen, there was something off with her personality. Theo thought a goddess would be... more than Danu was.

Theo heard footsteps and voices in the hall. She ran back to the bed and acted as if she were still asleep. The door opened.

Why am I hiding? She thought to herself, yet didn't get up.

People shuffled around the room. Glasses clanked and something was set out on a table. After a few minutes, the door closed. Theo sat back up. Whoever came into their room left a tray of tea and food in the sitting room and three clothing bags on the back of the sofa. Between the kettle and tea cups, Theo found a note.

She read aloud, "Good morning, daughters. Eat breakfast, and join me in the throne room. The appropriate attire has been provided."

"Huh?" Julia yawned and stretched. "Man, I must have passed out."

"What am I doing down here?" Victor grumbled.

Valera tumbled off of Gideon's lap. "Oh, I'm so sorry. I didn't mean to fall asleep. Are you all right?"

Gideon rubbed his legs. "Pins and needles... I hate pins and needles," he complained.

"I don't know what happened. One minute we were talking, and then nothing," Valera said.

"Muscle cramps." Eli hobbled around the room.

Theo picked up a crumpet and examined it. Her stomach growled, and there was no need to deny it breakfast. It appeared normal and smelled delicious. She chomped down on it and sighed.

"I think we were under a spell," she said between bites.

"Mmm, food." Eli gulped down an entire crumpet in one bite.

Julia opened one of the garment bags and pulled out a shimmering silver dress, much like Danu's. Theo cringed. She wasn't one to wear dresses, let alone sparkly dresses. She'd just gotten her t-shirts and jeans back. All three bags held the same dress.

"Has anyone else noticed that we don't stink?" Julia asked.

"Eww, Julia," Valera scolded.

Julia picked at her shirt and inhaled. "Seriously, I was filthy yesterday, but, now, I'm clean and my clothes are perfect."

"I guess you're right." Valera shrugged, looking in the bottom of the clothing bags. "No shoes?"

"Shoes are the least of our worries," Theo replied. "What are we going to do?"

Victor stood up and stretched. Theo's heart thumped in her chest. Danu couldn't be all bad. After all, she had healed Victor. Ever since his miraculous return, he'd seemed so different. He was happy. She caught herself staring, and so did he. His emerald eyes sparkled, and he smiled. She hadn't realized how much she missed him. He came up to her and leaned close to her ear.

"Can we start over?" He whispered.

She felt as if her smile would split her face. She looked up to him and nodded. Valera clapped.

"I knew you would work it out," she squealed.

Theo's cheeks burned. Victor slipped his hand in hers. She felt right again, until Julia gagged.

"Seriously, this is not the time. Get dressed. We'll have to face Mother Dearest sooner or later. Might as well be now."

Theo threw a crumpet at her. "Food first."

"We don't know what kind of ingredients are in these," Julia murmured, sniffing the delectable pastry. "Well, maybe just one. I don't want to starve."

Julia ate three of them, and then tossed one of the dresses to Theo. She caught it and slumped. There was no way Theo was getting into this thing. Danu would just have to deal with her normal clothes. Julia threw her hands on her hips and glowered at Theo as if reading her mind.

"We can't make her mad," Julia said.

Theo rolled her eyes and went into the bathroom. She slipped the dress over her head and looked into the mirror. The silky fabric kissed her skin. The slinky nature of it made her self-conscious. The neckline draped down to her lower back, the straps hung off her shoulders, and the slit in the side went too far up her leg. What she wouldn't give to put her jeans and a tee shirt back on.

"Open up," Julia yelled and banged on the bathroom door.

"No way."

Valera shook the knob, "Don't hog the bathroom. I need to get dressed too."

Theo relented and cracked the door, pulling them inside. Valera slipped out of her clothes and threw on her dress. Theo's mouth dropped. At least Valera filled it out. On Theo it was a like a sack, but Valera had curves. When Julia put it on, it made Theo even more self-conscious. The dress set off her white-blonde hair and ice blue eyes. Theo couldn't compete. Julia whistled at herself in the mirror.

"I look hot."

"I'm not leaving this bathroom," Theo declared.

"Don't be silly you look beautiful," Valera gushed, swirling in the mirror. "You might want to take the socks off though."

Theo looked down at the black socks on her feet and sighed. She balled them up and threw them on top of her other clothes. There was no help for it, she had to go. They stepped into a cacophony of applause and hoots from the boys. Their *enthusiasm* didn't help Theo's nerves.

"You should wear dresses more often." Victor nudged Theo's side.

She gave him a death glare. He laughed. Offering his arm, he ushered her out of the suite and down the corridor. The doors to the throne room opened before they got there, and Theo froze. The palace was filled with people. Danu sat on her throne, smiling over her court.

"Her Highnesses Theo, daughter of Maera, Julia, daughter of Ealga, and Valera, daughter of Aeda."

A blue tattooed man, wearing the pompous garb of the former wealthy elite, announced the girls as they entered. The room broke into applause as they walked down a green carpet toward Danu.

"Who are all these people?" Theo whispered to Victor.

He shrugged. "Go with it."

"Ah, my children. You are lovelier than ever. Come to me."

Danu waved them forward. Dr. Lawless sat cross-legged on a pillow next to Danu's throne. The girls curtsied and the boys bowed at the base of her throne. Victor, Eli, and Gideon moved to the side. The goddess hugged Theo and kissed her on the head, moving down the row to all three girls. Once again the room erupted with cheers. Danu snapped her fingers and three smaller chairs rose out of the stone in front of Danu's throne.

"Our devoted disciples exalt our rebirth, daughters. Sit and give them your blessings."

Danu returned to her throne, and Theo sat in the first chair. Serpent men brought baskets and set them beside the girls. Although, Theo wasn't about to deny Danu, she felt uncomfortable with all the pageantry. The situation felt so wrong.

The first three people to walk up to them were a Subterrian family. Their whitish hair and pale skin were giveaways. It was clear that they didn't fare well in the civil war. Their clothes were dirty rags, and they smelled as if they hadn't bathed in weeks. The man put a silver coin in Theo's hand and bowed. Guilt gnawed at her gut.

"I can't take this," Theo muttered.

The man looked up at her horrified. "It's all we have. Please, don't be angry with us."

She shook her head. "No… I mean… I'm not angry."

Danu's eyes blackened, and she leaned forward in her chair. The man gasped and shrank away.

"Is there a problem, daughter? Are you not satisfied with their tribute," Danu shrilled.

She pointed her claw-like nail at the man. He shrieked and begged, doubling over in pain. Theo stood up and turned to face Danu.

"No, Mother, please stop. I'm very satisfied with his tribute. He doesn't deserve this," Theo pleaded.

The man returned to normal, and Theo helped him stand. He looked at her with a blank face. He limped back to his family. Theo took her seat and made a point to drop the coin in the basket. Danu stood over them, grinning again. The man stuttered as he spoke.

"Mother of all Aether, Daughters of Danu, we surrender ourselves to your majestic will."

The Subterrians stood there expectantly. Theo had no clue what to say or do next. She was terrified that Danu would lash out again.

Danu cleared her throat. "Your sacrifice shall be rewarded my children," she said and nodded her head at the Subterrians.

They fell on their knees, said "thank you," and wept. Theo couldn't believe her eyes. Danu had just tortured the man, and now he pledged himself to her. The servants returned and dragged the family away. The ritual continued for hours upon hours. It seemed as if everyone from Subterria had returned. Theo made sure to accept and bless each person, so that Danu didn't punish them. The baskets filled up over and over again. Each time, the servants removed them and brought empty ones in return.

Theo recognized a few people from her time with Lazarus. The wealthy citizens who were once draped in riches were like all the rest – in rags weeping on their knees. They'd come to Lazarus' ridiculous Christmas ball and offended her with their atrocious concept of the human world. Even as horrible as they were, they didn't deserve this.

A woman with long grey hair and a robust figure walked toward them. Theo wanted to cry out. This was her friend. The leader of the circus who saved Theo and Vivi from Lazarus.

"Harmony?" Theo whispered.

Like all the rest, she stared at the girls with a blank face and repeated, "Mother of all Aether, Daughters of Danu, we surrender ourselves to your majestic will."

"Harmony, it's me Theo. Are you okay?"

Harmony's eyes glistened, and her jaw clenched, but she didn't move or say anything. Danu repeated her speech about sacrifice, and like everyone else Harmony fell to her knees and was carted off. She didn't even try to fight. Theo knew something was wrong. Harmony was one of the most willful people she knew. Right behind her were Benji, Adora, and the other freak show workers. It took three servants to pull Benji away. Theo couldn't take it any longer.

Not wanting to raise Danu's ire, she worded her question carefully. "Mother, where are they being taken?"

"The strong will be put to work rebuilding our empire," Danu said.

"And anyone who isn't strong?" Julia asked.

Danu's smile touched only her lips. "Only the strong are worthy to serve a goddess. Do I not deserve a world of perfection?"

Theo swallowed hard. She tried to keep the shakiness from her voice. "Of course, Mother. We're just surprised that there are so many people. Subterria seemed empty last night."

"Aetherians heed my call, and all will prostrate themselves before me." Danu stood up. "I've grown weary of this. It's time that you learned the true power of your abilities. Come."

Her dress swept across the stone floors as if she were floating. Theo looked around for Victor, Eli, and Gideon, but they were lost in the crowd. The girls followed Danu down a corridor to an empty alcove. With one finger, Danu drew a symbol over a blank wall. Behind the image, Theo heard a grinding stone. Cracks formed in the solid rock wall, forming a doorway. Danu touched it and the door opened. She swirled her hands and formed a glowing ball of aether. Throwing it toward the ceiling, it hung in the air and illuminated the newly formed room. The girls stepped into the grand hall. The walls and floors were polished into a mirror-like sheen.

"Theo, show me what you know of aether," Danu said.

Theo concentrated on her power. Holding out her hands, she created an arc of electricity between them. She pushed herself until the arc grew far above her head.

Danu scoffed, "You are not reaching deep enough."

Danu touched Theo's shoulder. A jolt of aether, stronger than she'd ever felt, flowed through her. Just like the night on the dock after Valera was taken, a swirling black cloud of aether surrounded Theo's body. Purple bolts of lightning shot from the cloud, scorching walls. Theo's muscles trembled. She felt as though she would lose control of the aether at any moment.

Do not fear aether. It is a part of you, Danu whispered inside Theo's head. *Be at peace.*

Theo calmed her nerves. She let aether flow through her uninhibited. Lifting her hands above her head, she made the cloud grow until it filled the whole room. A surge of pure bliss warmed Theo's body. She didn't want to let it go.

"You don't just control lightning, Theo. You control the tempests and the tides. You were born of the Moon," Danu said. "Release."

The second Danu said "release," Theo lost aether. She felt as if the entirety of the world fell on her shoulders. The ecstasy she felt disappeared, leaving an equal feeling of loss. The dark cloud fizzled and dissipated. Theo wanted to cry. She looked at Danu's smiling face. The woman seemed to delight in Theo's pain.

"You did well, child." Danu touched Theo's cheek. "Valera, you were born of the Sun. You control the flames and the mountains. Step forward and show me what you can do."

Valera did as she was told. Theo stood back and watched as Valera created a fissure in the ground. Danu helped her pull lava to the surface. Valera moved it around as if it were Play Doh. She gave birth to a mountain inside the chamber, and just as quickly made it crumble. Valera learned to heat and cool the earth. Then Danu took it all away with one word. Valera gasped, and tears welled in her eyes. The ground closed, and it was Julia's turn.

"Julia, my little warrior. You were born of the Earth. You control the beasts and plants. Your ice brings life and death."

If we control the earth and everything on it, then what do you control? Theo wanted to ask, but hesitated. She was more scared than curious. Danu's eyes bored into her. She seemed to loom over them. With a wave of her hands, Danu created a black void within the room. Stars formed. Gases spiraled and dust collected. It was as if they all stood inside of space itself.

"I was born of the universe. I control all. I create life. I bring death."

CHAPTER TWENTY-TWO

Julia

"You are my strongest child, Julia. You are the blade I wield against my foes," Danu heralded. "You can call upon the animals of the earth for aid."

Danu snapped her fingers and a rat skittered into the room. Waving her hand over the animal, she made it perform tricks.

"Now you," she said.

It took a few minutes for Julia to gain control over the rat. She had to go into its tiny brain and speak to it, much like she did when speaking to Theo and Valera telepathically. Eventually, she had him dancing across the floor. Then, she released it.

"You also have control over the plants."

Danu held her hand parallel to the floor and closed her eyes. The ground trembled, and then cracks. A seedling grew from stone. Julia copied Danu's movements. After a few tries, a sapling grew… and grew… and grew until it became a tree.

"Very good, Julia."

With one touch from Danu, the tree turned black. Leaves shriveled and fell. The trunk curled in on itself and disappeared. Julia noticed wrinkles forming on Danu's forehead, and the goddess seemed to weaken. She, on the other hand, felt rejuvenated.

"I shall retreat to my chambers for a time," Danu announced, leaving the girls in the grand hall.

This was the first chance they had to speak in private. They searched for the boys in the throne room, but everywhere they went people bowed and reached out to them. The whole scene irked Julia. Subterria was a proud and strong city, but now the people groveled like beggars.

"I see them," Theo whispered.

Sure enough, Eli, Victor, and Gideon were huddled in a corner away from the crowd. Julia waved Eli down and motioned toward the left wing. He nodded. The girls made their way to the doors. Someone grabbed Julia's foot, making her stumble to her knees. Theo and Valera were swallowed up in the people. A mass of hands groped at her – some trying to help her, while others just wanted to rip off a piece of her. The hand still gripped her ankle, mumbling that strange mantra over and over again.

"Daughters of Danu, we surrender ourselves to your majestic will... Daughters of Danu, we surrender ourselves to your majestic will... Daughters of Danu, we surrender ourselves to your majestic will..."

She tried to kick the person away, but only managed to get tangled in her dress. Fingers scratched her arms and pulled at her hair. She shrieked in pain.

"Hold on, Julia," Valera's voice drifted over the crowd.

Julia reached for aether, and let herself grow cold. The hand around her ankle released her. The tugging and grabbing lessened, but the force of the people pushing down on her kept her from standing. Finally, she saw someone fall to the ground, and two hands lifted her away. Eli had her in his arms. Julia hid her head in the crook of Eli's neck. Victor and Gideon fought a path through the people, until they reached the hall. Danu's serpent men kept the mass from passing through the doors.

"Thanks for helping, when I was being crushed," Julia spat as Eli passed a guard.

He grinned and hissed. Once a snake always a snake. Eli carried her to her room, and Theo did her best to heal the worst sprains and scrapes.

"What is wrong with everyone? And where did they all come from?" Julia grumbled.

Theo got a cold cloth and put it to Julia's face. "They've got to be under some kind of spell. Harmony wouldn't bow to anyone."

"We need to find out what's happening to the ones who are being taken away." Valera wrapped her arms around Gideon's waist.

"We can't go out in these dresses. We'll be trampled." Julia muttered. Somehow her dress had survived the attack without a single tear.

"Okay, then we disguise ourselves," Theo said, grinning.

Ditching the dresses, they put on their old clothes and smudged their faces with charcoal to look like the beggars.

"We look ridiculous," Julia groaned. "I have a better idea."

First, she wiped the junk from her face. She remembered how Danu's appearance changed from one minute to the next. Julia figured it had to be a spell. She went into the bathroom and stared in the mirror. Channeling aether, she reimagined her features. Danu had said that all they had to do was imagine a place, well why couldn't she imagine a look. She formed a picture of Theo in her mind. Her reflection shimmered and changed. She grinned, but lost the disguise. It took a lot of effort and concentration to finally keep the trick in place. After a few minutes, she stepped into the room.

"Theo?" Victor asked, looking at Julia.

"Ha! It worked," Julia cheered.

Theo walked around Julia, touching her face. The illusion faltered, but Julia maintained it.

"Well, that's disconcerting. Could you please put someone else's face on?" Theo asked.

Julia dragged the girls into the bathroom and showed them what to do. Valera chose to look like a model from one of her old human magazines. Theo did her best to look like her mother's teacher's assistant. Julia decided to try something harder. She formed an image of an old English teacher from Boulder High School in her mind, and used all her strength to project the aged woman's features on her face.

"Do we look different enough to slip past people?" Theo asked.

"We won't know until we try. Eli and I will go through the palace. You four look around Subterria."

Julia opened the door and slipped out. Eli shook his head at her.

"Is it weird that I'm suddenly attracted to grandmothers?" He smirked.

"Yes, and gross," Julia hit his arm.

The six of them split up inside the throne room. Without the gowns, people seemed to overlook them. Even the serpent men ignored them. The crowd knelt with their eyes fixed on Danu's empty throne. Julia led Eli to where people had been taken away earlier. She froze. Lawless stood next to two non-serpent men guards. He babbled at them. They looked bored. Eli moved in front of Julia and approached the three men.

"Hello, Dr. Lawless," he smirked.

"Eli, I was just regaling these men with the glory that was Danu's awakening," Lawless gloated.

"Yes, it was glorious." Eli played the part perfectly. He acted as mindlessly enthralled as everyone else. "Continue your tale, Doctor. I'm just taking this ugly, decrepit woman to the others."

Julia wanted to punch Eli, but she acted like an old lady. The guards didn't question Eli's passing. She supposed it was because Lawless knew him. Julia tried to keep her eyes down cast, but made the mistake of looking at Lawless. He paused and frowned. After a few seconds, he continued to exaggerate his part in the story. Apparently, he single-handedly saved Danu from the throws of torment and death. And then he carried all three daughters to safety as the tomb crumbled.

Julia rolled her eyes. Eli nudged her down a stairwell to what used to be the Order's dungeon, where guards separated the strong from the weak. Those who were healthy were moved into a second room, where Julia heard rushing water. The outcasts were put into cells in the dungeon area. Julia walked past rows and rows of the old and sick. Julia tried to avoid looking at the bodies on the ground. She didn't know if they were alive or dead, but they weren't moving.

Children were sent to a different set of rooms. A horde of stern-faced women watched over them. Like the adults, the children were empty shells. They stood in lines, moving through life like Aetherland's automatons.

"What are you doing here?" One of the women yelled. "You should be over there."

"Got lost, sorry," Eli quipped.

"She goes with the rejects," the woman sneered.

Eli took Julia's arm and nodded. Her Parmelia disguise had become a liability, so she released the illusion and resorted to rubbing mud on her face. Julia and Eli lined up in a group headed into the other room, where the strong were washed and given work tools. In one of the lines, Julia saw Benji. She slid into his line and tapped him on the shoulder. He turned to her.

"Benji, what are you doing here?"

"I surrender myself to Danu's majestic will."

"What's wrong with you? Where's Harmony?"

"I surrender myself to Danu's majestic will."

Eli grabbed Julia's hand. "It's no good. They're all the same. We need to get out of here."

He motioned to the serpent men coming their way. Together they slipped out a side door and ended up at the front of the palace. Lines of people spilled out of the doors and onto the street, waiting to pledge themselves to the goddess, while workers were being sent all over the city. The silence that had gripped Subterria just the day before was now a symphony of construction and a chorus of chants.

"Julia, over here," Theo called.

As Eli and Julia met up with the others near a half-burned building, Julia reported, "People are being sorted like cattle. Some are in cells and others are being deployed out here. This whole thing is so messed up."

"They're erecting a giant statue of Danu in the city center," Valera added. "This isn't at all like the stories Mother used to tell me. Danu was a benevolent, loving, ruler. This isn't right."

"I need to speak to my grandmother. She will know what to do," Julia said. "I think I can manage to teleport."

"It's too dangerous." Eli took her arm. "You've never done anything like this. Maybe if all three of you go, it would be safer."

"We can't all go. I need them to stay behind and cover for me. Eli, I have to do this."

"You should go to the surface and try it. Starting in open air might be safer," Theo suggested. "Just make sure you don't teleport yourself into the ocean instead of Pacifica City."

"Thanks," Julia deadpanned.

Theo and Valera went back to the palace to clean up and prepare an excuse in case Danu were to awake before Julia returned. Julia and Eli made their way to the surface. The island above Subterria appeared as if everything was normal. The cows still grazed in pastures. The wind still blew. The sky was still blue. There was no indication of the insanity happening below.

Eli held Julia against him. He whispered in her ear, "Come back soon."

She nodded and stepped back. With all her energy, she focused on the glass building in Pacifica. She knew she had to get it right, or risk drowning a hundred feet below water. She imagined the dome, the port, the streets. She formed the image of the Elders' Tower in her mind and willed her way through time and space. She kept her eyes closed and took a deep breath –just in case. Her skin prickled from the rush of cold air. She stopped in midair, falling a few feet to the sandy ground. She landed on her bottom in the middle of the street inside the glass dome of Pacifica.

"Watch where you're going," a woman shrieked, and then stammered, "Oh… I'm sorry…" The woman dropped to her knees. "Forgive my outburst, Hero of Pacifica."

Ignoring her, Julia hurried to the Elders' Tower. She was surrounded by a mob of citizens, all of them vying to gain her attention. She waded through them, until the crowd became so thick that she couldn't move.

"Let me pass," she grumbled. "I have to speak to Parmelia."

Her body temperature dropped, and the hands of the people touching her froze. Frost crept up the glass building like fungus.

Grandma help me, Julia shouted in her mind.

A platoon of white robes ran from the tower forcing a path for Julia and holding the mob away. Parmelia stood in the tower's door with open arms. Julia grabbed her grandmother and hugged her. She didn't want to let go. The Elders' council flocked to Julia's side. Julia's heart pounded in her ears.

"Julia, relax," Parmelia soothed. "It's okay. What's happened?"

Slowly, Julia was able to let go. Parmelia led her inside the tower and closed the doors. The crowd still chanted outside, but the white robes kept them out.

"Parmelia, we need your help," Julia said breathlessly.

"Come with me, tell me what's happened," her grandmother whispered and took her hand.

"Danu is free."

Parmelia and the Elders gasped. The room broke into a shouting match. Julia's head ached. She held her hands out and caused spikes of ice to shoot out of the floor.

"Quiet!" she yelled.

Everyone stopped in stunned silence. Julia took a deep breath and continued.

"We made a mistake by going to the island. There were... traps... and we beat them, but at a cost. We weren't going to release her, but Danu was stronger than we. She... forced us. She's in Subterria now. Parmelia, we don't know what to do. She's not like the stories... she's insane."

"There is something we should have told you girls a long time ago. Come with me," Parmelia said.

The Elders' council took Julia into a back room in a large library. One of them locked the door, while another removed a book from a safe. Parmelia ushered Julia into a seat at an old wooden desk.

"This is wrong, Parmelia. We shouldn't be sharing this," one of the Elders groaned.

"We have no choice. The girl needs to know the truth, or else we're all doomed." Parmelia sat across the desk and opened the book. She pushed it toward Julia. "This is the true story of Danu. We've kept the truth a secret for centuries… perhaps that was a mistake."

Julia flipped through the book "This can't be true," Julia gasped.

"I'm sorry. We should have told you. Danu isn't a goddess." Parmelia touched Julia's cheek. "Only a few of us from each generation learn the truth, and we're sworn to secrecy. We thought we were protecting Aether."

Julia scoffed, "So you're telling me that Danu, or whatever her name really is, was a sorceress from an ancient time. That our whole world is built on a lie?"

Parmelia nodded. "She tricked a group of druids into worshiping her. They in turn created the world of Aether. She gave birth to three girls, who also possessed the power to manipulate aether. But Danu didn't want to share, so she enslaved her daughters. Ealga, Aeda, and Maera fought against her, but they weren't strong enough to kill her. Instead they imprisoned her and broke the key."

"And we just set her free! Why didn't you say something?"

One of the other Elders huffed, "It would destroy everything we've built. What do you think would happen if Aetherians knew their world revolved around lies? It would end in chaos and destruction. We've kept order for centuries, but you girls have ruined everything."

"All anyone's ever done is lie to us... our parents... you... The Order... The True Followers... Lawless... How were we supposed to know?" Julia railed. Then, she covered her face and cried. "What have we done?"

"Enough, what's done is done," Parmelia growled at the Elders and wrapped her arms around her granddaughter. "It's okay, Julia. We can help."

"How?" Julia wiped her face with the back of her hand. "You don't know how evil she is."

The persnickety Elder scoffed, "Ealga, Aeda, and Maera couldn't fix it. How are we supposed to? We should all admit defeat and beg for forgiveness from Danu."

"You don't understand. She's already enslaving people and using them to create an empire. More of them flock to her every day." Bells rang out in the distance. Julia looked around the room. "What time is it?"

One of the elders looked at his pocket watch. "It's a half past four."

"I need to go. She's going to wake soon. I don't know what she'll do if she finds me gone."

"We'll research what to do about Danu. Go back and warn Theo and Valera. Whatever you do, don't let her know that *you* know the truth," Parmelia said, kissing Julia's cheek.

Julia thought about the fields, the village, and the skies. Closing her eyes, she soaked in aether and focused on the island of Subterria. Teleporting felt easier this time, and she landed on her feet close to the abandoned village near the entrance to the underground city. By the position of the sun in the sky, she thought she'd made it back in time. Then she saw *her.*

Danu stood in the fields nearby. The woman spoke to the cows and basked in the afternoon sunlight. Her smiling face looked straight at Julia. She walked down a hill, and, although she seemed happy, the grass under her feet blackened and burned.

"Julia, I was worried. I awoke and you were gone." The quiet tightness in her voice made Julia's nerves spark. "Although it lightens my heart to see your powers grow, you shouldn't leave without my knowledge."

Danu reached out and touched Julia's muddy face. She pinched a bit of sand between her fingers and frowned. Julia's shoulders slumped, and she grinned sheepishly.

"I... I'm sorry, Mother," Julia said the word as if it were numbing venom on her tongue. "I was worried about my ailing grandmother. She hasn't been well and needs help. I did a few chores for her while I was there. I guess I got a little dirty."

"Of course, I understand." Danu's eyes turned to slits. "Perhaps, we should bring her here. I could heal her... She is one of my children after all."

Julia struggled for an answer. She knew what Danu would do to Parmelia. Julia saw the old and sick in the cells. "I'm sure she'll be here soon. I told her all about your... greatness. She wishes nothing more than to meet you. She's preparing as we speak."

"All in good time then. It won't be long before the entire world is here, at my feet. Let us dine and speak more about your family." Danu walked down a wide ramp, leading to a massive gate. "I thought it a more fitting entrance to my palace."

"It is indeed," Julia muttered.

The streets of Subterria were sparkling clean as if the civil war had never happened. Danu's slaves had scrubbed and rebuilt half of Subterria within a day. The city was transforming into a monument to Danu. Everywhere Julia looked, she saw tributes and totems, statues and sculptures all dedicated to the *false* goddess. In less than two days, she'd managed to erase everything that was Subterria. And it made Julia sick.

CHAPTER TWENTY-THREE

Valera

When Valera saw Julia coming in with Danu, she felt a brief moment of relief. She and Theo had barely had enough time to poke around, clean up, and dress before Danu woke up. When Julia hadn't returned, Valera thought she'd drowned. Danu had come straight to the girls' rooms, and Valera was certain that she knew of their deceit. She must have been wrong. Julia whisked past her with a small nod and disappeared into the living quarters.

"I guess everything is fine," Valera whispered to Theo.

"I don't know. Danu looks annoyed," Theo said, watching Danu snap at Lawless before sitting on her throne.

The man was right back on Danu's heels the second she had entered the room. He was even more annoying when he was groveling, and if Valera could blast him into oblivion, she would.

Danu whispered to one of her servants, then commanded, "Daughters, come."

Valera hated being summoned like a dog. She almost missed the days of being trapped in Aetherland. Nevertheless, Valera, along with Theo, curtsied at the base of Danu's throne. She gestured to their seats in front of her, and they sat. They were more decorations than daughters. At least the mobs of worshippers had been reassigned. Now, only a few faithful courtesans – people who didn't need to be mind-wiped to swear fealty to Danu – milled around the throne room.

Valera could barely keep her eyes open, she was so bored. Her butt hurt from sitting on the stone chair. Her head hurt from stress. Finally, one of Danu's serpent men came into the room.

"Mother of All, Daughters of Danu, your feast awaits," the man declared as if they were at a ball.

Theo and Valera fell in behind Danu. The grand hall they'd used for training was now decorated with the longest dining table Valera had ever seen. A roaring fire inside of a mysterious new fireplace lit up the entire room. A chandelier cast a soft blue light from the ceiling. Gold dishes lined the silver tablecloths. More food than Valera had ever seen was presented around huge floral centerpieces. Danu sat at the head of the table and positioned the girls all around her.

Where did all of this come from? Valera wondered.

Danu smiled at her. "These are the gifts from my people, Daughter."

Valera hated when Danu knew what she was thinking.

Lawless leaned over Valera's shoulder and laughed. "She has a gift for you too," he whispered in her ear.

"Lawless, enough," Danu said.

He pranced over to her and glued himself to her side. Danu lifted a hand, forcing the man away. "Find a seat at the other end of the table."

Lawless looked like a scolded puppy. He plodded to the far end of the table and plopped into a chair, gazing at Danu with adoration and sorrow.

"Are we having guests?" Valera asked, noting the dozen empty spots at the table.

"Yes, I've invited my most loyal servants, as well as a surprise for you." She waved her hand and Victor, Gideon, and Eli strolled into the hall along with a few well-dressed people. "These are my true followers. They diligently fought for my return, and now they will reap their reward."

Valera hated the term "True Followers." The courtesans filed into the room, chatting and sitting near Lawless. A familiar face popped up in the crowd. Professor Scrod grinned and waved to the girls. The poor muddle-headed woman had no clue what she was getting herself into.

Julia walked in dressed in the silver gown. Valera smiled at her, but Julia refused to meet her eyes. She sat next to Theo and whispered in her ear. Theo's expression changed from melancholy to shock and her eyes teared up.

"Surprise!" A young girl's voice sang.

Valera spun around and looked at the door in horror. Her little sister, Vivi, rushed into the room wearing layers of pink silk. Behind her, Valera's mother and Theo's parents entered the room. Vivi ran into Valera's arms.

"What are you doing here?" Valera tried to keep the pain out of her tone.

"Danu invited us to surprise you! Victor!" Vivi ran to the other side of the table and plopped onto her brother's lap.

"Welcome, my children. Please have a seat," Danu declared. She turned to Valera and Theo. A red glint flashed in her eyes. "I thought it fitting that your families come stay with us."

Victoria sat next to her daughter. She and Theo's parents held the same blank stare on their faces as all the other people flocking to Subterria. Vivi and the courtesans seemed to be the only ones not affected. Valera fought back tears.

"Let us feast," Danu said, waving her hand in the air.

The lids on the dishes flew from the dishes exposing a decadent meal. Roast beef, chickens, turkeys, and hams filled platters. Bowls overflowed with steamed vegetables. Rolls and croissants dripped with butter and honey and smelled delicious. Valera's stomach rumbled, but she couldn't eat. Not with her family in danger. She picked her way through the meal, glancing at Theo and Victor from time to time. Neither one of them ate anything.

"My little darling, come sit with me," Danu said to Vivi.

Valera's little sister danced across the room into Danu's arms. With a snap of her fingers, Danu created a plate of cakes, pastries, and sweets. She doted on Vivi, feeding her the desserts by hand. Valera cringed. Vivi was clearly enamored with the woman.

"You're so pretty," Vivi chirped.

Danu laughed and kissed the top of Vivi's head. "Sweet child, I think I shall keep you."

Valera wanted to scream, "No!" She wanted to teleport her family away. She wanted to kill Danu. The only thing she could do was sit in her chair and fume. Danu doted on Vivi, until the little girl fell into a gluttonous stupor.

"Daughters, I shall give you time with your families. I must confer with my disciples." Danu dismissed them.

Victor picked up a sleepy Vivi and carried her to one of the rooms, to which Valera and Theo also escorted their comatose parents, setting them up near the hearth to keep them warm. Once Vivi was tucked away, they met in the adjoining room.

"She brought them for insurance," Theo ranted, pacing across the floor. "With them here, she has leverage against us."

Valera sat on the floor with her head in her hands. So far her family had been safely hidden in Aetherland. Now, reality set in, and she had to face that the danger to the people she loved – to the whole world – was her doing. She looked at Theo and Julia, and a switch went off in her brain. No, it was *their* fault. Theo's pacing grated on her nerves. An irrational urge to scream bubbled up in Valera. Everything felt so out of control.

"Would you stop, Theo? You're driving me crazy," Valera blurted out.

"What's your problem?" Theo scowled at her. "My family's here too, Valera."

Valera scrambled off the ground. She was so angry that she shook. Julia stood between them.

"Both of you, calm down. You're just scared," Julia grumbled.

Leave it to Julia to take Theo's side. What did Julia know anyway? She always acted as if nothing got to her.

"Of course, I'm scared, Julia. Not that you care. You don't care about anything," Valera snapped. "Why is it that your family is safe? Huh? I saw the way you were talking to Danu. Strolling back to Subterria as if you were her best friend…"

"What are you talking about?" Julia griped. "Why are you acting so weird?"

Valera felt like clawing Julia's face off. "I am not. This is your fault!"

Theo grabbed Julia's hand and channeled aether. Valera thought they were going to attack her. Instead, they formed a barrier of aether all around the three of them. An explosion of clarity struck Valera. She grabbed her head between her hands. Why was she so angry? Theo touched her shoulder.

"Feeling better?"

"I don't know what just happened. One-minute I was fine, and then... I was just filled with rage... I am so sorry," Valera cried.

The door opened, and all three girls held aether. Valera had a fireball in her hand ready to scorch whoever came through. Eli, Victor, and Gideon walked into the room and froze.

"Maybe we should leave," Eli smirked with his hands in the air.

"No, don't. I don't understand what's happening to me," Valera sobbed.

Gideon wrapped an arm around her. She wept into his shoulder until her eyes burned. Valera listened to Gideon's heart beating in his chest, the fire crackling, and the others talking.

"I think Danu cast a spell on her or something. I've never seen Valera that angry," Julia whispered.

"The aether drove whatever it was away," Theo added.

"It had to have been Danu. She's trying to manipulate us."

Valera didn't remember any event that took place. If it had been a spell, then she never felt it coming. She shuddered. Danu could make anyone do anything, and now she had Vivi.

"Victor, you have to take Vivi away. Warn the others not to come," Valera said.

Victor looked at Theo and shook his head. "I can't leave you and Theo behind. Not again. We should all go. You three can teleport everyone away."

Julia scoffed, "She knew I left. If we took everyone away, she would know for sure. And she'd come after us."

A knock on the door made everyone jump. Gideon got up and answered it, smiling when he saw the visitor. Professor Scrod shuffled in. Her aqua eyes darted around the room as if something were going to jump out and scare her. She flattened her bushy brown hair with a hand and cleared her throat incessantly. Valera was ready to burn the woman to a crisp. She was one of Danu's people. She was with Dr. Lawless. Theo sparked up, Julia iced up, and Valera lit up.

"Whoa, calm down," Gideon said before anyone made a move. "Let's just hear her out."

"Thank you, Gideon... I... I'm here to help. I swear I had no idea... how dark the goddess really was... until I came here," Professor Scrod squeaked.

"Danu is not a goddess." Julia jumped up and pointed a finger at the door. "How could you have studied her and not known?"

"What are you talking about?" Valera asked.

"When I went to Parmelia for help, she told me the truth... the real truth about Danu. She's not a goddess. She's a sorceress that enslaved a group of humans who worshiped her. She turned on her daughters. They had to imprison her. Danu's nothing but an evil witch."

"Evil bitch is more like it," Theo hissed.

"I didn't know. But I can help..." Professor Scrod muttered. "You need to go warn people. I'll create a diversion."

Valera heard a scratching sound in the hallway. Theo must have heard it too, because she stood up and held a finger to her mouth.

"Everyone, be quiet."

Someone coughed outside their door, then footsteps dashed down the hall. Theo went to check on her family. Victoria and Theo's parents were still sitting unmoving in Vivi's room. The little girl was fast asleep. Returning to the others, she stormed toward Professor Scrod. The woman slunk away like a sewer dog.

"Were you followed?" Theo pulled on aether. "Are you working with Lawless or Danu?"

"No, I wasn't followed... I'm not working with anyone..."

Victor held Theo's arm. His presence was the only thing that kept her from lashing out. He wrapped his arms around her and pulled her back. Eli looked out the door and shut it.

"There's no one there," he said.

"Let go, Theo. Not here," Victor whispered.

She relaxed a little. "There was someone outside."

"I heard it too," Valera added.

Finally, Julia stepped forward. "We don't have time for this. We need to get help. The next time Danu sleeps, Valera will return to Aetherland. She can warn Nessie and the others, and take Vivi back with her. We can't risk taking everyone, but Vivi shouldn't be here. Theo and I will go to Pacifica and rally the Elders. Hopefully, they'll have found a way to stop Danu by then. Professor Scrod and the three of you can keep Danu distracted."

"I'll do my best," Professor Scrod whispered and left.

Valera went straight back to her mother. Kneeling down in front of her, she took Victoria's cold hands. Channeling aether, she warmed the room. She took a blanket from the back of the sofa and wrapped it around her mother's shoulders. Even though their relationship was tenuous at times, seeing her mother under Danu's spell broke Valera's heart.

"Don't worry. I'll fix everything," Valera whispered.

Her mother smiled and brushed a piece of hair out of Valera's face. "I surrender myself to Danu's majestic will"

Valera sighed, "I'm sorry, Mother. This is all my fault."

Victoria partially snapped out of her stupor. "Do you think Danu will come visit with us? I should clean up." Victoria stood up and walked around the room tidying up. "Come now, Valera, we must look our best for Danu."

Valera took her mother's arm. "It's late. I don't think she'll be coming tonight. Why don't you get some rest?"

She led her mom to the bed where Vivi snored. Her mother sat on the edge and let Valera remove her shoes. Valera gently pushed her mother to lay down and covered her up.

"Of course, you're right. I want to look my best," Victoria yawned.

"Yes, you want to look your best."

Valera kissed her mother on the forehead, and the woman drifted off into a deep sleep. Valera stayed with her, watching over her family until she too fell asleep. She jumped when a hand touched her shoulder.

"It's just me," her brother whispered. "How are they doing?"

Valera shrugged. "Under Danu's spell, like everyone else. I'm sorry, Victor. This should never have happened."

He squeezed her arm. "The truth needed to come out. Aetherians have been living in a lie for centuries. We've been deluded, thinking we were somehow more evolved than humans."

He shook his head and closed his eyes. Valera hugged him. Her twin had always been there for her, and in return, she was ruining his life. She sobbed. He stroked her hair and patted her back.

*

Valera woke the next morning on the foot of the bed. Her mother and Vivi were already gone. She stretched out the kinks in her muscles. She was still wearing the silver dress. Although she'd slept in the gown, the fabric remained perfect. She was growing tired of perfection. If she could get away with it, she'd burn the dress to ash. She'd burn the whole palace down. Instead, she straightened her hair and went to the throne room.

Danu was in her chair with Vivi on her lap. She patted Vivi's head as if she were a prized poodle. Her mother was on her knees next to Theo's parents and Dr. Lawless. Theo emerged beside Valera and growled.

"I hate seeing my parents like that."

"Danu's proving a point. We're at her mercy," Valera sighed.

Julia grabbed both their arms. "Just play along… for now."

The three of them swept into the room and bowed in front of Danu. The woman grinned and waved her hands toward their miniature thrones.

"Sit," Danu commanded.

They did. The girls spent the day watching their families grovel and fetch. Danu lavished Vivi with gifts, endearing the girl to her. Each minute made Valera more anxious for the time when she could fight back. She couldn't wait to free her sister, but worried about the bond she was forming with the evil witch.

"Victoria, I should like to keep this child as my own."

Vivi giggled.

"Mother of all Aether…" Victoria strained against saying the words. "I surrender… myself to your… majestic will."

Valera smiled. Her mother was stronger than she'd ever thought. Theo's parents also seemed to fight the spell. Her mother cringed at the mantra every time she heard it. Danu scowled at Victoria and waved a hand over her head. Once again, Victoria was a good little puppet. Danu's illusion of beauty fluctuated. Valera saw dark circles under her eyes, and fine wrinkles creased her forehead. She stood and sat Vivi on the throne.

"Am I the queen, now?" Vivi squealed.

"Yes, child. You are queen... for now. I should like to rest." Danu glared at the girls. "Keep watch over the palace, daughters."

Although she looked at the girls, Valera knew she was speaking to her guards and courtesans. Danu left the room with Lawless on her heels. A thick haze fell over the palace. It was the same spell she'd used before to make them sleep. This time, Valera knew Danu's tricks. She held aether around herself and Gideon, forming a protective barrier against Danu's influence. Theo and Julia did the same over Eli and Victor. The courtesans dropped where they stood, falling into a deep sleep. Valera kissed her mother's cheek goodbye and picked up her sleeping sister.

"Remember to ask for help. Return here before morning," Julia said before teleporting away with Theo.

Gideon kissed Valera and stepped away. Valera formed the image of Aetherland in her mind, pushing away all worries about leaving Gideon and her family behind. The world seemed to blast by her. When she opened her eyes, she stood in the center of four tapestries inside her home. Danu's smiling face looked down at her from the cloth. The image was a betrayal.

With a single look, Valera lit the bottom of the tapestry on fire. She watched the fibers fizzle and burn until Danu's face was nothing but a blackened string. She extinguished the fire and went upstairs and laid Vivi in her bed.

"What... are you doing here?" Joe yawned behind her.

"You're back!" Valera hugged him.

"Yeah, Parmelia and Nessie's crew came for us after we didn't return. Turns out, the Blowfish's tracker box was still intact. Enough about that though. We've been worried sick about you girls."

There was a shuffle behind him, and a brunette with severe bed head popped up behind him. She pushed Joe aside and blinked through her glasses.

"Valera!" Theo's Auntie Grace squealed. "Is Theo with you?"

"No, she went to Pacifica to ask the Elders for help. We're in trouble."

"Go get Nessie and meet us in the library," Joe said.

Valera went to Nessie's room.

"Nessie? Are you in here?"

The room was quiet. The bed made. No doubt, Nessie was sleeping on *the Cornelius* or at the village pub. Nessie would have to be informed later. Valera didn't have time to track her down. She waited for Joe in the library, pacing back and forth. CHAD-4's gears whirred as it came into the room. He bowed. Valera didn't realize how much she had missed the mechanical butler. She hugged his cold metal body.

"Mmmm...mistress Valera, how may I serve you?"

Valera shook her head. His cold automaton voice reminded her of her mother's blind devotion to Danu. Being back in the mansion, she felt foolish for ever believing it was a prison. Danu's palace was the real prison.

"CHAD-4, I need you to stay with Vivi in her room. Watch over her, and don't let anyone near her. Keep her safe," Valera said.

CHAD-4 bowed and left the room. He wasn't built to fight, but knowing he was with Vivi brought a little comfort. Valera crumpled to the floor.

"Valera, is that you?" Nessie stumbled into the room.

Valera's aunt fell to the ground in front of her and grabbed her shoulders. The strong odor of ale and sweat made Valera's stomach turn, but she held onto her aunt. Nessie's short, cropped red hair stuck out in every direction. She missed Nessie's boisterous attitude and terrible sense of humor.

"Valera, I thought… I thought you girls were dead… Am I dreaming?" She pinched herself in the arm and yelped. "You're here… you're really here," she slurred. She pulled away, tearing up. "I have some bad news. Victoria and Vivi are missing. I've looked for them everywhere, but they just disappeared overnight. Poof!"

"Danu kidnapped them. Mother's in Subterria, but I brought Vivi home."

Nessie blinked until the information worked its way past her inebriation. First, she smiled. Then, she growled.

"Danu's ass, I should have known… only… I don't understand. What would a goddess want with our family?"

"Oh, Nessie. Everything is so messed up," Valera blurted. "Danu's no goddess. She's evil. She's holding our family hostage to keep Theo, Julia, and me in line. We have to do something, and soon. Before she has the world at her feet."

"Well, it's a good thing you came home," Auntie Grace said, marching into the room with Joe and Theo's Uncle Falen.

"It's good to see you again, Valera," Falen said.

"Wow, you look much better than the last time I saw you. Looks like your stint in the Order of the Azure Serpent's dungeons didn't leave any permanent scars." Valera smiled. Then, she turned serious. "I can't stay for long. I have to get back before she realizes I'm gone."

"You can't go back. Let Joe and the others take care of it," Grace said.

"You don't understand. I have to go, but I do need your help. You have to gather as many people as you can. When the time comes, we'll find a way to fix everything. We need you to be ready with an army."

"An army?" Auntie Grace gasped.

"Danu's taken over Subterria. Some people are faithful to her. Some people she forces to be faithful, but it will take an army to beat her." The clock on the wall chimed three times. Valera's time was running out. "I have to leave. Just please get everyone you can... and stay away from Subterria until we signal you. It's not safe. Grace, please take care of my sister."

Valera stood up and prepared to travel. Nessie grabbed her arm.

"Wait! Bring Joe and Falen with you." Nessie turned to the two men. "Keep hidden, but watch over the girls."

Her aunt kissed her forehead. Valera took the hands of both men and pictured her room in Danu's prison. Before she teleported out, she heard Nessie's voice shouting to her.

"We'll get you an army, Valera. I promise."

CHAPTER TWENTY-FOUR

Theo

Shortly after Valera blinked out of existence, Theo and Julia teleported to Pacifica City. They arrived directly within the council chambers, where Parmelia and the scholars poured over stacks of ancient books. The girls' sudden appearance in the room sent everyone into a panic. The scholars scattered like insects in the girls' presence.

"You're already back!" Parmelia hugged Julia.

Theo cleared her throat. "Sorry to interrupt. Danu's taken our family, Parmelia. We're out of time."

"I'm sorry, child." Parmelia reached out to Theo. "We think we may have found something useful."

They gathered around a table where old yellow-paged books were open. Parmelia scanned her finger over a passage and smiled.

"I believe we found a counter spell to Danu's persuasion. This book was copied from Maera's journal. Read this passage." She pointed to a paragraph of gibberish.

Theo couldn't even begin to process the language. Julia smiled and stepped in.

"I learned old Irish at the Academy. You really should have gone to the Academy. Aside from the uncaring staff, the dreadful living conditions, and the constant life and death battle for control, it was a great place to go to school." Julia quipped, and then read the passage. "De réir an cumhacht ag an Tríonóide, beidh thoghairm Danu bheith adh. Roughly translated, it says 'By the power of the Trinity, Danu's summons be silenced."

"Well okay then. How does it work?" Theo asked.

Parmelia turned a few pages back and read, "Only together were we able to protect the people from Danu's persuasion. By laying hands on the person and speaking the words, they were deaf to her summons. However, once under her spell, the victims were immune to the counter spell until Danu was entombed."

"So there's nothing we can do for my mom and dad?"

"Not until Danu is defeated," Julia responded.

"And how are we supposed to do that?" Theo snarked back.

Parmelia put her hand on Theo's shoulder and squeezed. "I know this is hard, but you three must stand together. I had something made for each of you."

She waved to one of the scholars. He left the room and returned a minute later with three ring boxes and a large bundle wrapped in cloth. Parmelia opened one of the boxes and held it up to Theo. A silver ring with a blue stone shimmered inside.

"It's a rare aether stone. It will help you absorb and control aether, which might give you an edge over Danu."

Theo slipped it onto her finger and felt the sweet jolt of aether flow through her. She removed it, put it back in the box, then tucked the box into her pocket.

"There's one more thing I need to give you. I picked these up when we found Nessie and the others at the tomb." Parmelia unwrapped the cloth and revealed the three relics of Danu and the Trinity Key.

Theo grinned. "You have them! They were useless around Danu."

"Not if you can bind her powers long enough to use them. With the rings, you may be able to weaken her…"

Theo felt something slither into her mind. She tried to push it away, but the persistent tugging didn't relent. Danu was waking. Julia's eyes widened. She felt it too. Theo grabbed the relics and the rings.

"We have to go, now!" Theo screeched.

She closed her eyes and didn't wait to say goodbye. Within seconds, she was back in the room at the palace. Valera, Falen, and Joe were waiting. Julia appeared beside her.

Daughters, come to me…

Inside her head, she heard Danu calling. Theo tried to sound tired as if she had just woken up.

Yes, Mother. I'm awake, but so tired.

Ah, Theo, my child. Bring your sisters to the throne room. I've something to show you.

"Uncle Falen, Joe," Theo hugged them both. "It's not safe here."

"We'll stay hidden," Joe rumbled.

"Theo, we should test Parmelia's spell on them," Julia said. "Valera, we'll need your help too."

Theo nodded and put her hand on Joe's shoulder. Julia put her hand on his back. Valera touched his chest.

"Repeat after me," Julia said. "De réir an cumhacht ag an Tríonóide, beidh thoghairm Danu bheith adh."

Theo and Valera repeated every word, although a bit awkwardly. They said it three times over, and then did the same to Falen.

"Did it work?" Falen asked.

"I don't know. Nothing really happened..." Julia said. "Do you feel any different?"

"Not really."

Daughters, come...

"We have to go," Valera yipped.

They left the men behind, hoping that their spell worked. Theo's hands shook. She could feel Danu's anger building, and she worried about her family and Victor.

"Valera, have you seen the boys?" She asked.

"No, they were gone when I got back."

CHAPTER TWENTY-FIVE

Julia

Julia was the first one to enter the throne room. The instant she saw Danu's frown, she knew they were in trouble. Danu's face twisted from a dark scowl into a fake smile. The glint of red in her eye sent ice through Julia's veins. Dr. Lawless sat at her side, giggling like a fool. Danu hissed at him, and he stopped. Julia looked around for the boys, but didn't see them or Theo's parents anywhere.

"Come my daughters, I've been waiting for you," Danu's singsong voice trilled.

The girls walked slowly to her throne. The courtesans chittered behind their hands. A sense of anticipation blanketed the room. Julia followed Theo's lead, trying to appear half-asleep. She rubbed her eyes and yawned.

"Good morning, Mother. What time is it? It feels so early."

"Poor, child. You look as if you hadn't slept at all."

Dr. Lawless erupted in laughter. He rocked back and forth on his heels until Danu glared at him. He threw his hands over his mouth, but his eyes lit up in glee. The crowd tittered. Danu snapped her fingers and two of her guards disappeared.

"I, uh, had bad dreams," Julia stammered.

Danu's smile faded. Her illusion slipped, revealing blackened eyes and sharp teeth. Julia shuddered. Danu knew. Every part of Julia told her to run, but she stood with Theo and Valera.

"I grow tired of this charade." Danu whispered. Her court held their breath. "Did you not think I would discover your treachery? I've given you everything, and yet, you turn against me?" Danu screamed.

Her two guards dragged a battered Professor Scrod into the room. The woman whimpered in agony and fell onto the ground in front of Danu's throne. Her clothes were stained with blood and torn. Her face looked as if someone had used a bat on her. Dr. Lawless poked at her like a child poking a dead animal.

"Not so special now are you, *Professor*?" He sang.

She curled into the fetal position and groaned. Danu's eyes blazed. She made a fist and squeezed. Professor Scrod shrieked and writhed on the floor. Danu's gaze stayed on the three girls. Julia heard Valera crying next to her. Theo covered her eyes.

"Stop it," Julia yelled.

"Traitors don't deserve mercy." Danu hissed.

With a final tightening of her fingers, Professor Scrod's body contorted and cracked. Every bone in the woman's body seemed out of joint. Her breath shuttered and stopped. Her lifeless eyes fixed on Julia. Dr. Lawless cackled. Angry, Julia lashed out at him with a blast of ice. One of the shards caught him in the shoulder, slicing through flesh and bone. Lawless held his shoulder and crumpled.

SAVE AETHER | 265

Danu's anger rattled the palace. "How dare you use aether against me!"

She threw a hand out to Julia, and a searing pain flamed through Julia's body. Julia fell to her knees. Valera dropped to the ground next to Julia and tried to help her. Instead, she got a jolt of whatever it was Danu was doing and shrieked. Danu released control over both of them and Julia's pain ebbed. Stepping down from her throne, the sorceress bent over, placed a finger under Julia's chin, and kissed her forehead.

"I don't want to punish you. You are my beloved daughters, but you must learn. I will not stand deception. Know that you've forced my hand."

She waved to someone behind her. Eli, Gideon, and Victor walked out from behind the throne and knelt where Lawless had been. In unison, they bowed to Danu. Julia's heart stopped. She crawled over to Eli. He wouldn't look in her eyes. Transfixed on Danu, he smiled.

"I live to serve you, my goddess."

"Eli, wake up. It's me, Julia."

He ignored her and waited for his mistress's command. Danu sat on her throne and grinned. She seemed to delight in the girls' pain. Julia wanted to lash out again, but held herself back. She returned to her position beside Theo and Valera. Her action seemed to bolster Danu's joy and ego.

"Traitors deserve no mercy." Danu hissed. "But I'm a benevolent mother. Take my daughters to the dungeon, so that they may reflect on their folly."

Eli stood and grabbed Julia's shoulders. His fingers dug into her flesh. She tried to jerk out of his grasp, but he crushed her arms. She couldn't use her power on him without hurting him. She glared at Danu, whose smug grin grew. Eli pushed Julia toward the doors. The courtesans cheered. She stumbled down the stairs and past the cells filled with the dying forsaken. The girls were taken to an area in the furthest, deepest part of the palace. They were locked in three separate rooms without light, without food, and without comfort. The last thing Julia saw was the shadow of Eli's smirkless face.

She'd been in a place like this before. She could do it again. This didn't affect her. She was strong. A foul smell filled the room, and Julia dropped to the cold hard ground. Her lungs burned in her chest. She scrambled to find aether, but couldn't grasp it. It was as if the room were devoid of air. Then, somewhere in the distance she heard her father's voice.

"Julia, get up. Stop acting like a child," Lazarus shouted at her.

"You're dead... Theo..." Julia couldn't think. Theo? Theo who?

Lazarus yelled, "What did you say to me?"

"Nothing Father," Julia warbled.

Her inside curdled. He wouldn't tolerate laziness or childishness. She stood up and saw her father's imposing form walking toward her. She couldn't remember the last time she saw him. She looked around the room. The dark cell was gone. She was in the Subterrian Order of the Azure Serpent Headquarters. She tried to remember why she was here. She looked down at her clothes and pulled at the blue academy uniform. This wasn't right. She remembered wearing different clothes in a different place.

"I'm not pleased with the reports I've been getting from your instructors. I expect better from you," Lazarus ranted.

She wasn't prepared for the pain of his hand striking her face. Her cheek stung. Taking a few steps away from him, she held in tears. He wouldn't tolerate tears.

"I'm sorry, Father. I tried my best," she said, standing at attention.

"You're best isn't good enough."

His words struck her seconds before his fist. She doubled over. A quiet whisper in the back of her mind told her this wasn't right, but she couldn't get free. She was afraid. He didn't tolerate fear. She recovered and put her arms at her sides. Her stomach churned. She swallowed the pain.

"I won't fail you again, Father," she coughed.

"You're right. You won't."

CHAPTER TWENTY-SIX

Valera

Valera watched Gideon leave. She heard the cell door locking and curled up next to a wall. She'd never liked the dark. The air felt thick, and she felt like she was drowning. She sank in warm water. It filled her nose and her ears. She sat up and gasped for air. Her eyes darted around the room, blurred by lavender soap. She rubbed them clear and saw her bathroom at Aetherland Isle. Her copper, claw-foot bathtub bubbled over.

"Valera, do hurry. We're having guests for dinner. I've laid your clothes out for you," her mother's voice drifted in from her room.

"Yes, Mother."

Valera stood up, looking at her naked body in the mirror. For a brief second, she remembered a sparkling silver dress. Shaking out her confusion, she retrieved a towel and dried off. She sat at her vanity and dried her hair, brushing it to a glowing sheen. She coiled it on top of her head in a tight knot just as her mother had taught her.

The dress on the bed was her least favorite. The somber black gown suffocated her. She cinched into a chemise and corset. *Pull it extra tight, we must be flawless.* Her mother's voice demanded in her head. She tightened the corset until she could barely breathe. *Not good enough.* CHAD-4 knocked on her door. He cinched the corset so tight, Valera felt her ribs crack. She had to look perfect, after all. The automaton helped her into the dress. Valera pulled at the high-necked collar.

"It's so scratchy," she whined.

"Stop fidgeting," her mother scolded. "Our guests are arriving soon."

Although she didn't remember leaving her room, she was now sitting at the dining table with her mother and Vivi. Vivi's bouncy curls were pulled into the same skin-ripping coif, and she was in the same body-breaking dress. Valera wondered why her mother had put her little sister in a corset. Something wasn't right, but she couldn't figure out what. Victoria tapped on the table. Valera sat straight up like the perfect doll she was meant to be. When the guests arrived, she stood and greeted them. A boy with white-blond hair and grey eyes bowed to her.

CHAD-4 introduced the man. "Presenting, Gideon Killian, Master Engineer of the Order of the Azure Serpents."

Valera thought he was the most handsome boy she'd ever met. He had to be the reason Mother had her dress up. Surely, this was her new suitor. She wanted to dance. Behind him stood an older man with moles on his face and crooked, yellow teeth. He wiped a hand across his running nose, and bowed.

"So you are the lovely daughter Victoria has told me about. My name is Fowler."

"Yes… I suppose so…" Valera stammered.

Her mother frowned at her and pinched her back. "Manners, Valera," she whispered.

The group sat at the table. Fowler sat next to Valera much to her chagrin. She wanted to sit with Gideon, but he sat in the farthest seat away from her. She sighed. Fowler leaned close to her and touched her hand under the table. She pulled away.

He addressed Victoria with a smile, "I'm quite agreeable to our arrangement, Victoria. After meeting Valera, I think it will be a great match."

Valera was agreeable to the arrangement as well. She'd be quite happy to spend time with Gideon. Fowler touched her leg, and she flinched. She couldn't understand why this disgusting man was at dinner. Crusty white phlegm flaked on the corners of his mouth when he smiled. Perhaps, he was Gideon's grandfather. Her mother had always said she would arrange an appropriate marriage at the right time. Valera smiled at Gideon. He looked bored.

"Should I not get to know him first?" Valera asked. "Gideon and I just met."

Her mother coughed and scowled. "Don't be foolish, child. Gideon isn't your equal. Master Fowler, on the other hand, will be a fine husband."

Valera swallowed the bile that rose in her throat. She stared at the man in question and gagged. Her mother couldn't possibly be sending her off to marry this man. He was at least four times her age and so... so gross. Everyone at the table laughed. Valera shook her head.

"This isn't right," Valera cried. "Gideon tell her."

Gideon stuck his nose in the air and scoffed, "Why would I settle for a homely creature like you? I have my eyes on a much finer prize."

He gazed at Victoria and smiled. Victoria blushed, and he kissed her hand. Valera felt like tearing her eyes from her head. She couldn't watch this any longer.

272 | L.M. FRY

"Get your head out of the sky, girl. Perhaps time alone with your future husband will help you learn your place," Victoria leered.

"No... this isn't right. This can't be right."

CHAPTER TWENTY-SEVEN

Theo

Theo stood by her locker in Boulder High, trying to appear invisible. Ever since her dad died, she was always alone. A memory of her dad showing her his mechanical heart flitted through her mind. She shook it out of her mind. Looking in the mirror, she adjusted the thick black eyeliner that had smudged beneath her left eye. Her mom didn't approve of her new emo goth look, but Theo didn't care what her mom thought. Her new style fit her mood – depressed and lonely.

A shadow loomed over her shoulder. Her worst nightmare appeared in the corner of the mirror. She swung around and slammed her locker closed. Maybe she could make a quick getaway. Charlie, the Boulder High linebacker, blocked her escape with his tree-sized arm. His friends howled behind him.

"Watch out, Charlie, she's a biter!"

Theo threw her best menacing glare in Charlie's direction. "Move."

"Aww, Theodora. I just want to talk to you," he chuckled.

"Move, or I'll… I'll make you move," she stammered.

In the back of her mind, Theo knew this was wrong. She remembered punching Charlie and breaking his nose. Yet, he stood in front of her arrogant as ever with a straight unbroken nose. Down the hall a boy walked by wearing a trench coat, a top hat, and goggles. She knew him… his name was…

Charlie's fingers brushed her hair off her shoulder. She pushed on his chest, but he didn't budge. This wasn't happening. She'd followed her mom into Aether, where her dad had been healed by the Steins. The artificial heart in her dad's chest ticked just like the clock on the wall. The clock on the wall marked the end of school The bell rang. She rubbed her forehead.

"What's wrong, Theodora? Don't you like me?" Charlie touched her shoulder.

She jumped back. He was in front of her. She could feel him. Her dad was dead. She was in hell.

"Leave me alone, Charlie. Please," Theo begged.

"Please, what?"

"Please, leave me alone."

Charlie's evil grin spread, revealing his perfect white teeth. They made Theo think of a lewd piranha. His friends laughed and urged him on. He leaned close to her ear.

"I'll make you a deal. You give me a little kiss, and I'll leave you alone."

She shook her head. He slammed his fist on her locker. Her body shuddered. She just wanted to go home. Every day she lived the same nightmare. He delighted in tormenting her. She sighed. She closed her eyes and puckered her lips. One quick kiss and she'd be free. Charlie's laughter erupted into an ear-shattering guffaw. He covered her face with his hand and pushed the back of her head against the locker.

"You wish, Goth girl. I'd rather kiss a corpse!"

Charlie and his pack strutted away in hysterics. Theo grabbed her bag against her chest and crumpled to the floor. Students passed by her without even looking. She was nothing. She cried until the halls emptied. Then, she stood up and walked home. The Victorian was cold and empty. Her mom was still at work. Throwing her bag on the stairs, she flopped down on the couch. She turned on the television and stared at snow. Every channel was static.

She thumped the remote against her palm and flipped to the next channel. Squinting, she peered into the static. Behind it, she saw a pair of emerald green eyes watching her. She touched the screen and felt a jolt. For a split second, the screen cleared. The boy with a long brown trench coat, a top hat, and a pair of odd goggles atop his head was smiling at her. She knew him. His name was… Victor. None of this was real.

CHAPTER TWENTY-EIGHT

Julia

Julia felt as though she'd been listening to her dad yell at her for days, and she was growing tired of it. She stared at the painting of her family behind his desk. The paint seemed to smear and discolor. She rubbed her eyes. The room transformed for a second. The painting was on the floor torn to pieces. Her dad's papers were all over the room.

"Are you listening to me, Julia? Wake up," Lazarus bellowed.

A spark of memory gnawed at her gut. Lazarus was dead. Theo killed him. She stared at the imposter in front of her. He frowned and lifted his hand to strike her again. She kept her hands at her sides. Beneath her fingers, she felt a hard square object. A box. A ring box. She didn't remember where it came from, but somehow she knew it was there. Lazarus's hand collided with her cheek. She fell to the floor. Anger rose in her belly. She stood and faced her father. He lifted his fist again.

With both hands out, Julia yelled, "No."

He froze in midair. "No? You dare say 'no' to me?"

She reached into her pocket and fumbled with the box. Lazarus stepped back. His face contorting in rage. Julia slipped the ring on her finger and felt the surge of aether flow through her body. The truth barreled toward her like a rampaging bull. She was in a room in Danu's palace. Lazarus didn't exist, but the aether in her veins did.

"You're not real!"

She blasted the room with frost. The hallucination of her father turned to ice and shattered. The room disintegrated. She was back in the real world. In the pitch dark, she stumbled to the wall and found her way to the door. She rattled the handle, but Eli had locked it before he left. She created a blizzard and chilled the walls. The metal door creaked. Under the jarring temperatures, it ruptured open.

She flew out of the room and collapsed into Joe. He held her up. Julia pulled back and threw her hands out at him. Her eyes struggled to focus in the light, and her mind couldn't process his face.

"Julia, it's Joe. Falen and I came to help you."

"How long have I been in there?"

"Three days," Falen said.

Julia gripped her head between her hands and squeezed her eyes shut. Slowly, her vision adjusted. Joe held a bag on his arm. The hilt of Ealga's Sword poked from the top of the canvas. Then, she saw Falen's hazel eyes. They reminded her of Theo's eyes.

"Theo? Where's Theo? We have to help them!"

"She's behind a door we can't open," Falen said.

Julia growled, "I can open it."

She couldn't imagine the hell Danu was putting Theo and Valera through. If she could bring back Lazarus, then who was tormenting her sisters? She ran to the next cell. With all her energy, she blasted the metal. Joe and Falen rammed the weakened door with their shoulders and burst into the darkness.

Julia found Theo huddled in a corner, muttering with her eyes closed. She tried to shake Theo awake, but Theo shuddered and pushed Julia away. Using her aether stone ring, Julia formed a protective shield around her friend. Theo's eyes shot open and blinked.

"Who's there?"

"It's me Julia. You're okay, now," Julia cooed.

"Where am I?"

"You're in a cell in Danu's palace. Joe and Falen are here with me."

"My dad is he... is he alive?"

Falen wrapped his arms around his niece. "Nathaniel is alive. Do you think you can stand?"

Theo's legs shook, but she got up. Julia helped her into the light. They moved to Valera's cell. Theo blasted the door off its hinges. Valera ran screaming from the room.

"I won't marry him! You can't make me," she shrieked at Julia.

Joe caught her in his arms and gently shook her. Beneath the protective shield, she came around. Tears streamed down her face. Valera tugged at her neck as if an invisible collar choked her.

"That was awful. My mother tried to marry me off to a horrid man."

She shuddered. Julia chuckled, eliciting a scowl from Valera.

"You were a bride-to-be, while I was being beaten by my dead father. Danu is sick, but you have to give her props for creativity."

"Girls, we need to get out of here. Danu will know you're free," Joe scolded.

"We can't go traipsing through the palace," Julia said.

"I saw some old clothes in a bin on my way down here. They looked pretty shabby, but you'll blend in with the people. Those silver frocks are kind of a give-away."

Falen left for a minute and came back holding rags. Julia surmised that they once belonged to Danu's worshippers who didn't meet her standard of worth. The girls dressed in the filthy clothes and messed up their hair.

"We can sneak out with the workers," Theo said.

"What about Gideon, and Victor?" Valera panicked. "What about our parents?"

Julia didn't want to leave Eli, especially not with Danu. Once she discovered they had escaped, she'd lash out at the boys for sure. Julia was determined to go back for them, but Joe stopped her.

"You can't. We'll have to come back for them later. You guys are more important."

"No, I won't go without him."

Theo took Julia's hand. "You're not the only one leaving someone behind. My parents and Victor are back there. We can't do this on our own. We need help."

Julia knew that they were right, although it didn't make leaving any easier. She set her mind on signaling Parmelia and Nessie. Joe led the way past the cells. Some of the captives looked at the girls and started talking. The brainwashed prisoners chattered and alerted the guards.

"Traitors!" Someone screamed.

Without time to waste, the girls ran for the exit. The workers turned on them and tried to stop them. Julia blasted the room with ice, pushing past outstretched hands. Theo shrieked when someone grabbed a fistful of her hair. Julia saw sparks light up the room and heard someone cry out. The smell of burnt flesh hit Julia in the face and made her gag. Joe and Falen knocked bodies to the ground and ploughed through the crowds. They forced their way to the exit only to find themselves confronted with Eli, Victor, and Gideon. The boys stood in their path along with an army behind them.

"Danu demands your surrender," Eli shouted.

Julia stepped forward, "Please, Eli, don't do this. I don't want to hurt you."

His eyes glazed over. Her words couldn't penetrate Danu's control over him. Eli pulled a pistol from behind him and aimed it at Julia's chest.

"Danu demands your surrender," he shouted again.

"Please, Eli, stop."

He pulled the trigger and a shot tore through the air. A streak of lightning shot out in front of Julia and exploded the bullet inches from her body. Before he could get another shot, Julia formed a wall of ice. A mob appeared behind them. They were surrounded. Julia looked at Theo and Valera. They put the aether stone rings on their fingers.

"Together," Julia hissed.

Theo blasted the wall of ice. Chunks flew out at the crowd in front of them. The power behind the blast knocked most of them to the ground. Valera hit people with fireballs. More people ran over the fallen. Julia saw Eli's unconscious body covered in blood. She wanted to stop and help him, but Falen urged her forward.

Julia made her way to the industrial district – the only part of the city still in ruins. The bomb-mangled door to the old graveyard was close. Danu's people recovered quickly. They gained ground. Julia felt aether being yanked away from her.

Danu stood on top of a building. The ground shook beneath Julia's feet, and a glimmer filled the air. The walls of Subterria crumbled in front of them. Julia drew on the aether stone and kept the falling rocks away with an ice tunnel. She reached the opening and waited for the others to pass. She collapsed the tunnel, and the cave-in of rocks blocked the exit. And halted Danu's pursuit.

CHAPTER TWENTY-NINE

Valera

Valera came to the end of the skull-laden catacombs. Light shone in from the crypt above them, but the exit was blocked by the broken door. Falen gave her a boost through a small gap. There was no way Joe or Falen would fit through.

"Back up. I'll clear the block," she shouted.

She grabbed a corner of the metal plate and heated it up. The steel glowed red hot and became pliable. With a tug, she bent the door out of the way. Far below, she could hear Danu's outburst in the form of explosions. A guilt-ridden worry crept into her thoughts. She'd left Gideon, Victor, and her mother behind. She knew the cost of Danu's anger and couldn't imagine what the sorceress might do to her family. The only way to save them now was to stop her.

The serene landscape around her betrayed the torrential storm that she'd just escaped. They only had a short time before Danu would surface with her army. Running across the pastoral fields of cattle, they made it to the abandoned village on the island. The humans had evacuated long before Danu's awakening. The ground was littered with the remains of the refugee camp for Subterrians, who were now Danu's slaves.

Valera entered a tiny shop, which used to house the liaison between Subterria and the rest of Aether. They rummaged for something to eat and something else to wear, since the old rags couldn't protect them from the harsh climate of the island. In the back of the shop, Theo found three old oversized flannel jackets. Valera slipped into one, then searched for the telecommunication device. An old rotary phone sat on a desk. She picked up the receiver, hoping for a dial tone and found silence.

"It's dead."

"The power's down all over," Theo said. "I think I can help."

Theo stepped outside. A bright flash of purple blinded Valera. Seconds later, the lights flickered on and the buzz of electricity filled the store. Valera picked up the receiver and heard the glorious beep. She dialed Nessie's telecom and waited.

"This is Captain Vanessa of the AV *Cornelius*." Nessie's booming voice sounded like heaven.

"Aunt Nessie, it's Valera. It's time." Valera cried. "Please hurry."

"Hang in there, kiddo. The cavalry is on the way. We came early, and I brought your army." The line went dead and cut their call short.

Valera dropped the phone. "Nessie's coming."

"We should get away from the village. It's the first place Danu will look," Theo suggested. "We should make a run for the cliffs to the west."

A thunderclap erupted in the sky. Valera didn't know if it was natural phenomenon or Danu's hissy fit. The downpour that followed turned the road to mud. They slogged through, although the thin coats did little to shield them from the rain and wind. Valera touched aether to surround herself in warmth, but Julia stopped her.

"Don't. It will give us away. We have to wait for the right moment," Julia said.

Valera nodded and tucked her blue fingers inside the pockets. Behind the thunder and rain, she heard the song of the waves. The road ended, and they continued over the hillside. The ocean crashed on the rocks below with such force that their mists crested the cliffs.

"How will Nessie see us in this weather?" Valera chattered.

"I'll try to calm it. Danu did say I had control over the tempests and tides right?" Theo half-laughed.

Valera tried to smile, but her thoughts were on her family and their safety. Danu would use them against her. Danu would use her entire army against them – an army of innocent people trapped by her spell. Julia handed Valera Aeda's Sextant, and pocketed the Trinity key. With the sextant in her hands, Valera felt a connection to Aeda. The feeling bolstered her nerves. Aeda and her sisters imprisoned Danu once, which meant Theo, Julia, and Valera could do it again. Now, if only it would stop raining. The five of them huddled together. Joe and Falen kept watch for Nessie. The girls kept watch for Danu.

"I see her!" Joe shouted.

A strange, white fog appeared among the black storm clouds. The massive balloons of the *Cornelius* capped the unnatural formation. Her roaring engines drowned out the rolling waves. Dozens of flying machines flanked the ship. Single inflatables and dirigibles, two engine airplanes and metal-winged ornithopters fought the harsh winds. From the oceans below, two wings erupted from the ocean like a monster. The *Manta Ray* lead an army of submersibles and boats. The weather fought them back, making it impossible to reach the girls.

Valera, Julia, and Theo held hands and channeled aether. Their rings shone, enhancing their power. Theo raised her hands in the sky and shouted at the tempest. Little by little, the wind subsided and the waves shrunk. Valera sent a pillar of fire into the sky as a beacon to everyone. The *Cornelius* released two flares in acknowledgement. The girls cheered.

Grappling hooks grabbed the cliffside and men flooded the fields. Ropes lowered people from the skies. Valera recognized many of the mechanically-enhanced men and women from Aetherland Isle village. One ship deposited an army of automatons made in Aetherland's warehouse. Captain Stoddlemeyer raised a sword, and a swarm of Pacifica City men stormed the island.

Valera saw her aunt's cropped flaming hair fly down a ladder. She ran to her aunt and held her close.

"How did you get so many?"

"I've acquired a lot of favors," Nessie joked. She pointed at a mob of white robes and Elders. "Looks like the boring brigade is here."

"How can you joke around?" Valera scolded.

Nessie jabbed Valera in the ribs. "The skies are clearing, the waters are calming, and we're storming the castle. Life is grand."

Valera shook her head. Her aunt was a true sky pirate. Parmelia and the Elders approached the girls. Nessie and Parmelia were the only ones who didn't look as if the world was ending. Parmelia hugged each of the girls, and shook Nessie's hand. Captain Stoddlemeyer joined the leaders with his chest puffed, and his brass buttons polished. The always cantankerous Rusty walked alongside him.

"I still say she ain't nothin' on me poor Blowfish, may she rest in peace," Rusty grumbled.

"Pacifica City Naval Fleet at your service." Captain Stoddlemeyer bowed to the girls and Parmelia.

Nessie slapped him on the back and hooted, "Good to see you, old man!"

He huffed and stammered, "Yes... well... I'm pleased to see you as well, Captain Vanessa."

Valera detected a hint of a smile on Parmelia's face. The elder cleared her throat. Someone in the ranks shouted. Everyone froze. Valera looked up and saw Danu rising from the earth like lava from a volcano. Her army of slaves stood behind her.

"I hope you're ready, girls," Parmelia whispered.

Valera's whisper was barely audible. "I'm not."

CHAPTER THIRTY

*T*heo

Danu looked like the goddess she *believed* she was. Her dress flew in the wind as if it were her banner. Her hair was as wild as her pure black eyes. With a deafening roar, she approached. The free Aetherians formed ranks behind the girls.

"Remember that Danu's people are our brothers and sisters, who are under her spell. Try to save lives, not take them," Theo shouted to the people behind them.

Theo saw fear in their eyes. They were witnessing Danu's power for the first time, and it scared them. Only the heartless automatons were unmoved by her display. Theo reached for aether and created her own demonstration. She whirled Maera's Scepter around her and formed a huge whip of electricity. It crackled and charged the air. The Aetherians cheered.

Parmelia leaned toward the girls. "We need to protect these people from Danu's summons. Hurry."

"We've only done it twice," Valera squeaked.

"And on one person at a time," Theo added.

Parmelia grabbed Theo and Julia's hand. "We don't have time for that. You'll have to do everyone at once."

"We'll try," Julia said.

They took one another's hands and touched Parmelia. They recited the spell. Theo could feel aether passing from her to Parmelia. Nessie took Parmelia's hand, and the spell passed to her as well. One by one, people added to the chain. The girls continued to chant the spell and pull on aether. The energy it took drained the girls, but they kept going. Soaking more and more aether through them, they covered the entire army. Sweat beaded Theo's brow, and her palms dripped. Then, it was done.

Danu's voice floated on the breeze like a whisper. "Come, my children. Come stand at my side and be rewarded."

The Aetherians didn't move. Danu's face contorted into an angry grimace. A shrill scream flew at them. With a wave of her arm, creatures stirred from the ground. Beetles, spiders, and ants bubbled from the dirt. The insect swarm charged at the Aetherians. Before they reached them, Valera cast a wall of fire. The bugs popped and ruptured like popcorn. From the skies above came birds. They attacked the airships and swooped at the Aetherians.

Two of the smaller aerial vessels crashed into the seas, landing on the boats below. Theo could hear the screams of people trapped on the downed ships. She whipped at the birds with bolts of energy. Feathers rained to the ground. The Aetherians fought the animals off with blades and guns. Julia lifted a hand toward the animals and seemed to fight Danu's hold over the creatures with her own. Danu's hold on the animals waned, and they flew off.

"Move forward," Julia shouted.

Their army marched. Danu's followers charged. The two armies clashed on the fields. Theo did her best not to kill anyone, but she left a trail of injured and burned people behind her. Shards of ice flew past her head, hitting a man in the legs. He went down in agony. Rats poured from the gaps and crevices to the surface and attacked Danu's people.

"They'll help fight Danu's army," Julia said behind Theo. "We need to go after the witch."

Theo nodded and moved through the enemy. A herd of cows stampeded into the line of automatons, sending mechanical parts flying in the air. Even in pieces, the CHAD units fought back.

"Julia, the cows," Theo yelled.

Julia released them from Danu's grip. The herd slowed and stopped. The army washed around the tamed animals.

Gunshots rang out around the girls. Bullets whizzed past Theo's head. The ground shook beneath them, and Danu's firing squad buckled and dropped their guns. Valera formed cracks in the earth under the weapons, sucking them into the abyss.

Both the Aetherians and Danu's people fell to the ground. The clash of metal and the screams of people deafened the field. The Aetherians inched forward toward Danu, but the cost was high. Theo stopped to heal people with the scepter.

"There's no time. We'll heal them later."

Julia pulled Theo away. Theo sighed. Julia was right, they had to rid them of Danu's summoning first. Theo felt a sudden loss of aether. She could feel it flow in Danu's direction. Julia growled. Valera's fire dwindled. They halted and looked at each other. Danu lifted the ground beneath her, so she stood above the oncoming army. Theo saw her trying to hold control over her people. The amount of aether it took to keep them under her spell was siphoning too much power.

Her illusion of beauty fell, and the true Danu was revealed. Her skin wrinkled and shriveled. Her body shrunk. The luxurious hair that flowed down her back thinned and turned grey. Soon she'd have to give up or risk losing her vitality as well.

Theo held up her scepter and slammed it on the ground. Aether surged back to her like a tidal wave. Using the staff and ring both, Theo felt more power than she'd ever held on her own. Julia held up Ealga's Sword of Ice. She stomped on the ground and icicles ruptured from the earth. A pillar of fire blew from Valera's outstretched hand. It charred a line right to Danu's feet.

Danu shrieked. Theo saw fear in her face. Danu retreated, leaving her people defenseless on the field. The girls pursued her into Subterria. Theo took one last look at the field. She recognized several faces. Harmony, Benji, Adora… She was more worried about the people she didn't see – her family.

CHAPTER THIRTY-ONE

Julia

As Danu's power drained, so did her ability to maintain Subterria. The aether lights flickered, casting shadows all around the girls. Buildings crumbled under the force of the battle above. Julia led the way through the streets until they reached Danu's palace.

Julia's stomach dropped, when she saw Eli, Victor, and Gideon standing guard at the doors. Although Danu had revived them, she hadn't healed them. Blood flowed from a gash on Eli's head from where the ice had struck him. Danu's dwindling power held them in place. She stood behind them grinning.

Julia inched forward and put her hands up in submission. "Eli, it's me Julia."

"Kill them," Danu grit through her yellowed fangs and disappeared into the palace.

Theo called out to Victor, "You don't want to hurt us. I know you don't. You'd never hurt your sister or me. I know you, Victor."

He growled at her, but a flash of reluctance crossed his face. Julia could see him struggling against Danu's persuasion. Eli took staggered steps forward. The pain on his face tortured Julia. Her smirking Eli was in there somewhere trying to break free. Danu's power dug in deep. With a shake of his head, he and Gideon charged at the girls. Using the sword, Julia encased them between four thick walls of ice. They smashed into the barrier, unable to break through.

Julia's action triggered Victor into action. He grunted and ran at Theo. With Maera's scepter in hand, she hit him with a thin jolt of electricity. His muscles contracted, and he fell over in a twitching mass. Theo knelt beside him.

"I'm sorry, Victor."

"He'll be okay. We need to get to Danu."

Danu sat on her throne smiling. Her illusion was back. Her courtesans and serpent men surrounded her. She'd outsmarted them. Her army above ground were the unwilling victims of her power. The army below was far more dangerous. They chose to fight for her. Theo's parents and Victoria stood in front of the throne like a living shield.

"I knew you'd come back to me, Daughters," Danu trilled.

The girls stepped closer. Danu lifted a finger, and Theo's mother fell to her knees, screaming.

"I think you're close enough," Danu yelled.

Lawless cackled beside her with his arm in a sling. "Kill them... kill them all."

The girls stopped moving forward, and Danu released Theo's mom. Marjorie sat on the floor crying and trembling. Danu leaned back in her throne and tapped a fingernail on the arm.

"You see, my children. I'm a fair and forgiving goddess," Danu cooed. "Come back to me, end this war, and we'll rule the world together."

Julia looked at the courtesans. "She's not a goddess. She's lied to all of you."

The courtesans and serpent men laughed at her. Danu joined them. Julia knew if they saw her true form, they wouldn't be laughing. She felt a slight pull and knew the sorceress was testing their strength. Danu's eyes fell on Julia's ring.

"Where did you get that?" she wheezed.

"It was a gift," Julia sneered. "From my grandmother... my *real* grandmother."

"Give the rings to me, or I'll kill them all," Danu hissed, pointing at their families.

Theo and Valera touched their rings while their eyes remained fixed on their families. Danu sneered. Valera's mother hit the ground with a sickening thud. Seizures contorted her limbs. Valera screamed, and Victoria's body went limp.

"Is she... dead?" Valera whispered.

A low moan passed Victoria's lips. "She's alive," Julia said. "We can't give Danu the rings."

Theo looked between her mother and father. She mouthed the words, "I'm sorry." Tears streamed down her mother's face, but she and Theo's father nodded at her and smiled. Theo sobbed, and released her ring.

"No," Theo shouted at Danu.

"What did you say to me?"

"I said NO!"

Danu's courtesans gasped and chattered. The serpent men hissed and growled. Danu was losing control of them. Her illusion of beauty slipped, and her followers cowered away.

Even when she replaced the spell, her faithful few scattered. Lawless was the last to stay at her side. Danu shrieked in rage. She struck down anyone who ran, including her precious Azure Serpents.

In a fit of fury, Danu lashed out at Theo's mother. Before Danu could hurt his wife, Theo's dad pushed her out of the way. He looked back at his daughter as Danu's spell struck him in the back. He fell to his knees, smiling. His mechanical heart pumped one last time and stopped. His lifeless body collapsed. Theo's mother crawled to him, weeping. Theo screamed.

Danu's last true follower attacked. Lawless slammed into a distraught Theo, knocking her down. He lifted a knife above her head. Behind him a gunshot went off, and Lawless dropped the knife. A gaping hole in his chest oozed. He rolled off Theo and died. Victor stood in the doorway, gun drawn. He ran into the room and helped Theo stand. Danu tried to flee the room, but Theo hit each doorway with a bolt, crumbling the rocks above and blocking Danu's escape.

In the fray, Julia took the Trinity key from her pocket. She held up Ealga's Sword to Maera's Scepter and to Aeda's Sextant. With the power of the rings, the key, and the relics, the girls called out to the three sisters. A mist rose from the ground. Julia felt Ealga's presence before she saw her form rise from the fog. Ealga, Maera, and Aeda stood with them. Danu's daughters stalked their mother. Danu struck at them with every ounce of power she had left, but nothing could touch them.

"I command you… I command you… to stop!" Danu yelled.

Ealga's ghostly form swept forward. "Mother, you no longer command… anything."

"It's time you came with us, Mother," Aeda touched Danu's shoulder.

Maera turned to Victor, "Leave now. Take them and go."

She nodded toward Victoria and Marjorie. Victor picked up his mother and urged Theo's mother away from her husband's body.

"I can't leave him like this... I can't leave Theo," Marjorie pleaded.

Theo kissed her mother's cheek. "Go, I'll be right out."

A tear rolled down Maera's cheek. She walked over to Theo's father and touched his head. In a beautiful display of lights, his body burst into particles of pure aether. The aether swirled around Theo and her mother before floating up through the ceiling.

"He is free now," Maera whispered. As Theo's mother reluctantly left with Victor, Maera touched Theo's cheek. "You must use the key. Put us to rest, forever."

Danu tried to run, but the sisters had a hold of her. Julia, Theo, and Valera held the Trinity Key between them. They merged their power with the key and each other. A cloud of pure aether flowed from them to Danu. She cried out in pain as the aether formed a block around her and her daughters. The first Trinity smiled at the last Trinity until the block of aether obscured their faces. Julia felt the remaining power of Danu snap. Julia placed the Trinity Key on the floor and struck it with her sword. It broke into three pieces.

Massive sinkholes formed in the ground. Without Danu, the palace couldn't stand. The ground above fell on the throne, smashing it to rubble. Julia grabbed the key shards, and the girls ran from the room. Theo stopped at the door. Dust and debris covered the block of aether. An earthquake rattled the city, opening a fissure under the crystal. It fell into the depths of the earth.

"Goodbye," she whispered.

Theo wiped her face and left. Valera melted the ice walls around Gideon and Eli. With Danu gone, her spell was broken.

"I'll explain later. Right now we need to run."

Julia grabbed his hand, and they made their way through the city. The monuments to Danu crumbled and fell. The already war-torn industrial district turned to dust. The aether lights went out. Thrown into darkness, they poured aether into their rings. The stones glowed, lighting their path.

The palace caved in. Fires broke out in the districts as machinery bled oil and ignited. The remaining buildings burned or disintegrated. A fissure opened in the streets, spewing hot gasses. Lava bubbled to the surface. It was as if the earth were swallowing all of Subterria.

Boulders and rocks blocked the main gates. The debris exploded under the power of the three girls. Sunlight streamed down the ramp, and Julia heard voices calling to them.

"Hurry," Nessie and Victor stood at the exit, urging them to move.

Julia stepped into the light. Both armies were gone. Only the dead littered the fields. The *Cornelius* hovered above them. Nessie led them to rope ladders. They grabbed hold and the ship lifted them before they reached the deck. The ground convulsed, and Subterria imploded. The island sank into the Atlantic abyss. Steam rose from the open wound as the seawater doused fires and solidified the lava.

Julia climbed the ladder. She wanted nothing more than to leave Danu behind forever.

The deck was filled to capacity. Subterrians stood there, still dazed from Danu's broken spell. Families looked for loved ones. A mass of children cried, and the forsaken elderly cared for them. The crew worked around the displaced and lost.

"After people came out of their stupor, we loaded the living on board the ships we had left. We'll travel to Aetherland Isle and figure things out from there," Nessie spoke behind her.

Julia turned around and saw her grandmother. Parmelia held Julia in her arms. "I thought I'd lost you."

"I'm here, grandma." Julia's voice quivered. "Danu's gone... for good."

After a few minutes, Julia stepped back and wiped her face with the back of her hand. There were so many people on deck, but she knew that they'd left people behind.

"How many got out?"

"Casualties were low," Nessie said. "Victor even brought out the children and old people."

"There were so many on the fields..." Julia murmured.

"You need to rest now," Parmelia said, leading Julia away.

She found a spot on deck for Julia to sit. While her grandmother doted on her, Julia looked around for Theo and Valera. Theo was crying in her mother's arms. Julia's heart broke for her. Nathaniel was a good man. Julia thought about what Maera had done for him. It made her think about her own parents, especially her mother. Perhaps, somewhere in the atmosphere, her mom was made of pure aether.

"Julia..." Eli's voice made her heart jump.

He inched toward her as if afraid to touch her. She scooted over and patted the ground. He sat down, and she examined his head wound.

"Ouch, that hurts, you know," he complained.

"Well, you deserved it," she teased.

His face grew serious. "I'm okay, really. Julia... I'm so sorry. I saw myself holding the gun and aiming it at you. I tried to stop myself, but it was as if I'd lost control."

"It wasn't your fault, Eli."

She cuddled next to him and dozed off to the voices of the survivors of Subterria.

*

Just as the Elders predicted, the world of Aether struggled with the loss of their goddess. As fake as she was, she gave them something to believe in. Without her, they didn't know who they were.

A week after Danu's defeat, Julia still reeled from the aftermath. When the *Cornelius* docked at Aetherland Isle, she saw firsthand the consequences of Danu's power. Several of the children from the cells didn't have family to take care of them. Victoria set up a temporary orphanage in the hopes of reuniting families, but too often they discovered that their parents died in the fighting or were taken to Pacifica.

With Subterria gone, hundreds of homeless left Aetherland Isle bursting. Refugees slept wherever there was room. Those who were sick or injured were taken to the warehouses, which became hospitals where people were healed by the best doctors in Aether. Theo did her best to use her powers, but even aether couldn't heal certain wounds. The death of her father had left her broken-hearted.

"Grandma." In the aftermath, Parmelia had shown what it meant to have family. "What happens now?"

Parmelia took Julia's hand. "We know we cannot control you girls. We can only advise you. Aether will turn to the three of you for help as they did Ealga, Maera, and Aeda. Although, it's up to you how you go forward."

"I don't know if I'm ready for that... going forward. Right now, I just want to go back. When things were simple."

Julia left Parmelia in the room. She needed to think. The Stein mansion was overflowing with people. During the day it buzzed, but at night it was quiet. Julia enjoyed the quiet. She snuck to the library where she found Theo and Valera waiting for her.

"You look terrible," Theo quipped.

"So do you," Julia shot back.

They both half-smiled. The distant memory of high school and slumber parties they'd shared as best friends made Julia chuckle. She almost missed those human moments. But they had to start over now.

Julia smiled at Theo and Valera. This time, they'd start over as sisters.

WICKED SECRETS

COMING IN MAY OF 2016

L.M. Fry

ELEAH Enterprises

EDMOND OKLAHOMA

CHAPTER ONE

Mom died before I was born.

Her death was plastered all over the news. *Car Accident Kills Pregnant Woman – Miracle Baby Survives!* The funny thing is, I don't feel like a miracle... I feel like a curse.

Tucking the faded newspaper article into my backpack, I take one last look around my empty room and suck back the torrent that threatens to let loose. I raise my chin and reluctantly make my death march to the 1994 Chevy Caprice. Dad bought the clunker after the company car was taken away, but the maroon tank may as well be a hearse as far as I am concerned.

For the past five years, Dad and I have been living in an upscale apartment in downtown Seattle. We've been a duo in everything we've done. Just the two of us. We were doing pretty well, or so I thought. I had everything I could ever want – a best friend, a boyfriend, money.

But three months ago Lunasoft, a company that Dad helped start, laid him off with some lame explanation about budget cuts. Last week we got an eviction notice, and two days ago he told me that we are moving. At first, I was excited because he said he had finally found a new job, but then the reality of it smacked me in the face. We are moving to Oklahoma. The place that, until now, was nothing but the funny, pan-shaped state.

Do they drive cars there, or do they still ride a horse and buggy?

Dragging my feet through the threshold, I close the door on my perfect life. Seattle is my home. I belong near the ocean, the mountains, and the city, not Oklahoma. Worst of all, we are moving to a tiny town that I've never even heard of named Carrsville. Literally, it's the place where the wind goes sweeping down the plains.

When I step out into the light, I look around for my boyfriend, Kyle. He rarely texts or calls, and when he does it's a one word response. So I thought maybe he'd come by in person to see me off, but I guess I was wrong. I shouldn't be surprised since he's been acting weird all week. Still, I thought for sure he'd at least say goodbye. *Maybe he's just stuck in traffic.* I bounce on my heels, stalling for time. Surely he'll drive up any minute. He'll exit his car and wrap me up in his lanky arms. He'll kiss me and beg me not to leave.

A few minutes later, Dad honks the horn. It sounds like a dying duck. I give up and skulk toward the hideous beast of a car with my hand over my face. George, our concierge, opens the huge door for me, and the look in his eyes screams, "Dead Girl Walking," as if I am on my way to the electric chair. Before I climb in, he touches my shoulder.

"Good luck, Emily. We're going to miss you around here," he says.

His feeble smile holds more pity than well wishes, and I bite the inside of my cheek, trying not to burst into tears. My mouth moves into what I hope is a grin.

"Thanks, George," I murmur and turn away before he can see the drops escaping my eyes.

The vinyl seat creaks and my gangly legs smack the dashboard as I sit, which makes the glove box pop open. I shut it only to have it open again. In a game of who's smarter than a glove box, I lose. Frustrated, I use my knee to hold it shut. The hinges screech as the door slams shut and locks me into my jail cell. George cringes through the window. I have just entered into my own personal hell.

Within seconds, my legs cramp. Since I have no room to stretch them out, I try to push the chair back, but when I lift the lever, the pressure from the boxes behind me forces the seat forward even more. No amount of pushing, screaming, or whining fixes my predicament. I'm stuck.

Resigned to my fate, I grab my seat belt. On my third attempt to buckle it, it clicks into place, but instantly the belt locks up and tightens with each breath I take. Totally frustrated with the way this trip is starting out, I fold my arms around my bag and glare out the front window without acknowledging my dad.

He sighs and turns to face me. "Kyle didn't show up, did he?" he asks.

I grunt my annoyance.

"Emily, I know it doesn't seem like it now, but I promise you Carrsville will be a good change for us. I'm doing this for you," he says.

I huff. We both know he's trying to convince himself as much as he is trying to convince me. When I don't respond, he continues his sales pitch.

"Your aunt Millie is there, and she is really excited to meet you. You'll like her. She and your mother were very close. And, I've been offered a dream job at Franks Oil Company. In fact, I was lucky to get it." His voice sounds like rusty gears grinding together.

"Okay, Dad." I exude as much sarcasm as I can muster.

He sighs again. As I study him, I can see how the stress has changed him. Dark sags make his pale blue eyes look sunken in and streaks of white peek through his dark hair. I know he feels guilty because, for the second time in my life, he's uprooted me.

He was nothing more than a stranger when he tore me away from my grandparents. I was ten years old when he showed up at his parents' door and begged to see me.

"You can't just stake a claim on her, Ryan. Not after everything that's happened," my grandmother cried as she closed the door in his face.

"I'm better now, and she's my daughter. I love her. You can't keep her from me." Dad shouted through the door, then stormed away.

No one knew that I was hiding under the stairs. I was fascinated by the tall, handsome man who claimed to be my father. My grandparents had told me that my dad was sick and couldn't take care of a baby. After I was born they took me home, and for ten years I thought that my father didn't want me. Yet here he was, eager to meet me. He loved me.

My elation was short-lived. My grandparents didn't trust my dad, so they refused to let him see me. Dad fought for custody and won. He took me away from my grandparents, and the bitterness that developed between them split the family in half.

Now five years later, he's forcing me to leave my home again and dragging me to Backwoods, No-where-ville. I may not have a choice, but I don't have to make it easy.

"Pffft... Right, Carrsville will be a great change for us. Famous last words, Ryan," I roll my eyes.

My words hit him hard and the skin at his temples tightens up, adding a few extra lines to his forehead. He hates when I call him by his first name, which is exactly why I do it. His shoulders slump forward, and a pang of guilt gnaws at me. I try to ignore it, but fail miserably.

"I'm sorry, Dad. I'm sure this will be fun," I apologize.

I feign a smile as I tug on the chest-crushing seat belt. Well, it would be crushing my chest, if I had one. But my fifteen, almost sixteen, year-old body is struggling to catch up with other girls my age. For example, my best friend Hailey already wears a C-cup and has curves in all the right places. I'm lucky to fit in an A-cup and my curves are none existent.

My apology makes Dad sit up, but he isn't smiling. "No, Emily, I'm the one who should be sorry. I'm yanking you away from your life and friends. If I had any other option, I'd take it, but with my history, it's been hard to find work. I'm doing the best I can for both of us. This is the only job I've been offered and our savings are gone."

"I know, Dad." My guilt grows. It isn't his fault he got laid off. It happens to lots of people. So I add in my best twang, "Hey, before you know it, I'll be wearin' cowboy boots and spittin' tobacco."

He smiles, "Yes to the boots, no to the tobacco. Deal?"

"Deal."

He turns the ignition. The car sputters, spews black smoke, and stalls. On the second try, the car wheezes like an old man before the engine quits. Dad grumbles.

"Well, I guess this is fate telling us to stay," I tease.

"No, no. The engine is just a little rusty. I just need to warm it up," he argues.

His fingers turn white as he strangles the pleather of the steering wheel. He pumps the gas pedal a dozen times and turns the key. Finally the car roars to life like a sickly dragon. Noxious fumes billow from the exhaust pipes, forcing everyone outside of the car to cough and swear at us. I cover my face in embarrassment.

"It's just you and me, kid. We'll conquer the road together. Right?" he asks like he always does when we face a challenge in life.

"Right, Dad." I smile for his sake, but I don't feel it.

"Oklahoma, here we come!" Dad crows triumphantly.

The rumbling engine muffles my groan. As we pull away from the apartments, my phone vibrates. A flashing screen warns me about an incoming text, and a picture of my friends dressed like cowboys and making goofy faces pops up. *We'll miss you Emily!* A loud sniffle escapes my nose. This is all I have left of Kyle and Hailey. A silly picture. Well, this and a slew of farewell cards, email addresses, phone numbers, and the promise of future visits. My dad squeezes my shoulder, trying to comfort me, but I shrug his hand away. I don't want his pity. Leaning my head against the seatbelt, I peer out the window and let the rush of tears flow. The gray reflection mutes my green eyes and blonde hair, and matches my emotions.

The day goes by in a blur of asphalt and fast food. The few texts I've sent Hailey and Kyle have gone unanswered, making me wonder where they are and if they've forgotten me already. When night sneaks up on me, a new nightmare begins. We stop in Boise, Idaho at a motel whose decrepit sign offers free _BO, a mini fridge, and, from the looks of the place, a generous supply of skittering roommates.

The second I step out of the car, my legs spasm. I hang onto the car as I stretch the kinks out of them, then limp into the office behind Dad. The attendant, a woman wearing a pink "Hot Mamas" tank top that matches her pink hair and black roots, looks at us as if we've committed some heinous crime by interrupting her. She glares over the top of her cheesy romance novel with the buff, bare-chested pirate on the cover.

"Sign here, cash only. You're in room thirteen. To the left by the ice machine," she barks and continues reading.

"Excuse me, ma'am," Dad interrupts.

The woman huffs. "What now?"

"The key?"

She slams her book on the desk, stands, and yanks the key off a board behind her. She scowls as she tosses the key at him.

"Anything else?"

"No thank you. You've been a delight." He gives her a mock bow, but her face is already planted back in her book. We get back in the car and drive around to park in front of our luxuriously awful accommodations.

Turns out, our room is not on the left by an ice machine, but on the right next to a pool filled with brackish water. Dad struggles with the room key, while I juggle our bags. When the door finally creaks open, I feel as though I am walking into a b-rated slasher movie. The décor is derelict chic with a brown-stained gray carpet, lumpy twin beds covered with threadbare lime green spreads, and a bathroom door without a handle. Before stepping inside, I turn around and pop the trunk of the car.

"Emily, what are you doing?" Dad asks.

"I don't know about you, but I am NOT sleeping under those blankets. I am going to use my own," I grunt as I dig through our packed bedding.

He scans the room and cringes. "Could you maybe get me a set too?"

"I am burning these after this trip. Who knows what diseased pests are lurking in this cesspool," my nose crinkles as a faint moldy smell circulates in the air. I hand him a blanket and some sheets.

"Oh, stop. This place isn't that bad," he scolds, and dumps his suitcase on a chair.

A plume of grey dust billows around him, sending him into a fit of coughs. He turns the faucet on to get a drink. To my horror the water spurts and fills his cup with a chunky green goo.

"Okay, so we won't be drinking this." He shrugs and pours the gunk into the sink.

"Or brushing our teeth. Or having a shower. Look at the bright side, even the insects will be repelled by us," I add as a wave of nausea grips my stomach.

"This is the best we can afford right now. I promise on the next road trip we'll stay at the Ritz." Dad gives me a weak grin.

The moldy smell grows stronger as I near the mini fridge. Black tendrils of mildew crawl through the door. I avoid opening it for fear of what goodies past occupants have left behind. I choose the bed closest to the window and notice that dark hairs poke through the fibers of the stained duvet. A shudder of disgust vibrates through my body as I cover the entire bed in a clean sheet. A cockroach skitters out from under the bed, across my foot.

"Ew, ew, ew, ew…"

"What's wrong?"

"A big bug is on my foot," I screech and kick it up and away.

When it lands on his bed, Dad squeals and bats at it with a pillow. The cockroach looks at him like he's crazy and runs off the bed. It scuttles under the dresser.

"I swear I just heard that thing laughing at you. A pillow? Really?"

"Let's just get some sleep," Dad growls.

During the night, our neighbors scream at each other. A loud thud shakes my bed as a woman shrieks and curses at a man. They finally quiet down after glass breaks and a door slams. Shortly afterwards, someone knocks on our door.

"Hey, what are you doing in my room?" a drunk guy yells through the window.

Dad gets up, clicks on the light, and cracks the door. The man shoves his face through, and I can smell the alcohol fumes from my bed. The man laughs and wheezes.

"Oh, this ain't my room, but hey, *she* sure is pretty." He grins, leering at me.

I shrink under my covers, and Dad firmly shuts the door on the man, who stumbles off. I hear yelling as the drunk bangs on our neighbor's door. Dad goes back to bed and falls fast asleep, snoring like a bear. Turning on my side, I notice two tiny red eyes looking at me from a hole in the wall. I throw a newspaper at them and they disappear. Later, I hear scratching in the walls next to my head, so needless to say, I don't sleep. An entire bottle of NyQuil couldn't knock me out.

Morning finally arrives, and as light filters through the dingy bent mini-blinds, I hear, "Good morning, Emily. Ready for breakfast?" Dad wakes up wide-eyed and perky.

"Ugh," I groan.

Thoroughly zombified, I slurp down a tasteless batch of pancakes and runny eggs for breakfast at the local greasy spoon. Dad has repositioned the boxes behind my seat to give me a little extra leg room, and I sleep like a bobble-head all the way to Denver. By the time we arrive, my neck has a crick and half of my body is numb. I check my phone for missed messages and find only one from Hailey.

Had so much fun last night. Went to a movie with friends. Totally missing you!

There's nothing from Kyle. My heart sinks.

"Want to stop for the night?" Dad asks over dinner at Gino's All U Can Eat Italian.

"Do I have a choice?" I mumble.

"You always have a choice, Emily."

"Then, I choose to go back to Seattle," I retort.

I smirk at my brilliance while slurping down a spaghetti noodle.

"Unfortunately, that isn't one of your choices," he sighs and rubs his forehead.

"Ugh, fine. Do we have to stop? I can't bear the thought of staying in another roach motel. Can't we just drive through the night?" I beg, cringing as my neck spasms at the thought.

"I don't know. It's dangerous to drive for so long. I'll have to drink some major coffee, so that I can stay awake. You'll have to help. I don't want to get in an accident because I fall asleep," he says.

"Let's do it," I say, satisfied that at least in the car I won't catch a disease.

Eleven hours, five coffees, and six energy drinks later, we get our first glimpse of an Oklahoma sunrise. A peach glow begins on the horizon, casting a golden light over an expansive sea of wheat. The land is so flat that the fields seem to go on forever. Rich red dirt swirls into an orange haze as the summer wind blows. If the situation were different, I would call it beautiful. Oklahoma is not what I expected. Then we stop at a gas station, and I get my first taste of the southern heat and humidity.

"Dad, it's stifling. I can't breathe, and it's only 7 a.m. Are we in some kind of extreme heat wave?" I whine as sweat instantly covers my body, soaking my clothes.

A raspy chuckle startles me. "Nah, darlin', this here's just a plain ole Okie month of June. I reckon you're not from round these parts?"

A wrinkled, sun-bronzed man sits just outside the gas station door. Like the quintessential cowboy out of a western, the Stetson on his head is well-worn and his brown leather boots are scuffed. A brass belt buckle the size of my hand catches the sun and blinds me. The thing must weigh a ton. I shade my eyes and squint at the man.

"No, sir. We're from Seattle," I stammer as my bladder screams at me, reminding me why I got out of the car in the first place.

"That's 'bout north as you can get. I s'pose," he says, scratching his whiskers. After a moment, he adds, "Ain't Seattle, where all that fancy coffee lattes come from? Y'all won't be findin' none of that spittle round here. We like our coffee good n' strong enough to put hair on our chests," and he spits a wad of brown goo into a bucket.

I swallow hard, "Umm, yeah okay. Do you have a restroom here?"

"Sure do, darlin'. Key's hangin' on the wall. Bathroom's round back," he says, pointing to the door with his thumb.

Half of his yellow-stained teeth are missing, turning his friendly smile into a misshapen grin. I slide past him into the small station. Sure enough a key hangs on the wall just inside the door. The key is chained and welded to a ten-pound tire iron. I guess they have a lot of bathroom key thefts around here.

Unlocking the bathroom door is an acrobatic feat as I juggle the tire iron, the key, and the sticky knob. I am about to give up, when the lock clicks and the door swings open with a bang. A putrid stench that smells like a mix of dead skunk and stale sewage wafts out, and I wretch. Covering my nose with the top

316 | L.M. FRY

of my shirt, I step into the tiny cubicle. Dried wads of discolored toilet paper are glued to the wall like a giant had a spitball party. The stall has no door, but it does have a curtain of black flies buzzing around it. One look at the toilet, and I'm done. I could hold it for another hundred miles, before I would touch any part of this hazardous waste dump. But as I turn around to leave, the door slams shut, closing me in. It won't open.

"Hello? Is anyone there?" I frantically knock on the door.

The light bulb flickers. Bitter panic rises in my throat as the room heats up like a furnace. The walls close in on me.

"HELP ME! I AM TRAPPED!"

With a pop the light bulb fizzles out. Fists banging on the door, I scream.

"DAAAAAAAAAADDDDDDDDDDD!"

Finally, I hear a noise outside, and the door handle shakes, "Just a second, Emily. The door seems to be stuck."

Like a living wall of yuck, the buzz of the flies behind me grows louder. Something whizzes past my ear. My palms feel like they are bleeding as I slap the door. The darkness chokes me. Sweat cascades off of my forehead, burning my eyes.

"Dad, get me out of here... now!"

"I am trying. I can't find the key."

"That's because the key is in here with me!" I wail.

"Then unlock the door, Emily."

His casual tone irks me. *Sure, just unlock the door as if it were that easy. Does he not realize I am about to die the worst death possible? Alone in a stinking gas station bathroom!*

"I've already tried that, Dad. It won't open," The words pour out in a mounting vibrato.

"I'll be right back. Just sit tight!"

"NO, don't leave me here alone..."

Something lands in my hair. Batting at my head, I slip on a wet spot and fall to the floor with a thud. The noxious fumes begin to fill my lungs as I hyperventilate. *This is it... I am going to die.*

Suddenly, pure, joyous sunlight streams in. I scramble off the floor and throw myself through the door, landing on my hands and knees. Fresh air bombards my senses as I happily draw it in. Blurry-eyed, I look up at a shaded figure standing in front of me.

"Are ye ever gonna fix this door, Jimmy? This toilet isn't fit for an animal, let alone a human being. Hey, are ye alright?" A rich Scottish accent melts my ability for coherent thought.

"Huh?" I wipe the sweat from my eyes.

"Are ye okay?" the voice chuckles.

A finely-muscled hand reaches out to help me up. When the sun hits his face, sparkling deep blue eyes twinkle at me. My heart flutters. His strong fingers wrap around mine, turning my arms to jelly. Once I am on my feet again, I gaze up at the Adonis who rescued me from the nauseating chamber. Sun-bleached hair, and a cute, crooked smile greet me. He looks roughly my age, maybe a little older. My mind screams at me to say something smart and witty.

Instead, I mumble, "Uh, thanks."

"Emily, are you okay? You had me worried!" Dad hurries up to me and hugs me, squeezing until my eyes feel like they are going to pop out of their sockets.

After letting me go, he places his hands on my face and examines it. Then, he bops my nose like he did when I was younger and had a scrapped knee. It used to make me laugh, but now it's just annoying. I bat his hand away, and a twinge of hurt flickers in his eyes, but it disappears as a whiff of the bathroom escapes on a breeze. He gulps and turns toward my rescuer.

"Thanks for helping, son. My name's Ryan Brent, and this is my little girl, Emily."

He shakes the stranger's hand. Dad's words bubble up through my infatuated haze. *Geez, Dad. Really? Your **little** girl? I have to say something to fix this!*

"Yeah, Dad, as if I am little anymore," I snort.

My hero stifles a laugh. Heat rises into my cheeks. *Why can't I form a proper sentence, without sounding like a complete moron? Try to act normal.* I put my hands on my hips, then decide it isn't natural. I stick one in my pocket and throw my hip out. A stupid smile plasters onto my face.

The stranger grins at my gawkiness and introduces himself. "My name's Liam. My brother Finn and I run the Two Brothers Pub in town. Yer welcome to come by for a drink sometime."

His 'r's roll over me like water over river rocks.

"I don't drink," Dad says.

My jaw drops. I have to see Liam again. "Geez, Dad. I'm sure they have water or something," I bluster.

Liam smiles. "It's more of a restaurant than a pub. Ye can come for dinner."

"We'd like that," Dad shakes his hand again, then motions me toward the car.

Liam nods. He walks over to his red mustang and climbs in while I continue to grin like an idiot and giggle. *Liam is such a nice name. Liam and Emily.* I sigh.

"Emily? Earth to Emily."

A hand on my shoulder startles me.

"Huh? What?"

"I asked if you are ready to go. Your Aunt Millie is waiting for us. Are you okay? You're acting strange," he touches my forehead, as though to check my temperature.

"Oh, sure. Sounds good," I mumble.

"I think the heat is getting to you," he replies, then shuffles me to the car.

Suddenly, Carrsville doesn't seem like such a bad place to be.

CHAPTER TWO

As we near the outskirts of town, I can see five skyscrapers rising above the tree line. The buildings seem out of place amid the vast farmlands that surround the city. The Carney River splits the town into two parts – Downtown and East Carrsville. As we drive through the mini metropolis, I notice that Franks Oil Company is written over every door.

"Which one are you going to be working in?" I ask.

"I don't know. Probably in the main tower," Dad says off-handedly.

Leaving the downtown area, but still west of the river, Victorian-style mansions stand proud along tree-lined streets. Each house sits on a perfectly manicured yard. *No doubt they belong to perfectly manicured families.*

The river isn't the only dividing factor in Carrsville. East of the Carney, houses are noticeably smaller and the streets give off the "typical Main St. USA" vibe of every other small town that we passed on our trip. We drive up to a two-story brick building located in East Carrsville. Over the store front on the ground level, a neon sign flashes, MILLIE'S MASTERPIECES & MORE. Our car sputters and chokes its last breath as we pull up at the curb. The door to the shop swings open, and a thin woman with long, wild, blonde hair runs out as though she's been watching for us. This must be Aunt Millie. A warm smile and amber eyes greet me.

"Emily! I can't believe it. I've wanted to meet you for so long. You look just like your mom. Just like Emma. Oh sweetie, it's so good to have you here," she holds her arms out for me.

Reluctantly, I drop my bags on the ground and step into her hug. Her arms are stronger than I thought as she squeezes the air out of my lungs. She smells like freesias and incense.

"Hi," I wheeze.

"Come in, come in. I have rooms ready for you upstairs. It's not much, but I call it home," she grabs my suitcase and walks through the store.

The perfume of a thousand flowers surrounds me as I walk up a winding staircase. Everything in the building seems saturated with the smell. The stairs lead to a small apartment and open into a living room which displays a mishmash of artsy décor and retro furniture. A well-worn set of purple chairs and a matching sofa sit atop an orange shag rug. Florist magazines fan across an uneven, three-legged coffee table. A bay window serves as seating for a dining table. Tucked away in the corner, orange laminate counters and avocado-green appliances enliven a tiny u-shaped kitchen.

"I know it's garish as hell, but so is its owner," Aunt Millie chuckles.

A short hallway covered in abstract paintings and antique photos leads to the bedrooms.

"Who are these people?" I point to the black and white pictures.

"I have no clue. I just love the ambiance that comes from old portraits," Millie says.

"Oh."

Personally, the photos creep me out. *Why is it that the people in old photos never smiled?* A shiver runs up my spine. Millie stops at the door of a tiny bathroom.

"I'm afraid this is the only bathroom upstairs, but downstairs in the back of the shop there is a toilet and a shower. Feel free to use it if this one is occupied. Here are your rooms. They're probably not what you're used to, but hopefully you will find them cozy." She opens the first door.

Cozy is an overstatement. The entire bedroom is the size of my closet in the Seattle apartment. A twin bed almost fills the room, leaving only a sliver of space for a bed table. An open window at the head of the bed looks out onto an alley between Millie's shop and a bakery, and the yeasty aroma of bread wafts through. Millie opens a folding door to reveal the closet. The shoebox-sized nook is barely big enough to hold a pair of sneakers, let alone an entire wardrobe. I drop a box on the bed.

"Thanks. This is great," I force a smile.

A picture on the night table catches my attention. Two girls around my age are standing on a bridge holding hands. My finger traces one of their faces. She looks like me. The only other picture I've seen of her is the photo in the newspaper article.

"That's Emma and I when we around your age. I hope you don't mind. I left it in here for you." Millie looks longingly at the portrait.

"I don't have many pictures of my mom. Thank you."

"After our parents died, she was the only family I had left. She was my best friend..."

"Hello?" Dad's voice calls out from the stairs.

"Why don't you settle in? I'll show your dad around." Her hand touches my cheek. "You have her green eyes," she says as tears glisten on her face.

I close the door after she leaves and sit on the bed. The small metal frame is warm in my hands. Leaning back against the wall, I stare into the picture. Mom's smile is brilliant. She was far prettier than I am. Her body had more curves, and her hair had a golden sheen. I do have her green eyes, though. I dig through my backpack beside me for the article. Permanent creases line the paper where I've folded and unfolded it a million times. Her picture is smudged, but she has the same brilliant smile.

Footsteps pass by my door, making me jump. I quickly fold the article up and tuck it back in my bag. No one knows I have it. My grandparents had hidden it in a scrapbook, and I found it when I was eight years old. They told me that she died in a car accident, but that wasn't the whole truth. She did die in an accident, but it was my fault. When Mom was eight months pregnant with me, her friends threw her a baby shower. The article speculates that on her way home she lost control of her car and drove into oncoming traffic. She was declared dead at the hospital, and, forty minutes later, I was born via C-section. *Some miracle. I killed her.*

Dad opens my door and peeks in, "Hey, Emily. How's it going in here?"

"Okay, I guess," I murmur.

"I know the rooms are a little snug." He drops a box on the floor.

"Well, at least everything will be within easy reach," I retort, shrugging.

"In a few months, we'll find a place of our own. Until then, we'll make do. We'll conquer Carrsville together. Right?" he asks as always.

"Right, Dad," I respond half-heartedly.

He looks at the box on the bed. "Aren't you going to unpack your stuff?"

My entire life is crammed into two boxes and one suitcase. One box holds my books, music, and random memories of home. The other box holds my shoes and winter clothes. My suitcase has what Seattle-ites consider summer clothes.

"All my clothes are designed for summers in Seattle. I will boil in them down here."

"*Hmm.* I see your point. Can you wait until I get my first paycheck? Then maybe we can get you some new clothes."

"If you want, you can raid my closet," Millie's cheerful voice yells from the kitchen. The surprised look on Dad's face makes me laugh.

"Wow, the walls up here are thin," he laughs with me.

"There won't be any secrets around here," I agree.

"Do you want to have dinner at the Two Brothers Pub tonight?" Dad calls out to Millie.

"Love to," Millie calls back.

Dad turns to me, "Can you be ready in a couple of hours?"

"Sure," I say.

My insides flutter as I imagine seeing Liam again. I certainly can't go looking like I do now. As soon as Dad disappears through the door, I open the box on the floor and arrange a few items around my room. But that's as far as my unpacking goes, because facing the reminders of what I left behind in Seattle is just too painful.

Next, I go to Millie's room to scope out her wardrobe. Millie flops down on her bed as I look through her closet, which is huge and brimming with clothes. From the looks of it, she's never thrown anything away. Going through her clothes is like stepping back in time.

"Take whatever you want. We're close to the same size. I have more clothes than I could ever wear. I am kind of a shopaholic," she confesses.

I pull out a pair of bellbottoms and fringed leather vest which I hold up as I look at her quizzically. Millie smiles, making a peace sign with her fingers.

"I went through a flower power phase," she says.

Buried deep in the back, I find a yellow sequined jump suit.

"Disco phase," she laughs.

Still searching, I find clothes more suited to the current era. By the end of my closet shopping spree, my wardrobe is full, but my stomach is empty. A warm shower washes away the remnants of our hellish move, including my entrapment in the gas station bathroom. Feeling human once again, I put on one of Millie's summer dresses. The bust line is a little loose, but the rest of it fits well. The thin straps and knee length skirt reveal more skin than I am used to showing. I look for a cardigan to wear over it, but a blast of heat from the window changes my mind. My pale arms stands out against the blue dress like white beacons of light. *People are going to need to wear sunglasses around me. Oh, well.*

Dad is fast asleep on his bed, and from the looks of his room, he fell asleep while unpacking. His clothes are strewn all over the place, and his boxes are half full. He is grunting and kicking like he's fighting an imaginary enemy. I shake his shoulder, and he jerks awake with a frightened gasp, "Emma!"

"No, Dad. It's just me. Sorry. I didn't mean to scare you," I apologize.

This isn't the first time that he's had bad dreams about Mom.

"Ready to go eat?" I continue over the grumbling of my stomach.

He rubs his eyes and stares at me, "Wow, you look just like your mom."

"It's probably the dress. One of Millie's many outfits. I think she loves clothes more than I do." I grin.

"I didn't think that was possible," he laughs. "Just give me a minute, and I'll get changed."

While I wait for Dad, I check my phone. Nothing. I begin to wonder if the friends I had in Seattle were imaginary. I text Kyle. *Hey, I was just thinking about you. Miss you.* I stare at the screen, willing him to return my message. After ten minutes, I give up. *Maybe he's in the shower or something.*

Finally, we pile into Millie's delivery van. Dad sits shotgun, leaving me in the back seat with bags of organic fertilizer and empty pots. I brush off particles of potting soil from the seat and cringe as the stench of fertilizer permeates the air. The interior is as hot as an oven, making the smell worse. Great! The first time I met Liam, I smelled like a nasty bathroom, and this time I am going to be wearing Eau de Cow Patty. He's going to think I never shower.

"Could you turn on the air conditioner? It's pretty warm back here," I beg as beads of sweat drip down my face.

"Sorry, no air conditioning," Millie responds, rolling down the windows.

The blast of warm air does little to help with the heat, but it does help the stink. I sit as close to the window as I can, sucking down the fresh air as we drive through town.

Two Brothers Pub is in the old section of downtown Carrsville, beyond the four modern skyscrapers that make up the Franks Oil complex. The fifth building is much older. It stands in the center and overshadows the entire town. The architecture is a strange mix of gothic and art deco with tall pointed arched windows and an abundance of ornate detailing. Sitting along the topmost edge are four hideous gargoyles that look down on the city with disdain. Another cold shiver runs down my spine as we pass under them.

"Aunt Millie, why are there gargoyles on that building? It looks like some kind of medieval castle," I ask.

"Creepy, right? I'm not sure what the deal with the gargoyles is, but the building is part of the Franks Oil Empire," she answers.

The metropolis area looks like a ghost town. However, a mile past the Franks Oil district, when we enter old town, the world comes alive. Rows of historic buildings line the streets. Old- fashioned street lamps illuminate the faces of Carrsville. The entire town seems to be here.

We pull up just outside the front doors of the Two Brothers where a long line of people wait. Music pumps through outdoor speakers in beat with buzzing fans that blast cool misted air over the patio section of the restaurant. Every seat on the patio is occupied. People chat with each other in loud voices, calling out to friends in line. Everyone seems to know one another. I feel like I am in a different universe. Back in downtown Seattle, you were lucky to know your next door neighbors.

An apron-clad Liam steps out, juggling an array of drinks and platters in his hands. The fans blow wisps of his blond hair into his eyes, and I get the sudden urge to brush them out of his face.

"Liam!" I call out to him eagerly and wave, instantly regretting it, because for a brief second the entire crowd hushes and looks at me. I shuffle my feet in embarrassment and look at the floor. A few people snicker, but soon the crowd returns to their meals. When I lift my head again, I see Liam smiling warmly at me. He motions for us to bypass the line and follow him through the service doors.

A mosaic of black and white tiles leads us to the chaotic party going on inside. The noise level is deafening. A live band plays music from an open balcony on the second floor while boisterous customers laugh and eat. Lights reflect off the ornate tin ceiling like a disco ball, casting a rainfall of glitter around the room. We edge past the massive bar where every kind of liquor bottle imaginable glimmers in a rainbow of colors. Behind the counter a lean man, who looks like an older version of Liam, tosses bottles and mixes drinks with ease. People cheer him on as he performs daring maneuvers without spilling a drop.

Liam leads us to an office in the back, which, unlike the rest of the place, is relatively quiet.

"Glad, ye could make it. As ye can see, we're a wee bit busy tonight," Liam says.

"Is it always this crazy?" I ask as heat rises in my cheeks. *At least I can speak this time.*

The door swings open, and the bottle-flipping bartender walks in, wiping his hands on an apron. A handsome, brown-haired man in a chef's coat follows along behind him.

"Liam, are ye gonna introduce us to yer friends?" The bartender's accent is thicker than Liam's. His hair is a shade darker, but they have the same mischievous sparkle in their blue eyes.

"Aye, Finn. This is Ryan Brent and his daughter, Emily. And, of course, ye know the lovely Miss Millie," Liam says.

Finn takes Millie's hand and kisses it. A blush creeps up her face, and she giggles like a giddy child. I don't know why, but a small part of me feels envious. He stands and turns to face me. Finn flourishes a small bow, making my face burn.

"Millie, you are brighter than the sunniest of days, and dare I say young Emily bears a striking resemblance. Welcome to our humble pub. My name's Finn Findlay and this is my other half, Cody Matthers."

Cody wraps his arm around Finn's waist and smiles, "It's so nice to meet you. We don't get to see many new faces around here. Whereabouts do you stem from?"

"We just moved here from Seattle," Dad replies.

"I love Seattle this time of year. Everything is always so green and beautiful up there. You two must be frying in this heat. Liam, get them settled and I'll make them my specialty. It was so good to meet you," Cody says, then pecks Finn on the cheek before disappearing into the throng outside.

Liam immediately escorts us out to a corner booth where the music is only a dull roar. When he hands me a menu his fingers brush mine, sending a thousand tiny needles up and down my arm.

54407513R00202

Made in the USA
Charleston, SC
04 April 2016